BIG PINE
BOOK
AND
GARDEN
CLUB

C. T. MESSING

Minneapolis, Minnesota

www.sawmillpublishing.com

ISBN 978-1-7322677-0-1 (print)
ISBN 978-1-7322677-1-8 (ebook)
Library of Congress Control Number: 2018942781

Cover design: Carson Creative
Editor: Marly Cornell

The author thanks Rebecca D. and Jim M.
for your invaluable advice and encouragement.

Printed in the United State of America

Sawmill Publishing
Minneapolis, Minnesota
www.sawmillpublishing.com

CONTENTS

CHAPTER 1, ED

AN EARLY HOMECOMING

You could say the birth of The Big Pine Book and Garden Club came about as the result of actual labor pains. On Friday afternoons during fishing season I drive the forty miles from Big Pine down to Malmo, on the east shore of Lake Mille Lacs where my Navy buddy, Elliot, has a cabin. Elliot and I usually have an early supper at his house then head out onto to Minnesota's most famous walleye lake for an evening of fishing. Walleye eyes have evolved to be efficient for feeding under low-light conditions, which means nighttime hours are usually the best time to catch them. Mille Lacs is a big piece of water—surface area is around 200 square miles and, except for trout, it's home to most species of game fish found in Minnesota. But it's most famous for walleyes—in my opinion the best eating freshwater fish anywhere.

That May Friday we were just heading out onto the bay when Elliot's wife came running out of the house, yelling and waving her arms like she just won the lottery. When we got back to the dock, she told us she'd gotten a call from her pregnant daughter, down in the Cities. Her daughter's water broke, she said, and she and Elliot needed to get down there right away. They took off for Minneapolis to welcome their first grandchild, and I headed back to Big Pine.

From Malmo to Big Pine is a nice drive that runs through

almost every kind of North Central Minnesota landscape. Nearly 60 percent of the county acreage is classified as wetlands of some kind—lakes, bogs, marshes, and low-lying patches of woods, all threaded by creeks and rivers that eventually drain into the Mississippi. In the southern part of the county, down near Mille Lacs, the wetlands alternate with full-section-size corn and soybean fields. There's some oak savanna too. The oaks sit in beef pasture now, not in the original prairie grasses and flowers, but it still has the peaceful look of a savanna. As you drive north, there's less farmland and more woods, mostly jack pine and aspen—though aspen is usually called "popple" up here, and by the time you reach the town of Big Pine you are in what most Minnesotans describe as "up north."

The signs at our county borders read, "Welcome to Larkin County, Home of the White Deer." The signs could also add, "We're old, we're poor, and there aren't many of us." All true. Our county's sparse population has the highest percentage of people over sixty-five in the state, nearly 30 percent. Down in the Twin Cities Metro the figure is about 10 percent. We are also one of the lowest household income counties. One consequence of those dismal numbers is that the Larkin County Fair is held midweek—the concessionaires don't take in enough money to justify committing valuable weekend days. We're used to it, but I think midweek fair status is an invisible year-round drag on citizen morale. And though there are other Minnesota counties that are poor to the point of midweek fairs, Big Pine bears an additional demoralizing burden: the town was once home to the third-largest turkey processing plant in Minnesota, our high school mascot is a turkey and our interscholastic sports teams are The Gobblers and the Lady Gobblers.

What were they thinking?

When I got back home from the aborted fishing trip, I headed for the kitchen to get some ideas for a second supper. Elliot's wife is a nice woman, but if I was married to her we'd eat out a lot. I knew Doris wouldn't be home for hours. One Thursday evening each month she drove over to Hibbing with our friend, Chip Brakkman, to volunteer at the nursing home where Chip's wife, Ivy, spent the last months of her life after her stroke. As I stared into the fridge, I heard some bumping noises coming from upstairs. We don't have many burglaries in our town, but you never know, so I went up the stairs pretty softly to check things out. The sounds were coming from the guest bedroom. The door was only half-closed, and I saw right away that Doris and Chip weren't in Hibbing after all.

The bumping was the headboard hitting the wall. They were too occupied to notice me. Doris was on top, on all fours, with her knees on either side of him, and her hands braced on his chest. As she rocked back and forth she made some little gasps I recognized— though I hadn't heard them in a while. I watched them for at least half a minute, maybe longer, trying to fit what I was seeing into the world I thought I knew.

Guys from some cultures know what to do in those situations— go get their gun, maybe, or some other dramatic move. But I'm a Minnesotan, Swedish on both sides. We usually see sex and violence as separate activities. My version of a jealous rage would have been to say something like, "Gosh, Chip, I don't remember saying it would be okay for you to put your dick in my wife," maybe in a sarcastic tone of voice. But I didn't do that either. I guess I went numb and, strange as it might sound, I couldn't bring myself to interrupt them.

I tiptoed back downstairs and tried to figure out what to do. If I wasn't going to break things up, I also wasn't about to sit on my own front step waiting for them to finish. So I took some action: I drove the forty miles back to the Mille Lacs and got myself a spot on a charter launch for the night walleye bite. By then it was raining, and the lake was running a nice "walleye chop," the one- to two-foot waves that stimulate fishing action.

I must have looked as lost as I felt—the launch skipper asked if I was seasick. One of those wildlife artists who paint outdoor scenes like "Fall Mallards Landing on a Pond," or "Irish Setter on Point," could have done me as "Confused Cuckold in Spring Rain."

I replayed the scene with Doris and Chip about a hundred times; it seemed so unreal that I had to keep telling myself it happened. My fifty-eight-year-old wife launching herself into adultery? With Chip? And since when did Doris like being on top? It all seemed so darned unlikely—for Chip, even more than for Doris.

When I got home for the second time that night Doris was already asleep. I wasn't surprised—she'd had a tiring afternoon. I lay awake for a long time, listening to the crickets and looking at my sleeping wife. For thirty-five years I'd been in same bedroom in the same house with the same woman, and now everything looked different—like I'd been watching a regular movie that suddenly turned into 3D, maybe. I just could not fit Chip and Doris into the category of things that happened.

~

Chip started teaching at Big Pine High the same year I did, both of us hired right out of college—him to teach history, and me to teach biology and coach Gobbler wrestling. When our principal started to introduce Chip and me to the student body at the opening fall assembly, a girl yelled, "He's so cute!" which set off a bunch of squealing and shouting and laughing from other girls in the auditorium. Chip just stood there on the stage, blushing like a ripe cranberry.

He really was a good-looking guy—still is, I guess, but back then he could have been a model for a "Visit Norway" brochure. I'm pretty sure Hitler would have sent him to a breeding camp. After the commotion over Chip died down, the principal introduced me as the new biology teacher and wrestling coach, then ended his comments by saying, ". . . and he knows Russian."

The students didn't realize that was his show-stopper finish. After about ten seconds of silence, he recovered by asking me to say something in Russian.

I said, "*Das vedanya.*"

Then the principal started the applause that finally got me and Chip off the stage.

~

I'm a homegrown product, a graduate of Big Pine High School, but Chip's an exotic, an immigrant from over in Hayward, Wisconsin, "The Muskie Capital of America." His boyhood ambition was to be a muskie fishing guide, and he was already taking paid clients during his high school summer vacations. His dad's ambition was for Chip to follow him into the Lutheran ministry—Wisconsin Synod Lutheran ministry.

The Wisconsin Synod folks are a different bunch. Lutherans are not generally known for wild lifestyles, but the Wisconsin Synod people make mainstream Lutherans look like drunk fraternity boys at Mardi Gras. Even other Lutherans make fun of their conservative attitudes; the old joke is that Wisconsin Synod people don't "do it" standing up . . . they're afraid it will lead to dancing.

Teaching was the compromise reached when Chip finally convinced Brakken Sr. that he didn't feel a call to the pulpit. Teaching was a respectable compromise; it satisfied his minister dad, and it would leave Chip his summers for muskie fishing. That he landed in Big Pine wasn't an accident. Larkin County has almost as much good muskie water as the Hayward area, so when Chip saw the notice of the opening at our high school he was on it right away. There were other applicants, but his advantage was that he was a rookie— meaning the district could start him at the bottom of the pay scale. School money is tight here.

Chip always seemed as square as they come. I'd never heard him refer to sexual doings with anyone, including with his wife, Ivy. And he never joined in the teacher's lounge speculations about student sex, a topic of "concern" that some of our teachers never seemed to tire of addressing. Our shop teacher was disgustingly transparent; any time student sex was brought up he would sit there with his eyes closed, pretty obviously creating his own visuals to accompany the discussions. I hope his wife benefited when he screened them at home.

Chip, on the other hand, was like as not to change the subject. Ivy once confessed to Doris that she'd had to seduce him when they were in college. She'd intended to save herself for marriage, but she figured if some other girl reached into his Dickies ahead of her, Mr. Boy Scout probably would have felt he had to marry her. As far as I knew, Ivy was the first and only woman he'd ever been to bed with— at least until Doris.

Chip and Ivy, along with Stan and Maddie Keller, were our main couples' friends for three decades. We all had kids around the same time, we babysat for each other, we went down for weekends in the Twin Cities together. Until the X-rated scene in our guest bedroom, our sex with each other's spouses was limited to exchanging chaste kisses on New Year's Eve.

Then life bit back at us, hard. Ivy had a bad stroke when she was only fifty-four, and two years later Stan went into cardiac arrest in the kitchen of his Town Talk restaurant, dropping Big Pine's Jewish population to zero in the two seconds it took him to hit the floor. I really miss him.

The anonymous mash notes started arriving in Chip's first few weeks of teaching. He seemed genuinely shocked by them. He was one of those rare good-looking guys who really didn't understand how attractive they are to women. Or if he did know, he didn't seem to care. Sometimes he'd show me the notes and we'd try to figure out the identity of the smitten party. One arrived in an envelope along with a Magnum condom. Chip said the oversize condom was proof he hadn't ever fooled around with whoever sent the note; he had a Scandinavian sense of humor to go with his looks. There was also one non-anonymous submission. Only three words: "I want you."

And it was signed, "MH."

MH was Michelina Hamer, known as Mickey, the youngest sister of the most lusted-after girl in my own graduating class: May Hamer. If the yearbook had a "Likeliest Jail Bait" category, the title would have gone to Mickey. Her note shook Chip pretty good. There might not have been any girls like Mickey at the synod high school he attended or, if there were, they probably weren't around for long. Not that Chip considered taking her up on the offer, but it was hard to be around Mickey and not have a few prurient thoughts.

Any high school teacher who says they've never had an occasional fantasy about a student is just lying to you and to himself, or for that matter, to herself. Even clueless Chip must have wandered off in that direction a few times. Mickey was just too hard to ignore when she planted herself in the front row of your classroom, twirling her finger in her hair and leaning forward on her desk to give you the best possible view. She did it to me a few times, but it my case I knew it wasn't an offer—it was more like a taunt.

High school kids' attitudes had changed some since my own graduation seven years earlier, but for most kids it was more in the way they talked, rather than a dramatic increase in actual sexual behavior. With the Hamer sisters, it wasn't all talk.

Chip asked if I thought he should turn Mickey's note over to the school guidance counselor—the job Doris would take six years later, after our son, Charlie, started school. My advice was he should wait it out, and Mickey would eventually lose interest.

She did. Less than a month after sending the note, she was walking the halls hanging on the arm of Ned Cooley, the best wrestler in Gobbler history.

Over the following three years, he would make me look like a coaching genius. Three decades after that, he would save my ass.

CHAPTER 2, ED

A WEEK IN LIMBO

The morning after my badly timed homecoming, I was out of the house before Doris came down for breakfast. I left her a note that I was going fishing after school, and that I wouldn't be home until late. I packed some extra sandwiches and hooked the boat trailer to my pickup so I wouldn't have to stop back at the house after school. Even though Doris and I both worked at the high school, we didn't usually cross paths during the day—her counseling office was in the new wing, and my biology classroom was in the old part of the building where the hallways still smell like they did when I was a student there. Fifteen minutes after the bell ended my last class, I slid my boat into the water at Hamer Landing on White Deer Lake.

White Deer is a jewel. It's spring fed, and the water is so clear you want to drink it. It's a relatively small lake, just over a mile long from north to south and about a half-mile wide. Albino Point reaches out about halfway up the west shore. Of the 220-some lakes in Larkin County, White Deer is one of the least built up. The north end is mostly State Forest land, and much of the west shore was bought up in sizable chunks by a few old-money Twin Cities' families back before World War I, when Big Pine first became accessible by passenger train from Minneapolis. From the Big Pine station it was only a twenty-minute buggy ride to the lake. The Hamer family still owns almost a half-mile of shoreline on the east side, and Fosters' Lodge has another quarter mile, north of the Hamer place. The result of limited ownership is that White Deer's shoreline isn't cluttered with cottages and docks every fifty or one hundred feet, the kind of density that makes parts of some of our other lakes, including Mille Lacs, look like low-income suburbs. Also, most of the existing structures on White Deer are set back from the water, leaving the shoreline with a more natural look—what you see is mostly just pine and poplar on the elevations, and tamarack and cattail swamp in the lower-lying places. The lake must have had an elegant feel to it in the days before outboard motors. I was born too late to experience it, except once in a while before Memorial Day or after Labor Day when the loons and I are sometimes the only creatures on the water.

Once you've heard a loon, you will never mistake it for anything else. A loon call is a frictionless spear of sound that can arc across a mile of water and still penetrate right through the middle of your chest. It nails you every time. Each spring the lake is home to one or two loon pairs, but not usually more than that. Loons like a big chunk of water all to themselves, they tend to return to the same lake year after year, and they're not very sociable with other members of their own species. I have a lot of loon traits myself. I can't say I recognize individual loons, but I must have seen the same ones over many summers. They live as long as thirty years, so I like knowing it's at least possible that some of those I see now are offspring of young ones my dad and I watched riding on their mother's backs fifty years ago.

I began fishing White Deer not long after I learned to walk. Some of my earliest memories are of sitting in the boat with my dad, pulling sunfish out of the water. At first, Dad had to take them off the hook for me because my hand was too small to hold the spiny fins down while I worked out the barb. The best part was bringing the catch home to my mom. She'd greet me like I'd just saved the family from certain starvation.

By the time I was seven, I could handle a casting rod or a spinning outfit and unhook my own fish. At ten I considered myself a helluva fisherman.

Winter didn't stop us, either. We put our fish house on White Deer as soon as the ice was safe, and left it there until the mandatory removal date in mid-February. We'd sit, just the two of us, in the dark four-by-six-foot shack in the middle of the frozen lake. We had a propane heater, but unless it was deep cold, the kerosene lantern and the heat from our bodies was enough to keep the small space warm enough to shed our parkas. The odor of kerosene still takes me back there. In the shack I was my dad's son, but I was also his equal. We'd sit together for hours, each watching his slip bobber in the dark water, waiting for it to move; when it sucked down slowly it was probably a crappie or, once in a great while, a rare winter bass. A series of light bobs might mean a perch or a walleye and, when it shot down like an underwater rocket, it was usually a northern pike

We didn't do all our fishing on White Deer. In good years you can't beat Mille Lacs for walleye production, so we'd either tow our sixteen-foot Alumacraft fishing boat there or sometimes just drive over and get seats on a commercial launch. At least once a year, we'd go on an all-day Lake Superior charter out of Duluth for lake trout. The last time we made the Superior trip I was thirty and Dad was fifty-seven. He hooked a good-size laker that afternoon, fifteen pounds almost, but he was too weak from his chemo treatments to bring it all the way in. When he handed me the rod to finish bringing the fish up to the net, I think we both knew it was our last trip together. Doris and Charlie and I spread his ashes on White Deer the following spring.

I don't go over to Superior these days, and I gave up ice fishing on White Deer after Charlie went off to college. It hurts to say it, but I doubt Charlie misses fishing with me the way I missed fishing with Dad. I did put the shack out on the ice the winter after Charlie left home, but the first time I went out alone the circle of black water around my bobber looked like a porthole into the Big Dark, the place where Dad has already gone, and where I will go soon enough.

In summer though, White Deer is still my home. It's not only my favorite place on the planet, I also know it better than I know any other bit of geography. Just by eyeballing a couple of points on the shoreline, I can triangulate my position to within about ten yards and tell you within a foot how much water there is under my boat. I've been out there in every season and during every kind of weather— rain, sleet, wind, snow, sun, fog. I've used every type of live bait you can name—minnows, worms, frogs, leeches, night crawlers, plus artificial versions of all of them—spoons, jigs, rigs and plugs, including surface baits, sinking baits and bottom bumping baits. I know there are fishermen who are more skillful than I am but, if you're talking White Deer, I doubt you could find anyone who could guide your fishing trip as well as I could. Though, of course, I wouldn't do it. Albino Point, on the west side of the lake, is on the cover of our "Welcome to Larkin County Woods and Waters" brochure. The photographer caught a brown doe and her albino fawn standing on the point in a morning mist. It's a great photo. The mother and baby are framed by the few pines that managed to find root between cracks in the granite, and the mist gives the scene a timeless feel. It's also a lucky photo. I've fished White Deer at least a thousand times over the last half century, and I've seen deer on the point on many occasions, but I've seen albinos there less than a handful of times. The albino gene has been in the area for a long time—the local Ojibwe population includes a White Deer Clan of about fifteen families who can trace their history at least as far back as the eighteenth century. We sometimes go a year or two without seeing any albinos, but the trait is carried by enough of the local herd that we aren't often without one or two of them. I use them as examples in the genetics segment of my biology classes—how two brown deer, each carrying a recessive gene for albinism, can produce a white fawn. The albinos aren't protected by law like they are over in Wisconsin, but most hunters have enough self-restraint not to "harvest" them. There is a financial temptation though—a white buck with an eight-point rack can supposedly be worth ten grand as a mounted trophy—maybe more if the rack is exceptional.

After I came in off the lake that night, I stopped in for a couple at the VFW just to make sure Doris would be in bed when I got home. I talked fishing with a guy I've known for a long time, but it was almost impossible for me to focus on his words. Like the launch skipper, he asked if I was feeling okay.

I wanted to tell him I didn't think I'd ever feel okay again.

CHAPTER 3, ED

CONFRONTATION

Saturday morning, there was no way to avoid her. It was the day we scheduled to finish up our spring planting, or at least everything except Doris's tomatoes. We're only 150 miles north of the Twin Cities, but our growing season is about three weeks shorter up here. We can get hit with a frost well into June, and Doris doesn't like to take chances with tomatoes. She leaves the seedlings in our greenhouse for as long as possible—though calling it a greenhouse is kind of a stretch. It's basically just a plastic wrap lean-to slouched against the south side of our tool shed. It was supposed to be temporary, and if we saw it on someone else's property we'd say it was an eyesore, but it's been there so long it just doesn't register that way with us. I guess that given enough time we stop seeing a lot of things.

Gardening helps keep my natural pessimism under control. Doris says I was bit by the Curmudgeon Fairy when I was in my twenties, but I think I was born that way and that falling in love with her just jolted me out of it for our first couple years together.

The tag line under my grim graduation photo in the high school yearbook reads, "A Quiet Strength," but when I look at the picture it seems like "An Awareness of Doom" would be more appropriate. I always come across that way in photos. In my sophomore yearbook there's a group shot with the wrestling team. Except for our heavy-weight, I'm the tallest kid in the photo. I was already six feet, the height I am today, but I hadn't filled out yet. I competed at 145 that year and I looked to be built more for basketball than for wrestling. The doom look was already present, though—the same "thousand-yard stare" as in the senior yearbook photo. Doris always says black-and-white photos hide my best feature. When she really likes me, she calls me "Blue Eyes." She says that's what first attracted her.

Growing things helps me keep doom at bay and hang on to the illusion that life has reliable sequences, that things might end well. If I plant something and take care of it, I can hope it will ripen to look like the image in the seed catalog. When my baby sister died, I lost confidence about life moving along that way. Sarah was supposed to grow from a baby into a girl, then become a mother and a grand-mother. She didn't get anywhere close. Now, more than half a century later, things were still moving out of sequence—friends were disap-pearing or dying out of turn, and Doris and Chip had suddenly come on stage as characters I didn't recognize. Life was sprawling all over, and I didn't have a trellis to train it to. I was lost.

Doris didn't grow up with gardening. Her parent's backyard, in an upscale Minneapolis suburb, was landscaped with shrubs and flowers, a gazebo, and a peeing cherub fountain, all tended weekly by a yard service. But after we were married, Doris started gardening with me, and of course she threw herself all in, like she does with every-thing. I built her a couple of raised beds. I said they would make it easier on her back, but really it was to keep her from taking over completely. The raised beds are nothing fancy, just rectangles of two-by-twelve boards anchored at the corners with four-by-four cedar posts. Those few inches of added height also discourage rabbits. You'd think it would be nothing for a rabbit to hop up the extra distance, but they almost never do. It would be something different from what they know.

Because we grow different things, we can work in the garden together without much need of conversation. She does the greens, herbs, and tomatoes. Doris is tomato crazy. She studies seed catalogs all winter, then sends away for least half a dozen varieties, all the way from acidic little heirlooms to new hybrids that get as big as muskmelons.

I have to admit that I appreciate tomatoes a lot more than I used to. I do the rest of the vegetables, mostly ones where the home-grown versions are a lot tastier than store bought—pole beans, edible pod peas and, especially, potatoes. Some people put in foolish space wasters like melons and corn, but half the years, the season up here is too short for melons to ripen, and these days you can buy hybrid corn in the store that stays sweet for days after it's picked, not just for a few hours like the varieties we had fifty years ago. Besides, what's the point in growing it yourself if it doesn't taste any better? With enough work, a guy could probably cobble up a bad pair of shoes for himself too, but buying comfortable ones from a shoe store makes more sense.

In what little conversation we had in the garden that morning, Doris used the high-pitched, chirpy voice she takes on when she's pretending something isn't eating away inside her. When our son,

Charlie, was six he had a seizure, and the doctors found a growth on his brain. It turned out to be a benign meningioma. After it was removed, he was fine, but I remember Doris reassuring him before surgery, using that same fake voice to tell him everything was going to be okay. It didn't fool Charlie. He asked her—if everything was going to be okay, why she was so scared?

After we finished the planting, Doris made my favorite weekend lunch, popovers and bacon—thick chewy bacon, not like the paper thin, overdone stuff that so many people serve. Bacon should not crumble in your mouth like a potato chip. We were still at the kitchen table, finishing up our coffee, when Doris mentioned that I'd been a little quiet that morning. Was I feeling okay? I must have been waiting for an invitation. I unloaded the whole story about coming home early from fishing and seeing her with Chip. I couldn't look at her as I talked.

After I finished, she was quiet for what seemed like forever. Then she put her head down on the table and cried harder than I ever remember. I had to reach over and slide the butter dish out from under her hair.

She said she was sorry, that it was the only time, and that whatever else I thought she wanted me to know it was all her fault.

"I started it," she said. "I know he wanted to run away," she said.

"I'm sure that would have been painful for him, what with you having such a tight grip on his johnson," I said. It was mean, but I couldn't help myself.

"I needed someone to want me, Ed, to look at me and want me.

19

It's been a long time since you did."

She cried some more and said some more about how horrible she felt, and that I might not believe her but that it had only happened that one time—with anyone, ever.

I did believe that.

I don't think we've ever lied to each other about big stuff, but I didn't say anything. And she said again that no matter what, I should not blame Chip.

"It was my fault," she said, "I was the one who pushed it."

I told her that wasn't hard to believe—I said the position they were in squared pretty well with her being in charge, and that she seemed to be enjoying herself a lot. I could see her imagining what the scene had looked like to me standing in the hall, and I could tell that it added to her misery and humiliation. I was small enough to relish her pain. She said she wished she were dead, and she sounded like she meant it. Then she asked did I want a divorce?

Divorce? The question upset me as much as her infidelity.

"Yes," I said, "That's it, Doris. I want a fucking divorce. I've decided on a new start. I'm moving to Delaware. I understand there's a lot of opportunity there. A guy like me can write his own ticket, I hear. I'm thinking of going to medical school, or opening a department store. Maybe both. And of course I'll be starting a new family. I don't think sixty-two is too old for any of those things, do you, Doris? And just think, you won't have to fuck my friends in the guest room anymore—you can just bring them into our fucking bed and fuck them there."

I was pretty much screaming at her and, despite her misery, she had sense enough to reach behind her and push the back door closed. Probably spoiled the entertainment for everyone on the block. It's a quiet neighborhood.

I said I was going over to check on Uncle Pete, and then going fishing. I told her I'd be home late, if ever. She was still sobbing at the table when I went out the back door and slammed it so hard the bottom pane broke.

Like an idiot, I stuck my head back in and told her I'd fix it on Sunday if the hardware store had the glass in stock. That obviously revealed my hint about not returning as the limp threat it was. *Jesus*, I wasn't just an inadequate husband, I couldn't even make a potent bluff.

As I drove to Pete's the word "divorce" rolled around inside my head like a bowling ball. Was Chip so exciting that she'd already decided to dump me? I'd given her an opportunity to minimize my pain when I said it had looked like she was enjoying herself. She could have had the decency to say something like "It was no fun at all, Ed, not even close to how it is with you."

But she didn't.

CHAPTER 4, ED

MY UNCLE PETE

Pete was my dad's adopted brother, taken in by my grandparents when he was ten. I don't know much about his life before then, but it probably wasn't good. Dad said that Pete was an angry kid when he first came into family, always ready to fight, and that he was a terror with his fists. He was three years older than Dad, but they both en-listed in the Army on the same day, just after Pearl Harbor, and they were both in for the duration of the war. Dad never saw combat, but Pete's unit fought in North Africa, then became part of the first wave to hit Omaha Beach on D Day. Pete never even got into the surf that morning. As soon as the bow gate of the Higgins boat dropped, German machine gun bullets ripped through Pete and half his landing buddies. Pete was hit in the leg and the stomach. He was lucky the boat's pilot was able to back out and get to a hospital ship. Pete found out later that many of the guys who did get into the water joined the ones you see in old newsreels, washing up and back on the sand. He spent almost a year in a veteran's hospital, getting his insides put back in working order and learning to use his prosthetic leg. The Army gave him a Purple Heart and a 100 percent disability rating.

When he finally returned to Big Pine, Pete persuaded Otto Hamer to sell him the forty acres that butts up against Albino Point on White Deer Lake. Unlike other pulpwood operators, who bought just the rights to the timber, Otto bought the land as well, and he didn't usually sell it after he cut it over. It was only because Otto was a combat veteran himself that he made an exception for Pete. The sale was made with the understanding that Pete wouldn't build any structure that was visible from the lake or from Otto's house on the hill across the lake. Pete put up a three-room place, along with a machining and welding shop about the same size, and went back to repairing equipment, just like he'd done before the war. He never married, and I'd never known him to have a girlfriend. My dad said the war injuries left Pete disabled in that department.

Three or four times a year, Pete drove down to the Twin Cities for a few days or a week. He visited the VA Medical Center for checkups and to have his prosthetic leg serviced. A couple times they replaced it with a newer model. He said he spent the rest of his visits with guys he'd known in the Army, though to my knowledge none of them ever came up to see him in Big Pine. Beyond those trips, his social life all those years revolved around the Big Pine VFW and Sunday dinners at my parent's house, then dinners with me and Doris after Mom and Dad were both gone.

Some guys who live alone for a long time lose interest in personal appearance and grooming. Not my uncle. He had an ironing board permanently set up in his little living room, and when he went out to the shop in the morning he was always fresh shaved and wearing creased khakis. His forward-leaning walk made me think of an axe, standing on its handle, eager to bite into the day's work. He kept the shop squared away too, all the wrenches and other tools hanging in size order and the floor swept with grease-absorbent sawdust compound every night. You might assume the orderliness was a result of his time in the Army, but my dad said Pete was always particular about things, even as a kid.

When I got to Pete's that afternoon, Doris's mention of divorce still had me staggered. Maybe the visit would let me slide back into my previous reality for a while—the one where my longtime friend hadn't harpooned my longtime wife.

Pete must have noticed I was off balance because he asked me if I was feeling alright. I said I was okay. Of course, "I'm okay" in Minnesotan is a phrase that might be used in place of, "My cancer has spread to more organs, but the docs think maybe they can slow it down a little with radiation and chemo."

Pete didn't press me for details. Northern Minnesota guys are not big on sharing feelings. We are also not huggers. I blame all this nuisance hugging and male-bonding stuff on people like the guy who wrote about men hanging around together in "drum circles"—a guy who is, by the way, from *southern* Minnesota.

I'd known Pete my entire life, and we surely loved each other, but we managed to resist getting naked and beating tom-toms together. We also never hugged, at least not since I was out of grade school. If his house burned down, or if he got a terminal diagnosis, I might put my hand on his shoulder, maybe even give it a squeeze, but full-frontal hugging would not be part of the deal. There are other ways to handle things. That afternoon for instance, after we finished not hugging, I helped him lift a trailer axle and some other heavy stuff onto his welding bench—way more useful than an embrace or a naked camp-fire dance, and no loss of Scandinavian personal boundaries. (I know you could argue that wrestling requires boundary violations, and some hug-type moves, but there the goal is to defeat the guy in personal combat.)

As we were finishing up the work, Pete mentioned that he was almost done with his two-year probation and he was going to miss his probation officer. She was a nice woman—I'd liked her back when she was one of my students. On her visits, Pete had been showing her the basics of welding, and he said she was picking it up pretty good. If he enjoyed anything more than fixing broken stuff, it was showing other people how to do it.

The details of the incident that landed Pete in the corrections system have already been spun into a local legend. Pete just hated snowmobiles—though up here we mostly call them "snow machines" or "sleds." He hated the noise, hated the tracks in the woods, just plain hated everything about them. He wouldn't do a welding job on a snow machine for any price. Of course his land was well posted with "No Snowmobiling" signs, but that hadn't stopped a couple of winter vacationers on Arctic Cats who buzzed up the hill above Albino Point and onto Pete's property one January afternoon. When they stopped and got off to relieve themselves of accumulated beer, Pete opened fire. He put one 30.06 round into the engine compartment of each machine—nice offhand shooting, given they were more than a hundred yards from his back door. It turned out to be a good thing that Pete shot both of them, not just one. His lawyer argued against an attempted murder charge by pointing out that Pete hit both machines in the same spot, which showed he wasn't aiming at the riders. His status as an eighty-two-year-old disabled combat veteran helped too—probably helped a lot. He got off with a suspended sentence and probation. Now, there's a sign at the spot where Pete's targets crossed his property line: "Snowmobiles Have Been Shot On This Property." Not a threat, just a statement of fact.

After we got his work set up that afternoon, Pete got out a couple cans of pop and we talked about a book on the Battle of Vicksburg we'd both recently read. Like me, my uncle was a Civil War buff. His old black-and-white console television, probably the last one in Larkin County, served mostly as a stand for an oversize book of Civil War campaign maps.

I've always wondered why history is such a late-life magnet for men, including many of us who daydreamed through our high school history classes. I don't know the answer, but I do know that I enjoy my hours as a volunteer at the Big Pine History Center enough that, once a month, I give up a Saturday morning on the water just to poke through archives and artifacts from the time of my great-great-grandfather. His kepi cap and a couple of letters he wrote before Gettysburg were passed down to me.

"Great-great-grandfather" usually calls up an image of a white-haired old man, but Magnus Olson died when he was only twenty-four. A cannonball took his leg off at the Battle of Gettysburg and, according to the letter from his lieutenant, he bled into eternity within a couple of minutes. He had plenty of company. The First Minnesota regiment took 82 percent casualties on the second day of the fighting, the highest rate of any unit in the war. I always wonder if Magnus saw it coming. I've read that sometimes they could see an incoming round, especially if it was slowed by skipping along the ground a few times on the way toward them. It's hard to imagine a worse instant—seeing something that's going to kill you when it hits you and simultaneously realizing you can't move out of its way fast enough.

What strikes me most is the randomness of Magnus's death. It's not likely the crew that fired the cannonball saw him. They were probably just shooting in the general direction of the enemy. Maybe if he had paused a minute to blow his nose or to take a leak, he would have been six feet to the side of the cannonball's path. Or maybe a sharpshooter would have picked him off five minutes later. Or maybe he would have lived another sixty years and become an original investor in Coca-Cola stock. Everything changes everything.

The postmortem letter from his lieutenant stated that Magnus's last request was to tell his wife and daughters that he loved them, and that he looked forward to seeing them in Heaven. Pete thought that was likely just BS to make my great-great-grandmother feel better; my uncle ranked pretty high on the cynic scale. He liked to tell religious folks that if they expected to go to Heaven he could guarantee they weren't going to be disappointed. I don't know if any of them ever caught the intended message in his statement. He begged off my fishing invitation that afternoon, saying he had "an appointment in town," which meant he was going to ride his lawnmower the two miles into the VFW post to get buzzed and watch bowling. After his

DUI, it was either the lawnmower or have someone pick him up.

After I came off the lake that night, I stopped into the VFW myself. I wanted to be sure Doris would be in bed when I got home. For the next week, we didn't see much of one another. My workday started and ended an hour before hers, which gave me time to get home and head out for evening fishing, and then to the VFW until around midnight. By the time I got home, she'd be asleep or at least pretending to be asleep. Occupying the same bed after what happened might seem strange, but there weren't any other good choices—the guest bedroom was the scene of the crime, our living room sofa was only five feet long, and if I'd taken a room at Big Pine's only motel it would have been the headline news at the Town Talk's 9:00 a.m. geezer gathering. Besides, if one of us was going into exile I felt it should be the harlot, not her cuckolded husband.

Sleeping was tricky, though. We had only a standard double at the time, which meant we practically had to hang off our own sides of the bed to avoid accidental contact. We were careful in the mornings too. If she was in the kitchen and I needed something from the fridge, I didn't just brush by her—I waited for enough clearance that there wouldn't be any chance of us touching.

CHAPTER 5, ED

THE PAIN OF THE CUCKOLD

That week after our breakfast table explosion was miserable. I spent every evening sitting in my boat, alternately mourning and raging over what I'd lost—what our marriage had lost. One impulsive act by Doris had changed everything. What gave that act so much power? It wasn't that my loss was anything measurable. As one of the guys on the pulp crew used to say, "You can't wear it out." A crude way to put it, but pretty much true. Doris's fling with Chip wasn't anything I'd ever have been aware of if I hadn't walked in on them. Chip just made use of what economists call "idle capacity," though my professor at the U used the example of schools that sit empty in the summer, not unoccupied vaginas. So if my wife's sexual usefulness and her availability to me weren't diminished by her romp with Chip during her "idle" time, why was I so upset? Why are guys always upset, sometimes to the point of murder? It sounds like a stupid question, until you try to answer it. I've thought about it a lot.

The biological explanation is pretty simple. Evolution programs us to make sure our line continues. The only way a male can be certain that his genes are successfully passed along is if his mate is 100 percent faithful. Consequently, males, whether humans or Whitetail bucks, will fight and even die to make sure anything in their mate's womb is theirs.

Females don't have the same genetic motivation, even if paternity is uncertain, females are 100 percent certain to pass along half of their own genes to their offspring. In a purely biological sense then, a man's infidelities are less important to his mate. Maybe that's why fewer women than men murder their unfaithful partners.

But there's more to it than just ensuring that our genes are passed along. If that was the only concern, men wouldn't care what our female partners did once they were beyond child-bearing age. But we do care, usually a lot. There's the pain of betrayal and loss of trust. Doris took a vow to be faithful, and now she'd broken that vow. That she had been faithful for so many years made it all the more painful and shocking for me when she became unfaithful. And of course there's humiliation, especially if it's public humiliation. That might be what makes guys, and even some women, homicidal.

I'm ashamed to admit it, but one of my early reactions was fear that other people would find out about the situation, and I'd look like a pathetic, impotent fool. Not that guys would make wiggly finger horns at me in the tavern, but I could imagine the whispers: "Hey, did you hear? Doris Olson is playing hide the weenie with Chip Brakkman. I guess Ed actually walked in on them."

That kind of thing gets around a small town fast. In my more rational moments, I was pretty sure neither Doris nor Chip was going to tell anyone about their affair, but even without the fear of public knowledge I was still left holding a pail full of male insecurity.

Doris wasn't the only person who was hard to avoid that week. Her Norwegian mount's classroom was one floor above mine, and there was the risk of bumping into him in the stairway or the parking lot. My first reaction to seeing him and Doris in bed had been numbness, but even Swedes boil over—we just simmer longer before if happens. I believed Doris when she said she'd been the initiator, but Chip could have said no. Did he think that would hurt her feelings? What about my feelings? He was my friend, and friends don't fuck friends' wives. I worked up to a fantasy of walking into his classroom and putting an arm bar on him—a wrestling hold with considerable potential for damage. I'd make the students quiet down so they could hear his elbow snap. Then I'd tell them to remember the sound if they ever found themselves thinking about screwing a friend's wife. But I just couldn't sustain it.

Deep down, I knew Doris was telling the truth when she said she was the aggressor. Chip just didn't have that kind of move in him. So instead of disjointing him, I spent the week timing my comings and goings to minimize chances of meeting him in the hall, and I stayed away from the teacher's lounge.

Then, at the end of the week, Doris lobbed a stick of dynamite across No Man's Land.

~

I'd hit the VFW, just like I had every night that week after the drama at the breakfast table, but when I got home on Friday, Doris didn't pretend to be asleep. As soon as I was in bed she said, "Do you want a divorce, Ed?"

That heavy, terrifying word again. She'd already sent me out on a spacewalk, and now she wanted to know—did I want to untether and drift off into the void alone? Forever? *Jesus,* what I wanted more than anything was to reel myself back to the ship, but I couldn't say it. Instead, I just lay there like a damn mummy.

Then she said, "Do you want to fuck me?"

She'd never, ever, used that word in bed before, and it was 220 volts, straight to my dick. When I pulled her over underneath me, it wasn't to "make love." Fucking is exactly what it was, something I was doing to her, not with her. I held her jaw with my hand to keep our mouths locked together. It wasn't kissing so much as telling her that Ed, her husband, still had exclusive rights to every part of her body. But if I was trying to punish her, it didn't quite work out that way. At first it was all me, but after a couple minutes she was into it the same angry way I was. Sometimes she orgasms when I'm in her, and I think she would have that night if I could have kept going just another couple minutes. Most of the time though, I do something afterward— or sometimes before. But when I started to slide down that night, she held me back and said I didn't need to do that.

"I haven't had a shower today," she said.

I kept moving down. She god damn well wasn't going to say I hadn't fulfilled my husbandly duties. Once I'm in place, it usually doesn't take long, and that night she pulled the pillow tight over her face within just a few minutes. She's always been gratifyingly noisy at the end. She started using the pillow when Charlie was a baby, so her she wouldn't wake him up or scare him.

Afterward, we lay quiet for a while. Then she said, "Tell me what's going on with you, Ed."

Doris the Counselor. She's probably used that phrase on kids in her office a thousand times. It worked with me. I told her I was angry at her, that I was scared, and that I loved her, all mixed together. Then I started crying. It was probably the most honest statement of feelings she'd ever heard from me—I'm usually the guy they're making fun of in the old line about "the Swedish man who loved his wife so much he almost told her."

Doris cried too and said how much she appreciated me being willing to talk. She said she loved me, and that her guilt and shame over Chip was hugely painful, but she said she also realized she'd been angry with me for a long time, and she wanted more than anything that we should work that out together.

I said I wanted that too—and I said I appreciated that at least she'd taken Chip into the guest bedroom. We kissed good night, and the middle third of the bed was no longer off limits.

~

The school year had less than a month to run. It's not an easy time to get kids focused in the classroom, and that spring wasn't an easy time for me to focus either. One solution for the kids is biology class field trips, including the annual trip to the "The Lost Forty Acres."

The Lost Forty is located about two hours north of Big Pine, and it's the last remaining stand of the virgin White Pines that once covered most of Northern Minnesota. On the bus ride up I always have the driver stop at the little creek that trickles out the south end of Lake Itasca. The kids can cross it on stepping stones and then tell people they walked across the Mississippi River without getting wet.

Up until the late nineteenth century, white pine covered the northern third of Minnesota and beyond, stretching hundreds of miles up into what are now the provinces of Ontario and Manitoba. Before Europeans arrived, there were large pine forests in the eastern US too, but the Civil War and Reconstruction ate up most of what remained of that stock and, by the late 1870s, Minnesota held the largest remaining source of good building timber in the country. Logging then became the first major driver of our state's economy and attracted our first big wave of immigrants.

To early European settlers, those trees must have seemed an inexhaustible resource. A 200-year-old, 150-foot-tall "white" yielded enough lumber to build a nineteenth century home, and Minnesota had millions and millions of those trees. "Had" is the operative word. Now the Lost Forty is all we have left, spared only because of a surveyor's error. Sometimes I wish I could give him a posthumous medal; other times I wish he hadn't left us a reminder of what we had, not much more than a hundred years ago.

When we first get up there, I have the kids just wander around for a while, and I ask them to imagine what it felt like to live there before we showed up. One of oldest human remains in Minnesota was found not far from the Lost Forty. She was a girl, about fifteen, who lived nearly 8,000 years ago—roughly 2,000 years before the Earth was created, according to the parents of about half of my students. It's likely she drowned—she was found in a dried-up lake bed, not a burial site. At the time the girl lived, Minnesota had more large lakes than it does today. Big Pine itself sits on the now-dry site of a twenty-mile-long post-glacial lake, one of the puddles left by the largest lake ever to exist, Lake Agassiz, to the north and west of us. Agassiz was formed as the glaciers retreated at the end of the last ice age, and it covered Northern Minnesota and a big chunk of Canada.

The girl's bones tell us she wasn't yet a mother, but someone valued her—she died wearing a necklace of conch shells from the Gulf Coast, a thousand miles away. It had to be a rare and prized item. How did she come to have it? How did it travel to our area? Was it a gift from a lover? I ask the kids to imagine the two of them together. Did he make her laugh? How? Funny animal imitations, maybe? Was he there to try to save her when she drowned? I do my best to get the kids to see her as a real person and to feel the world she lived in.

Sometimes I'm too successful in bringing the girl to life, and some students get emotional thinking about her disappearing down under the water. But presenting her as a real person is part of getting them to see the natural world through her eyes, so they can under-stand how much of it has been lost, and how important it is to hang on to what remains. I ask them to think what animals she saw, what she ate, how she stayed warm when it was thirty below. I have them imagine her looking up through the pines at a flight of a hundred million passenger pigeons, blocking out the sun as they passed over-head. That sounds like an impossible number, I know, but biologists have estimated there may have been flocks as large as a *billion*. Once in a while a kid, usually a boy, will point out that there must have been a blizzard of bird shit coming down. There was. I tell them that in the nineteenth century, the downtown buildings in Chicago turned white when a big flock of passenger pigeons went over the city. The idea of all that bird shit is always a big hit.

At the end of the trip we look at black-and-white photos of Larkin County in the late 1890s, twenty years after the first loggers arrived. In some photos the landscape looks like an endless cemetery of tree stumps, and the houses like mausoleums scattered in the ruins. The stumps were stubborn—The History Center has a woodcut of a man behind his horse-drawn plow, working a field dotted with them. Pulling large pine stumps was difficult, oak stumps more so. Pulling a single oak stump could take a man and a horse an entire day. For people who could afford it, dynamite became the shortcut. The Center has a copy of an early twentieth century DuPont brochure, "Farming with Dynamite." Unfortunately, there were people who also used it for fishing.

Nowadays the second- and third-growth forest makes the scenery around Big Pine look a lot less stark and brutal than it did in those old photographs taken after the clear-cutting, and there are supposedly as many deer now as there were in those early days. That's because the forest floor underneath the tall, old-growth trees didn't have much of the vegetation that provides food and cover for rabbits and rodents and deer—and also for the bobcats and coyotes and wolves who eat them. Young forest is thicker, busier territory.

If man disappeared tomorrow, it would take hundreds of years to regrow pines the size of those cut by the first loggers—trees that could be hollowed out to carry twenty or thirty members of the drowned girl's clan. But even if the trees grew back, there still wouldn't be any clouds of passenger pigeons overhead. The last survivor was Martha, named for Martha Washington. She died alone, at the Cincinnati Zoo, in 1914. Zookeepers said she always seemed nervous, which is understandable—she'd spent her early years in a cloud of millions of her own species, and she probably wondered where the hell everyone went. Between about 1880 and 1915, we clear-cut the largest stand of timber in North America and wiped out the most plentiful bird on the planet. I try to impress on the kids that it all disappeared in about one half of an average human lifetime. I want them to understand how fragile the natural world really is, and how we need to protect what we have left. What I don't tell them is that I think we're already fucked.

I do have to work at keeping my natural pessimism hidden, especially from the kids I'm supposed to inspire. My mother used to call me "E. O." which, given my nature, pretty quick became "Eeyore," after the depressed donkey in *Winnie the Pooh*. I suppose I am an Eeyore, and my poor wife has borne the brunt of it. But she's also come up with some strategies to counteract it. Early on in our marriage, Doris started calling me out on my gloomy comments about life, and eventually she came up with the Eeyore Rule. When I say something especially negative she'll say, "Okay, Eeyore, that's over the line, I'm calling it."

Then I have to give her an example of something, anything anywhere, that's getting better. It's harder and harder to come up with examples. There were easy ones at the beginning—automobile tires and TV picture quality have improved, and John Denver's "Rocky Mountain High" finally dropped off the charts, but I went through most of those gimmes a long time ago. The Rule is that I have to keep finding new positives. Not my strong suit, but that's why it's a good exercise for me. It reminds me there are sometimes positive changes. One of Doris's recent challenges got me to thinking about the ugly issue of wife beating, something that was fairly common up here, and not that long ago.

I told her that when I was a kid, there was a woman who sometimes showed up in Hansen's Grocery with a black eye and other marks on her face. I imagine there was worse under her clothing—word was that her husband used his belt on her, not uncommon back then. She didn't try to say she'd fallen, or that she ran into a door jamb. She knew that everyone knew. She'd buy her groceries without saying anything to anyone, without making eye contact, then head home to the guy. The attitude of most people in those days was that if a woman survived a beating without hospitalization, then marital violence was "none of our business."

Now it is "our business." Now cops arrest the guys, even if the wife doesn't want to press charges. Now there's a battered women's shelter up in Big Rapids. That's definitely better, and Doris liked the example.

CHAPTER 6, ED

RECOVERING

Our Friday night reconnection didn't magically erase everything. I still had moments of feeling angry and betrayed, but I also felt more connected to her than I had in a long time. In our emotional confrontation after her fling with Chip, Doris had accused me of not wanting her sexually. My first impulse was to tell her that wasn't true, and that of course I still wanted her. But that would have been a lie. The truth is the truth, no matter how hard it might be. Now, I really did want her. We had sex four more times in the next two weeks, about matching our total for the previous year. And for the first time in a long while, I didn't need a fantasy and a couple of beers to get me going. When we had sex, I was having sex with Doris, my wife.

What changed? A cynic could say my revived passion was just a cover for my insecurity, my need to regain alpha status and take back harem rights over my one-woman harem. I'm sure those possibilities crossed Doris's mind too—she's smarter than I am to begin with, plus she has a master's degree in psychology. No doubt my insecurity and possessiveness were part of it, but they weren't the whole of it. Our canoe had gone over a Niagara-size falls, and all the emotional cargo we'd stowed away over the decades was churning around down in the plunge pool along with her infidelity. Both of us were trying to figure out what to try to hang on to, and what to let float away downstream.

I'd been forced to see Doris as someone other than the woman I thought I knew. Forced for sure—nothing about the start of our adventure was voluntary on my part. But I think she was forced to look at me in a new way too. Everything was up for review and revision. Over the next weeks I could sometimes tell she was watching me while I read the paper or sat in front of the TV. I did the same to her, trying to figure out who she was now, what she was thinking, and what she wanted. It was unsettling as hell, but at least we were alive to each other again. For a long time we'd been seeing each other more as cardboard cutouts than as complete human beings. Now I was more often aware that I really did love her. I hoped she felt the same way about me.

~

The Chip crisis was the second time in my life that a shock forced me to reinterpret everything I thought I'd known. The first time was when my dad sucker punched me, just a few weeks after he died. I found the bundle of letters in the bottom compartment of an old tackle box full of beat-up wooden fishing plugs. The plugs were paint chipped from fish strikes, and the attached treble hooks were rusted from freezing and thawing in our unheated garage. The rust had run off onto the stationary, making the letters look older than they were. In fact, one letter made reference to my dad's leukemia— which meant he received it in the last two years of his life. The writer told him how much she wanted to be able to be with him during his illness.

The letters spanned nearly twenty years. One of the earliest made a sympathetic reference to my Navy enlistment in the spring of my senior year of high school. The writer told Dad she knew he would miss me, but that he should take comfort that I would probably not be going to a war zone. In the same letter she said how much she was looking forward to being together with him at the upcoming Minnesota Education Association conference in St Paul. *Jesus*, I remembered his MEA trips. Now I knew that he spent those nights away from home in a hotel bed with a woman who wasn't my mom. My first reaction was that the woman was a crazy person, writing about relationship that existed only in her mind. That had to be it—otherwise Dad was someone I'd never really known, and my memories of him and my mom were no more real than the Cleaver family on television.

Of course the woman wasn't crazy, and it wasn't hard to figure out her identity. She's in her late eighties now, long retired from her teaching job in Big Rapids. I haven't seen her in many years but the Big Rapids phone book still has a listing for her. After I found the letters, I spent years trying to weave their long affair into our family history in a way that let me believe that my dad had still loved my mom, despite his secret life. I'd never told Doris about the letters, but during our reconnection after Chip I did tell her. It seemed like the right time.

Discovering my dad's long affair was the first time it really hit me that, for most of us, the real love lives of our parents, our grand-parents, and everyone who came before them go unmentioned in our family histories. We might get a sanitized version, but nothing like the exciting, confusing, messy mix that was more likely the reality.

Parents tell their children how they *should* lead the sexual parts of our lives, but not how they led theirs. Your mom might tell you that her first date with your dad was at the Steamboat Days dance, but she's unlikely to tell you they first went all the way on New Year's Eve—or that he wasn't her first lover. Fathers aren't any more forthcoming. I heard Dad describe his first car many times, right down to the upholstery and the hood ornament. I know all the details of his first deer, including the weather conditions, the time of day, and how much it weighed dressed out. But he never told me about the first time he got laid, an event that was surely as important to him at the time, and as clear in his memory, as his first car or his first buck deer. I don't even know if my mom was the first, but whoever she was, and however Dad felt about her, is lost forever. How did he and my mom decide they were the "ones" for each other? Did they really choose each other, or were they just carried along into marriage by biology and custom? I'll never know.

Looking even two generations back, the chances of getting any real relationship history, especially sexual relationship history, are pretty much zero. Try to imagine your white-haired grandma telling you that, while your grandfather was at his bachelor party, she had a final hot tangle with two guys from the carnival. Maybe she told her best friend about it, maybe not. Either way, it would have been a memorable event in her personal history—just not one that would ever be handed down to her children or grandchildren. Or what if she and Gramps were involved in an earlier version of Big Pine Book and Garden? How would we ever know?

The closest any of my grandparents came to acknowledging that sex existed at all was my one grandmother's fondness for naughty stories. For her generation, traveling salesmen were a common subject, and Grandma's favorite was about a traveling tie salesman who has bronchitis. He knocks on a door, and when a woman opens it, he says in his hoarse voice, "Is your husband home?" The woman whispers back, "No, come on in."

Grandma would start laughing even before she got to the punch line. I don't remember that my grandfather thought she was all that funny. Maybe it was a touchy subject.

If Dad had destroyed the letters before he died, I wouldn't have known one of the most important stories of his life—though at the time it wasn't a story I wanted to hear. I doubt that our son, Charlie, would welcome hearing the full story of his parents' love lives either, but that shouldn't mean we should scrub them from history. Our children, and maybe even our grandchildren, might be uncomfortable with a real account, but I bet our great-grandchildren will be fascinated. They might even learn something useful. I realized that I wanted someone, sometime in the future, to know about our Book and Garden adventure, and that the most important thing we can pass down is the truth about our own lives.

~

My last school responsibility that spring was Success Day, an annual event hosted by the high school Entrepreneur's Club. Success

Day always features a Big Pine graduate who comes back to town to talk about his own wonderfulness and how he (only one female up until then) succeeded, despite the unspoken handicap of growing up in Big Pine and attending Larkin County schools. My own entrepreneurial experience consisted of running an honor system worm and night crawler stand when I was a kid; but when the club's faculty adviser, our Business teacher, went down with a heart attack while shoveling wet March snow, the principal volunteered me to fill in for the rest of the school year.

Success Day hasn't always been a success. In fact, it has some ragged history. A few years back, our featured speaker was the creator of a multilevel cosmetics marketing scheme. I remembered him as a fifteen-year-old con artist in my biology class, and Success Day proved he hadn't changed a bit. For a week after his talk, he conducted nightly seminars offering "Master Dealerships" to Big Pine-ites willing to stock three thousand bucks worth of dimple putty and such. The principal's wife bought a Master Dealership. Things did not go well. The Minnesota Attorney General shut down Mr. Success less than six months after his appearance on our school stage. I don't know if our principal and his wife recovered anything in the subsequent litigation—it wasn't something anyone was brave enough to ask him about—but since then, the district has been a little more careful about allowing speakers to offer financial opportunities to our residents.

The spring of Chip's and Doris's adventure, it was my shitty bad luck that our speaker for Success Day was to be an even worse scoundrel than the cosmetics peddler; I would be welcoming Joseph

Otto Hamer, Attorney at Law, a.k.a. Joey Hamer—the worst human being I have ever known.

CHAPTER 7, ED

THE HOT WATER SURPRISE

Two weeks after Doris and I had our midnight reconciliation, Maddie Keller was our Sunday dinner guest, a regular occurrence after Stan died. Beyond our relationship with Maddie and Stan as a couple, Doris and Maddie were best friends, and Stan and I had been almost as close. The Kellers bought the Town Talk Cafe the year before I returned to Big Pine as a teacher. Under the old ownership, cuisine quality had peaked at "okay" sometime in the past, and it was well below that high-water mark by the time Stan and Maddie took over. Almost right away we all knew that Big Pine finally had a good place to eat. Stan wasn't in the restaurant business just to make money; he loved to prepare good food, and he loved introducing people to new good food.

Maddie came from what she called a "tuna fish casserole family" (I happen to *like* tuna fish casserole—especially with a potato chip crust), but after she met Stan in college she became a food fanatic herself. She also developed into a helluva cook in her own right. Stan said she was better than he was, but Maddie also liked the front-end work—waiting table and the back-and-forth with customers—so Stan did most of the cooking. Any time the two of them traveled, they looked for new dishes, then worked on reproducing and modifying them in Big Pine. I'm obviously partial, but I don't think there are many small-town restaurant owners anywhere as open to new ideas as Stan and Maddie were.

Kellers Town Talk was likely the only restaurant in the country that served both lutefisk and genuine kosher corn beef sandwiches, though not on the same days. Lutefisk was offered only on December Wednesdays. Despite my Swedish heritage, I admit that I hate lutefisk. I think most people hate lutefisk. It's just one of those nasty traditions, like self-flagellation or circumcision, that people think are necessary to maintaining their ethnic identity. Lutefisk starts out as perfectly good codfish, then ends up as something that has to be soaked in lye for six days before you eat it. And when you cook it, it doesn't turn flaky like other fish; it turns into fish Jell-O—and believe it or not, that's the desired result.

Stan wasn't a lutefisk fan, but he felt he should keep up the holiday tradition. In private he said the best cooking method was to place the lutefisk fillets between two pine boards and grill everything until the boards are charred black. Then, he said, you toss the lutefisk and eat the boards. He was evenhanded though—he said gefilte fish was almost as disgusting.

The corn beef sandwiches were an entirely different deal. On Fridays, Stan had the corn beef and the rye sent up by Greyhound from a friend's deli in the Cities. He loved it when vacationers from Minneapolis or Chicago would see Kosher Corn Beef Sandwich on the menu and ask if it could possibly be the real thing.

"Try one, then you tell me," Stan would say. He served the sandwich with a dill pickle that made your eyes water. It took a while for native Big Pine-ites to adjust their minds to the notion of a seven-dollar sandwich, but eventually third- and fourth-generation Scandinavians were calling in midweek to reserve one for Friday night. The corn beef usually ran out by Saturday lunch.

Besides being a popular menu item, the corn beef was Stan's nod to his Jewish heritage. A hundred years ago, there was a sizable Jewish population on the Iron Range. Logging drew the earliest immigrants, but loggers were like locusts, forced to keep moving as they ate up the forests in front of them. Miners were the ants who stayed in one place, raising families that needed to be schooled and doctored and provisioned. Those miners' needs were what drew Jewish immigrants to our area. Some were doctors and dentists and other professionals, but most were merchants, including Stan's great-grandfather. By the 1920s, Keller Mercantile was just one of an entire block of Jewish owned businesses in Hibbing, and there were more than a thousand Jews spread among four Iron Range congregations. That was the peak. Stan's great-grandfather was orthodox, but by the time Stan was growing up his family was almost completely secular. He said the only times he was very aware of being Jewish were when other kids teased him about it. The last synagogue closed in the 1980s when it no longer had a *minyan*, the ten adult men necessary for an Orthodox congregation. Most of the businesses are also gone now, and many of the children and grandchildren of the early Jewish merchants have migrated down to the Twin Cities and other urban centers.

Maddie and Stan operated the restaurant for almost thirty years, right up until Stan let us all down by dying too young. Maddie said she knew right away she didn't want to run the place by herself.

Less than a year after Stan died she sold to a young couple from Minneapolis. Part of the sale agreement was that Maddie would stay on half-time for the first year to make sure the transition was smooth. It worked out. Big Pine still has a good restaurant.

No one expected Maddie to stay single if she didn't want to. In addition to being warm and funny, she still looked good. She wore almost the same bob haircut she had in high school and college, the difference being that she's gone salt and pepper now. I like that look. It reminds me of Billy Wiederholt's mom, the star of some of my earliest erotic fantasies. Maddie's a little plumper than she was at twenty, but she still has whatever it is that guys respond to—including a nice round butt. Right up to her last waitressing days, an occasional visiting hunter would give it a pat. Anytime Stan saw it happen, he came boiling out of the kitchen and told the guy that the waitress's ass was not on the menu.

After dinner that Sunday afternoon, Maddie went upstairs to use the bathroom. She called down after a minute to say the hot water faucet was stuck. Doris said I should go up and see what the problem was, but when I got upstairs Maddie was standing in our bedroom, not the bathroom. The next thing I heard was Doris calling up to us, saying she remembered she had some shopping to do and that she'd be gone for a couple hours. I was going to tell her it was rude to leave when we had company, but the front door clicked shut before I could get it out.

Maddie smiled at me, then reached out and hooked a finger into one of my belt loops and pulled me toward her. When she started unbuttoning my shirt, I must have looked like a cornered squirrel. Maddie said not to panic, I should just relax, that she and Doris had worked it out together.

Later, Maddie told me she knew the story about me coming home early from fishing. She said Doris told her how much she appreciated the way I'd been trying to work through the crisis. Maddie wasn't very clear about who first suggested the ambush, but she said she told Doris that she'd always found me kind of appealing and that she missed the physical side of things quite a lot. She'd also pointed out that I would be only the third man she'd ever been in bed with. Doris already knew that of course, but it was a detail that appealed to her. And I guess that was it.

Before she left, Maddie said how much she enjoyed our time together.

"All-time top three?" I asked her.

"Absolutely" she said. And then she said she hoped things might work out so this wouldn't be the only time.

I said I hoped so too. In fact, I was pretty much ready for the next time that minute.

Maddie was gone by the time Doris walked in, carrying bags of groceries from the Red Owl in Hibbing.

"Were you two able to entertain yourselves without me?'

"We did fine," I said.

"There are more groceries in the car," she said.

That night in bed, Doris and I started to talk about all that had

C. T. Messing

happened in the past few weeks. We didn't get very far into it before Doris said she could still catch the scent of Maddie's hairspray on the pillow. She said it was a little bit exciting to know what had happened there a few hours earlier. That's when I finally confessed that, looking back, the scene with her and Chip had an erotic element for me.

"Really?" she said. "Oh my goodness."

When she slipped off her nightgown there wasn't much doubt that the world we'd lived in for so long had slipped away as well.

~

That Sunday afternoon wasn't the first time Maddie and Doris knocked me off balance. A few years earlier I was in my pickup when I heard on the radio that the woman who used a butcher knife to harvest her abusive husband's penis was found not guilty.

When I got home Doris and Maddie were sitting at our kitchen table, having coffee, and I relayed the news about the verdict.

Maddie slammed her hand down on the table so hard the cups jumped, Doris punched her fist in the air, Black Panther style, and they both shouted, "YESSSSS!"

Made a guy want to start sleeping on his stomach.

Their raw celebration reminded me of a *National Geographic* article I read that was written by a woman anthropologist who'd spent decades studying a group of Polynesian islanders. She photographed the group, first as young people, then again twenty years later. She pointed out that in the young group photos the faces of the men look fierce and aggressive, while the women's are soft and diffused.

In photos of the same group, twenty years later, the situation is

51

reversed—the men's expressions look softer and the women's fiercer. I'd seen some of that transition in Doris. The first year we gardened together, before I built the raised beds, she found a nest of baby rabbits under the hay mulch around one of her tomato plants. For the next ten days she didn't water that plant for fear of getting the babies wet.

Nowadays she might or might not evict them, but I know her tomatoes would get watered, drenched baby bunnies notwithstanding. It's not that she's become hard exactly, but she looks at life and people a little differently than she did when we first met. She'd probably say she's more of a "realist" than she was at twenty.

~

Two evenings after Doris and Maddie sprung my Sunday surprise, Doris and I had the conversation that probably marks the real beginning of The Big Pine Book and Garden Club. That night after supper, Doris told me Maddie was all for continuing the adventure, and they both wanted to know how I felt about that possibility.

When I didn't answer right away, Doris said she had no problem sharing me with her best friend once in a while—no matter "what else" we might decide on.

Of course, "what else" stood for Chip's participation. It also implied the answer to a question I hadn't been brave enough to ask— did she want to continue with Chip? She seemed to be telling me she did.

"I guess you must have had a good time with him," I said.

Doris tries hard not to hurt people, but she also tells the truth when someone asks.

"I won't lie to you, Ed. It was exciting. It was new, and that was exciting all by itself. How could it not be, after thirty-five years? You can't tell me Maddie didn't have the same effect on you. But most of all it was exciting because he was really turned on by me, by my body. I haven't moved you that way for a long time."

"You do now," I said.

"I know that, Ed, and you're a good lover when you're into it. Since everything blew up, sex with you has been wonderful—the best we've had in a long time. I do love you, and I'm happy to go back to just you and me for the rest of our lives, if that's what you want. Of course Maddie will be disappointed, but wherever we go from here is your decision."

Doris's psychological genius at its finest—she acknowledged enjoying sex with another man, but she did it in a way that protected my fragile ego. And the kicker about Maddie's potential disappointment was brilliant. I'd been reliving Sunday afternoon to the point I'd gotten daydream erections while I was monitoring study halls. I wasn't exactly a tough sell, especially after Doris had defused at least some of my anxiety about competing for stud ratings.

I told her I'd been thinking about it a lot. In the first days after her infidelity I saw it as a wound to our marriage, a thing that needed healing. But I also said I'd come around to realizing it might have been the price of coming alive to each other again. I told her I was open to taking at least take a few more trial steps in a new direction.

Doris started laughing, and I deserved it. "All in the name of science, right, Dr Kinsey? You just can't wait to get back in bed with Maddie again, can you? Transparency, thy name is Ed Olson."

"How do you plan to bring Chip in?" I asked. "And are you sure he'll want to be in?"

"Trust me," Doris said, "he'll want to be in."

That confidence was something new. After a lifetime of self-doubt, she was finally seeing herself as hot. She always was but, thanks to her horror of a mother, she'd just never believed it when she was young. Now, at fifty-eight, she finally did. And she was right—I still saw guys sizing her up in that way where you know they're speculating on what it would be like to bang her—not twenty-year-olds maybe, but for sure guys my age. Now she was sizing them up too.

Life was inside out—in less than a month we'd dumped any moral notions about marital sexual exclusiveness and set off on a path we couldn't have imagined just a few weeks earlier. Or at least I couldn't have imagined it.

I was sitting on the sofa with her when she called Chip to invite him to dinner. I couldn't hear his end of the conversation, but I could tell he was trying to wiggle out of it. Doris told him she knew he felt bad about what happened, but that it was her fault and what was he going to do? Avoid us forever? She told him Maddie would be there too, that everything would be fine, and she wasn't taking no for an answer.

Chip caved, and they set a night.

CHAPTER 8, ED

MY HISTORY

No one who knew me in my youth would have figured me for a future libertine. If anything, I was even less sexually accomplished than most of my classmates. Like most high school boys in those more innocent days my sex life was exclusively solitary. Many boys used girly magazines or *National Geographic* for inspiration and, if those weren't available, every household had a Sears catalog. The Sears people did their best to desexualize the young lady models, but how do you show them in bras and panties without calling attention to what's being covered up? Unlike most of my friends, though, I didn't use pictures for inspiration. My fantasies were always about girls or women I knew, and Billy Wiederholt's mom was right at the top of my list. I wasn't the only one of Billy's friends who thought she was sexy; guys would say right to Billy's face that he had the best-looking mom around. You could tell he didn't like it, which was understandable. Who wants to know that his mother is the star of some other kid's jerk-off fantasies?

Unfortunately for Billy, Mrs. W was undeniably hot. If there were ten women shopping in Hansen's Grocery, every man in the store would manage to think of something he needed in the aisle Billy's mom was browsing. Mrs. Wiederholt was in her late thirties then, but already she had salt-and-pepper gray hair, a look that has turned me on ever since.

In summer she favored denim short shorts and a blouse with the ends tied just above her waist, leaving an inviting little swath of belly flesh showing. One of my favorite fantasies involved a plague that wiped out much of humanity, with a disproportionate number of male casualties—Mr. Wiederholt and Billy included. After the disaster, Billy's mom and I are assigned to help with re-population. It starts with me untying the ends of her summer blouse, and concludes with her tearfully saying she knows she'll have to share me with the other female survivors, all of whom also happened to be hot. That's the best thing about solitary sex—you get to have it with whoever you want.

Along with Mrs. Wiederholt, May Hamer guest-starred on my bedroom ceiling more than a few times, but I always figured she was way too cool to be interested in me in real life. May had been the "it" girl for my cohort ever since we were in grade school, though by her last year of high school she mostly dated older guys. She was sometimes referred to as "easy," but you knew that any guy who described her that way had never gotten to first base with her. For one thing, you didn't choose May—she chose you. Big difference. You could be voted Best Looking, and be captain of the football team, but if May Hamer decided you were a wrong number, you were going nowhere. I think most of us respected that in her.

May's cool was hard to exaggerate. In our junior year, we rode the same school bus along with sleepy-eyed Willis Niemi, an otherwise low-energy kid who had one remarkable super power. It's no secret that the amount of sexual energy residing in the loins of any sixteen-year-old boy is substantial, but Willis was in a class by himself.

I don't remember him as being anything noteworthy in the locker room, but he had an amazing talent he would sometimes entertain us with on the bus. He'd put a couple of text books in his lap—heavy ones, like American History or Biology. He'd close his eyes for a minute, looking like he was in a trance, then say, "Watch this," and the books would rise and fall at least an inch, two or three times. It was a stunning demonstration of phallic power. Willis said just the vibration of the bus was usually enough to give him a hard on, but that it was even easier if he thought about the new art teacher. One afternoon he did the trick while May Hamer was in the seat across from us. May didn't get all squeally or pretend she didn't see it, the way some of the other girls did.

"Very impressive, Willis," she said, "too bad you're still a dork."

Like I said, May was cool. Seamlessly cool.

The last time I saw Willis was at our thirty-year class reunion. I wanted to ask him if he remembered the textbook trick, and if he thought he could still do it, but his wife was next to him every time we were together and I didn't think I should bring it up.

My non-solo high school sexual experiences were minimal. I did have a girlfriend for most of my junior year. We went to school dances and movies and spent a fair amount of time making out in my '51 Chevy. She did like making out, but that was as far as she'd go.

Another problem was that her folks liked me. They'd probably figured out, correctly, that I was too lacking in seduction skills to be a threat to their daughter. They were always inviting me to join them in wholesome family activities. Unfortunately, one of the wholesome activities was group singing. The first time they got out a songbook I wanted to die. Singing in front of people is my phobia. I don't sing, I can't sing, and by that I mean I really, truly cannot carry a tune. I would rather have lowered my virgin member into a blender than sing in front of an audience. I remember the girl's parents saying things like, "Oh sure, you can sing, you don't have to be good, just open your mouth and let it come." But they could have promised me their daughter would start putting out for real, and even that wouldn't have got me singing.

My senior year saw the arrival of the only girl in our class who would rival May Hamer for top spot in the Ceiling Movie category: Inge, our new Swedish exchange student. She was blonde, like May, but her appeal was more the innocent milkmaid variety; May came across like experienced Kitty from *Gunsmoke*. Inge's looks alone were enough to stir up any guy, but I'd read an article in *Playboy* that made the idea of a dating her even more exciting. According to the writer, some Swedish parents allowed teenage couples to sleep together on overnight visits—at home, *with parents in the house!* It took about a nanosecond for my seventeen-year-old brain to transmit the information to my groin. Not that I could imagine my mom saying, "Have fun," as Inge and I headed off to my room, but just the fact that somewhere, some parents, maybe even Inge's parents, were okay with it was an incredibly erotic thought.

Naturally there was a lot of competition for Inge's attention. Most of my male classmates were also figuring angles for getting close to her. I began my own campaign by getting a couple of library books on Sweden and memorizing a few facts that I thought I might be able to drop into conversation. In retrospect it would probably have been tricky to bring up Gustav the III's Russian War or 1960 Swedish Herring Production numbers in a casual chat, but I was willing to try. The problem was creating a one-on-one opportunity where I could make her aware of what a cool guy I was.

Then, when I finally got my chance, I literally blew it.

My opening came when I managed to position myself immed-iately behind Inge in the cafeteria lunch line and then successfully trail her to a table. When I asked if I could join her, she said, "Why not?"—a clear indication she was hot for me. She did most of the talking as we ate, and every time she said anything remotely interest-ing or funny I responded with knowing nods and sophisticated nose laughs. Unfortunately, one of the laughs launched a moist booger out of my sophisticated nose. It came to an abrupt, sticky stop in the middle of the Formica table surface. It was probably an ordinary, unremarkable booger, but I recall it as being roughly the size of a cantaloupe. That was when I first realized that arrows streaming out of people's eyes, the ones you see in comic books, are a real life phenomenon. I shot my hand out in a lightning swipe to clear the disgusting thing off the table, but all I managed to do was transform it into a gummy smear. I honestly have no memory of the rest of my lunch with Inge. PTSD, probably.

Later that year, I did go on a few dates and touched a bare female breast for the first time, though it wasn't a unique achievement. My conquest was well known for allowing her boobs to be caressed on the second or third date. It was also well known that you could take her out ten more times without ever reaching third base. Beyond that, nothing happened in my senior year that I would have been afraid to tell a girl's dad about.

Fortunately I had another outlet for much of my adolescent energy: wrestling. Wrestling didn't completely suppress my sex drive, but it came close. Football can be hard work, but wrestling is always hard work—puking-level hard work. Many nights I was too tired by nine o'clock to play even a five-minute May Hamer movie on the ceiling. More than anything, wrestling success was the basis of my fragile self-esteem. I had a very good season my senior year; I won twenty-one matches, eleven by pins, and lost only three, all by decisions. I thought I had a shot at the state championship. In the regional round of the tournament I drew an easy opponent, a kid I'd beaten a half-dozen times over the years. By the third period, I was ahead on points, 7 to 1. I could have just ridden out the clock, but I made one last effort to pin the kid and managed to tear my left biceps. Foolish Ed, a stupid injury. The tear was only a partial, but it was still a six-to-eight week recovery. That was the last time I was on a wrestling mat as a competitor. I received my high school diploma without having achieved either of my two most important goals: winning the state championship and getting laid.

~

By the spring I graduated, Lyndon Johnson had Vietnam going full bore, and the draft quota was around 40,000 boys each month. My dad hated the war. He said he'd rather see me head to Canada than to have his only son come back from Southeast Asia in a body bag. We finally compromised on the Navy. Dad's idea was that I would probably be away from the fighting, I might learn something useful, and I'd have college benefits when I got out. I signed up under a ninety-day delayed entry program, leaving me one last civilian summer to change my status as a virgin. I also hired on with Otto Hamer.

Working on one of Otto's crews marked transition into manhood for many of us Big Pine boys—at least in our own assessments. Pulp cutting was miserably hard work in those days before the job became mostly automated. In college I read a quote from a famous economist to the effect that, after growing up on a dairy farm, nothing had ever again seemed like work to him. I think a couple of July days in the pulp woods might have given him a little different perspective on the hardships of farm work.

Cutting and piling up eight-foot pulp sticks is not only hard physical work, it's also dangerous as hell. A chainsaw has as much conscience as a shark, plus its teeth revolve. If a shark wanted to gently nibble you without doing damage, it probably could. A chainsaw nibble is an arterial disaster, which means smart guys do not work in the woods alone. In the summer months, the heat and the bugs made the job even more hellish. Mosquitoes, gnats, no-see-ums, deer flies, hornets, and wood ticks all did what they could to drive us crazy. The ticks you didn't find until you got home, by which time they'd already buried their heads under your skin—anyplace under your skin. On even the hottest days we always covered up with long-sleeved shirts and trousers to repel bites and stings and thorns, but the sawdust and the ticks still ended up inside. Add in the tune of three-or-four snarling chainsaws, and you have a work environment nasty enough that even guys who did it year-in year-out usually worked only six-or-seven-hour days.

Most of the guys on Otto's crews had a little more rough bark on them than your average working men—and none had more of it than Otto himself. Otto was built for work, not for show. He had the slope-shouldered look of a standing bear and, stripped down to his old style undershirt, he didn't trail the bear by a lot in the fur department either. Otto had more hair on the backs of his hands than most guys have underneath their shorts. He also had the worst-looking mouth in Larkin County. Lack of dental attention in childhood, plus a two-can-a-day Copenhagen tobacco habit as an adult, left Otto with a smile that might send a suburban high school into lockdown.

The guys on Otto's crews were a mixed bunch. Some of them cut pulp to fill in between construction jobs or during the winters when they weren't working on the docks or on the ore boats over on the Duluth/Superior harbor. For others, guys without a trade or another skill, it was what they did because it was all that was available to them. And then there were the alcoholics, the ones who might have other skills but who couldn't hold down regular jobs because they couldn't make it to work on Monday mornings.

One guy on my first crew never saw his check—his wife came to Otto's shop every Friday to pick it up. Otto understood that it was the only way she could count on getting money for herself and the kids before her husband took off on a bender.

That summer I experienced the some of the hazing and humiliation that comes with being the youngest guy in a crew of working men. Naturally, my name became "The Kid."

"Darryl, why don't you take The Kid and start cutting over by the creek?" or,

"Jesus, Kid, that's not how I showed you. You do it like this!" or,

"I can't do it right now. I gotta take a dump. Have The Kid do it."

What made the physical exhaustion and the bottom rung status worthwhile was that, in addition to the money, I could swagger into the Buckhorn Tavern at the end of the day as part of a crew of manly men who had just finished a day of the manliest kind of work. I even wore my hard hat into the bar the first few times, just to underscore my Manly Crew Member identity. Then one day one of the older guys asked me if I was afraid the ceiling was going to collapse. I still cringe when I think of it.

Another advantage of working in the woods was that our days started and ended early. Even if I stopped into the Buckhorn for an hour with the crew, I still had time to get home and clean up and eat before I headed out on my mission to unburden myself of virginity.

Summer was the season of hope for Big Pine boys like me. Vacationers doubled our population, including our young female population. Every June, girls from the Twin Cities appeared in Big Pine like an overnight mayfly hatch: resort workers, camp counselors, girls dragged up to family cabins by their parents, all of them potential prey for us teenage would-be carnivores. Even girls who had steady boyfriends at home were functionally unattached for the summer. How could a guy miss? My hopes were sky high, and it happened that I didn't have to wait long for my big opportunity. I met her at the Steamboat Days street dance.

CHAPTER 9, ED

THE OPPORTUNITY

Steamboat Days is our town's annual festival, held in late June. It's a tribute to the era of steam on the uppermost reaches of the Mississippi from about 1880 to 1915. The word "steamboat" usually calls to mind the 300-foot-long boats of the southern Mississippi. The ones they show in movies are always loaded with handsome gamblers and good-looking women in gowns, all of whom appear to be daily bathers. The steamboats that plied our area were runty little eighty-to-ninety footers. Anything longer couldn't negotiate the oxbow switchbacks up here—there are seventy of them between Big Pine and Big Rapids, fifty miles to the north. Our boats carried no gamblers, no *Gunsmoke* type dance-hall girls; and the only way a passenger got a bath on the trip was if the boat sank, which was a frequent occurrence. The History Center has a record of one that went under four times in four years. The last time it happened, the owners salvaged what they could, including the boiler, and left the rest where it went down. The boiler became part of the heating plant for one of our first schools. But they were boats propelled by steam and paddle wheels, and they were the best thing we had to base a festival on. It could have been Gobbler Days.

My opportunity was up here from the Twin Cities for the weekend. She was with another girl and a guy who seemed to be the other girl's boyfriend. Every time I looked over at her, she smiled at me, until I finally got up the courage to ask her to dance. She wasn't shy. When the band played a slow song she started grinding into me—a maneuver known in those days as "pushing box." After a few dances she asked if I had anything to drink. I did—I kept a six pack and a half-pint of vodka in my trunk for just such an unlikely occasion.

An hour later we were on a blanket in the woods near Hamer Landing, drinking gulps of vodka, chased by warm beer. I could not believe my luck. After about fifteen minutes of hot making out we were still technically dressed, but most everything was unbuttoned, unzipped, or unhooked. When I slid my hand under the back of her jeans, she raised her hips to make it easier for me to slide everything off. It wasn't a fantasy—she really wanted to go *all the way*. I had her jeans almost off when she put her hand inside my shorts. I realized too late that was way, way more than I could handle. I was done about two seconds later. As she wiped her hand off on my shirt I was enveloped by a thick, slimy cloud of self-loathing and humiliation. It was the most abysmal moment of my youth, and I had no one to blame except myself. I was the Wile E Coyote of seduction. Barring a miracle, I'd be entering service to my country as a cherry.

CHAPTER 10, ED

THE MIRACLE

Back then, just like today, Veteran's Park on the east bank of the Mississippi was the town's main summer socializing spot—that's if you don't consider the taverns. The park is ten acres of green space, with picnic tables, a brick bathroom building with running water, permanent barbecues and a softball diamond. Unless you're from northern Minnesota, the river up here isn't the river you probably visualize when you hear the word, "Mississippi." In Larkin County, it's still narrow enough that ten-year-olds with decent arms can play catch across it—and if the ball falls in the water they can retrieve it without worrying about carcinogenic chemicals or flesh-eating bacteria. The park is a wonderful gathering place, and on any warm evening there are always a few dozen townspeople hanging out, picnicking, barbecuing, and playing or watching softball until sundown. It sounds corny, but I'm sure the scene is one Norman Rockwell would have loved. Those evenings are the warmest memories of my youth.

The softball games were as much social events as they were competitions. Teams were made up of whoever was on hand, and they were almost always mixed, young men and young women mostly, but with a few older guys too. I remember people worrying out loud that overweight Merl Hansen might have a coronary trying to impress the women. Merl wasn't yet a known adulterer, but early in my marriage he confirmed my wife's uncanny powers of observation:

Doris and I had shopped together at Hansen's Grocery and, after we left, Doris said she thought there was something going on between Merl and the woman who worked at the register. When I asked her what made her suspicious, she said that Merl and the woman seemed just a shade too formal with each other. A year later, Merl's wife filed for divorce after she caught Merl cleaving the cashier on the butcher table in the back of the store. Everyone except Doris was shocked. I don't even try to lie to her.

That last summer before my departure to boot camp, our best girl softball player was May Hamer. Besides being hot, May was athletic, though until Title IX changed things, later on in the seventies, there weren't many team sport opportunities for girls. It was at those co-ed softball games that you could see what an athlete May was. She was the only girl who was credible at shortstop. None of the other girls—and only some of the guys—could field a grounder backhand and then get the ball to first ahead of the runner. May could zing it—not as fast as good male shortstop, but often fast enough to "get the out." She was deadly when she played second base, which leaves a shorter throw to first.

I can still see her, with her blonde hair stuffed up under her baseball cap, swaying back and forth at the ready, waiting for the batter to swing. Lots of times her dad, Otto, would umpire the games. Otto loved watching May play. We all did. She still topped my personal dream roster that summer, but she seemed as out of reach as ever—maybe even more than ever. We'd always had a friendly enough relationship, but that was the extent of it. I'd never been brave enough to ask her out. The aftermath could be dangerous, as I saw firsthand, earlier that year.

The guy was a tackle on the football team. He had one date with May and afterward started hinting to everyone that they'd gone all the way. I was walking behind him in the hall, between classes, when May came walking toward him from the other direction. She smiled and said, "Hi Asshole," then kicked him in the nuts. She caught him dead on. He was a big kid, but he was out of business the second she connected. Even after he was down, all doubled up with pain and spewing barf on the terrazzo, May danced around him kicking him any place she found an opening. "Don't ever tell anyone you got in my pants, you asshole. You know you didn't."

I thought she might actually kill him, but then she slipped on the vomit and went down herself, still kicking at the kid and screaming for him to tell everyone he was lying. A gym teacher finally grabbed her and wrestled her away. May got only a one-week suspension. Turned out she fractured her wrist when she fell, which probably seemed to the principal like a sufficient punishment.

The kid was so humiliated that he transferred up to Big Rapids for the rest of his senior year. He was lucky the Goth craze hadn't come along yet; if May had been wearing those leather combat boots he might really be dead. Like I said, she was too scary to ask out.

It was after one of those twilight softball games though, two weeks before I was scheduled to leave for basic training, that the

Miracle happened. In the socializing after the game May asked me for a ride home. I knew she had an older boyfriend, a college guy, but he wasn't around that evening. Once we were in the car she asked me to drive to someplace where we could be alone. I could think of only two possibilities. The first was that, for some unknown reason, she was going to kill me; the second was that something really, really good was going to happen. We ended up on a logging road, a hundred yards into the woods. After we parked, May asked me straight out if I was a virgin. I'm sure she knew that I was. I think I just nodded. She said she knew I was going into the Navy in a couple of weeks, and maybe even to war. She said no one should head off to that as a virgin unless they wanted to be one. Then she said I should get the blanket from the back seat. I told her I had a sleeping bag in the trunk.

"Perfect," she said.

I'd never seen a girl take off her clothes, but May did it without a hint of self-consciousness, then slid into the sleeping bag.

"C'mon, Ed," she said, "I don't bite."

I don't know how memorable the occasion was for May but, after that evening, I thought of her as one of the most generous human beings who ever lived. I saw her only one more time before I left for boot camp. She was holding hands with the college guy at a softball game, but she winked at me as I walked by them. It was the best wink I have ever received. Probably the best wink anyone has ever received. I imagine we're preoccupied with other things at the time, but I hope one of my final visions will be of May, lifting the corner of the sleeping bag to welcome me in.

Had it not been for May, my last sexual encounter before entering the Navy would have been delivering the surprise handful to the girl from the dance. Instead, I would be swearing in as a member of the Fraternity of the Laid. Stupid, I know, but it was a big deal to me at the time. One of the best things about getting old is not having to defend stupid stuff you did or felt when you were young. You have the freedom to just admit, "Yup, that was pretty stupid."

I like that.

CHAPTER 11, ED

SERVING MY COUNTRY

After boot camp, the Navy sent me to the language school in
Monterrey for ten months of intensive Russian. Then I was posted to
a lonely location I'm still not supposed to name (hint: the few women
in the area all knew how to cook seal meat). My job was translating
intercepted Russian naval communications. For the first few months, I
believed myself to be right on the front line of our nation's security.
Then at Christmas, I translated a long message that indicated a major
repositioning of the Russian Pacific Fleet. It seemed like a huge
intelligence coup, right up until I translated the final line of code. It
read, "And Merry Christmas to our friends at (naming our super-
secret base)."

My lieutenant thought maybe it was a cover, a bluff, and that
they'd just recently discovered we were listening and they wanted us to
think they knew all along we'd been listening, and that everything
we'd collected in the past was stuff they made up. Did they really
know that we knew what they were sending? Maybe our higher ups
knew they knew we knew they knew and were playing some kind of
game so complicated nobody really knew anything. What I knew is
that I no longer felt like a key to national security.

In my off-duty hours, I read Russian novels and learned to play
chess. Outdoor activities were limited by cold in winter, and billions of

hummingbird-size mosquitoes in summer. Fortunately we had a decent gym and an indoor basketball court. One of the other translators was a competitive judoka, and I worked out with him for the year he was there. My wrestling background gave me a head start on learning judo, and by the end of a year I could at least make things interesting for him. The extra activity also helped me keep weight gain to a minimum—Navy food is good, and they make sure it's especially good in remote billets like our base. Helps keep morale up.

After May's patriotic sacrifice, I lived in arctic celibacy for that first Navy year; but on a fifteen-day home leave to Big Pine, things turned for the better. For my first couple of days back, I basked in my status as a serviceman in a time of war. That I was based thousands of miles from any armed enemy didn't seem to matter much. Even the older guys I'd worked with on Otto's crew greeted me with some respect; I was no longer The Kid. Many of the classmates I graduated with weren't around to admire me, though. Some had joined the service or been drafted; others had left to find decent paying jobs in the cities, or just to get the hell out of Big Pine; and a few were away at trade schools or college—including, unfortunately, May Hamer.

On my third day home, I stopped into Hansen's to pick up some stuff for my mom. The lady in front of me at the register was asking Merl if he could think of someone who would come out to her cabin and help her wrestle her boat out of the shed and into the lake.

She was a good-looking woman I guessed to be in her late thirties. Not Big Pine late thirties, more like rich suburban late thirties. She had one of those horseshoe bands holding her hair back, and her sunglasses were tilted up on her forehead, both things I associated with well-off women from the Cities. I thought horny old Merl might offer to help her himself, but then he nodded at me.

I told her I'd have time after dinner.

Getting the boat out was easy, and after we had it in the water she asked me did I want a beer? She told me she was staying at the cabin while she and her husband worked out their divorce. Turned out she was forty-one. I didn't leave until about three in the morning. After that I saw her every night for the next week. We developed a stupid routine where I'd knock on the screen door and sing, "*Little pig, little pig, let me in,*"—and of course she'd sing back the "Chinny chin chin" line.

We knew exactly how many days we had before the certain end of our relationship, and that freed us to wring as much sensual pleasure as possible out of our time together. It was my first experience of hours of sexual time, not just hurried minutes—hours with a woman who was completely comfortable in showing me how to please her, and who also wanted to please me. It was a wonderful nine days. The tenth wasn't so good.

On my last visit to her cabin, I went straight from a friend's house instead of stopping home to clean up like I usually did. I knocked and started my "three little pigs" song, but this time a girl in cutoffs and a halter top came to the screen door. She looked familiar. A few seconds later her mother came running up from the beach, spitting out words like a machine gun—something like "This is Ed, Stefanie, he's been helping me with some chores. And Ed, this is my daughter Stefanie. She just finished her freshman year at the U, and her father dropped her off this afternoon, and I left a message your house that I didn't need you today, but I guess your mother didn't give you my message that I didn't need you today."

I obviously didn't get the message. I wished I had.

Before her mother finished speed babbling, Stefanie and I had placed each other. The last and only time we'd met ended with her wiping her hand on my shirt. Stefanie wasn't at all in doubt about the kind of chores I'd been performing for her mother, and I remember exactly what she said: "Mom, I know him. He's my age. You're fucking a boy my age, and I'm going to kill myself."

Stefanie ran into the cabin, her mom ran in after her, and I ran to my car.

Still, it was a great leave, and I didn't hear anything about a nineteen-year-old summer visitor killing herself that weekend.

The other oasis in my arid sex life should have been my leave in Thailand. Thailand was a major jolt—I'd gone from the surface of an ice planet to Paradise, in just twenty-four hours. A lot of American servicemen on R&R from Vietnam fell in love with the place. The beaches and the food were wonderful, and the jungle wasn't full of people trying to kill them. And most of all, they fell in love with the women. Guys fantasized about moving there, marrying a Thai woman, and living out their lives there. A few did but, for most guys, relationships with the women were short-term rentals.

The Thai brothel (the only one I've ever been to anywhere) was a circle of tiny hooches. If the woman wasn't busy inside, she stood outside the entrance. Once you paid the older woman in charge, you could, for an hour, pretend you lived there with the girl. Somehow I ended up with a comedienne—her first words to me were "Hello, Mister Sailor, that a pistol in your pocket or you just glad to see me?"

I knew right away I wasn't going to consummate the relationship. It turns out I am not suited for that kind of transaction. Passionless sex with a complete stranger just doesn't work for me, especially if the stranger is using Mae West dialog as the lubricant. I don't have to feel that I'm in love, but I need to believe that both parties are doing it because they have some genuine desire for each other—and there was no way to convince myself that, aside from my twenty bucks, there was anything the girl desired from me.

But I'd already paid the twenty, so I spent the time drinking tea and getting a shoulder massage. As I was leaving, she said, "Hey, Mister Sailor, do you know what the elephant ask the naked man? He ask him 'how you breathe through that little thing?'" Then she laughed like I'd told the joke and it was the first time she'd heard it.

On my second Thailand leave, I met a Navy nurse from Milwaukee who did seem to have some genuine desire for me. We kept in touch for the next year and agreed to explore things further back in the States, but that plan ended when Doris entered my world.

And that's it—my life and my sex life, pre-Doris. Not exactly a Casanova.

CHAPTER 12, MADDIE

ME, MADDIE

By the time we colluded on my seduction of Ed, Doris and I had been best friends for a very long time—we met during spring quarter of our freshman year at the U of M. We clicked right away, and we spent that summer working together at the big resort on Bay Lake, west of Big Pine. I'm even somewhat responsible for her marriage: it was early in that summer when I introduced her to Ed at a wedding dance.

They say long-married couples grow to resemble one another. Maybe it also applies to long-time friends. In recent years Doris and I have been asked, more than once, if we are sisters. We do wear the same dress size, and we've both let our hair go gray—though mine is grayer than hers. Beyond that, I don't see the sisterly resemblance. I think our faces are quite different—she has sharply defined features, where I see my own as a little doughy.

When I was young, I was "high school cute." Doris was long-term beautiful—not that she was able to own it. When she looked in the mirror, she just didn't see herself the way the rest of us saw her. It's hard to believe anyone so intelligent could be so blind to the obvious. When we first met, it was as if she worked at being unattractive. Clothes, hair, glasses, I could count on her to select the least-flattering things she could find. Once we became friends, I took over most of her fashion decisions, and I'm still in charge of that today. That's about the only area where my mind works better than hers. I'm intelligent enough to do what I have to do; Doris is scary intelligent. She also knows me better than anyone ever has, probably including me. She knew I'd been a "good girl" in high school, at least as far as boys were concerned, and that I'd been in bed with only two men before Ed. The one thing I'd never shared with her was the full story of my relationship with Sissy Hamer, my best friend from second grade on.

I don't know what brought Sissy and me together, but I don't think most people could say what it was that caused them to become best friends in childhood. It just happens.

Sissy lived in the biggest house in Larkin County, a white, three-story Victorian that still sits on top of the hill on the east side of White Deer Lake. During much of my childhood, it was as much my home as my parents' house. For me it was a fairy tale castle, and Sissy was my Snow White, Cinderella, and Sleeping Beauty, all in one beautiful, perfect girl.

At the time we became friends, Hamers had already been living in the house for seventy years, and Sissy's dad, Otto, was born in the same bedroom where he and Sissy's mom slept. The house was large enough that only the twins, Mickey and Joey, shared a room, and then only for a few years when they were little. In those days, most Big Pine kids, even kids from better-off families, shared bedrooms, and often beds, until they graduated from high school and went out on their own.

In most ways the Hamers didn't live rich, though they were—

at least Big Pine rich. But one thing they spent money on was dentistry. That was very unusual around here. Until Cal Peterson opened his practice, the nearest dentist of any kind was in Brainerd, thirty miles away. In those days many Larkin County kids didn't make the trip unless they had a toothache bad enough that clove oil didn't work. The result was a lot of bad teeth. In my junior year, our prom queen had enough dental issues that her mouth is closed in the official portrait.

But the Hamer children all had smiles you could use in a toothpaste ad, and Jo Hamer made sure they stayed that way with day-long trips to an orthodontist in Duluth. She also made all the kids brush after every meal, then come back and give her Cheshire-cat grins so she could inspect. I can still see Sissy's wonderful sweet mouth and her perfect little white teeth. I'm sure Jo's focus on her children's teeth was a result of her husband's ghastly mouth. Half of Otto's teeth were missing, and the ones he had left were all pitted and stained brown from tobacco. Those awful teeth, along with his beard, made him look like a nightmare creature when he opened his mouth. He was actually a very nice man, but it took a while to get used to his appearance. I couldn't imagine Mrs. Hamer kissing him.

Sissy's bedroom was the only one on the third floor, and it had a cupola with windows faced out toward Albino Point on the other side of the lake. I like to think that Sissy's grandfather built that cupola with the happiness of young girls in mind. Either one of Sissy's older sisters, May or Jessie, could have claimed it by seniority, but they both wanted to be closer to the second-floor bathroom, so Sissy and I had our own world up on top. There were seasonal prices to pay though; in winter the sheets were so cold that on sleepovers Sissy and I clamped onto each other like magnetic spiders when we first got into bed. July and August could also be uncomfortable; many people don't realize that Minnesota can have summer days and nights that are as hot as they are in Florida—just a lot fewer of them. On the hottest nights, we slept in just our underwear and hoped for a breeze off the lake. Back then, the only air-conditioned building I'd been in was the movie theater in Brainerd.

Early in grade school our main interests were Nancy Drew books, horse stories, and just about everything Sissy's older sisters did. At bedtime we'd read to each other for hours until Mrs. Hamer came up and made us to turn out the lights. We fell out every so often—in fifth grade we both had a crush on the same troublemaker—but we always got back together and pinky swore friends forever.

I was two months older than Sissy, but she was ahead of me in a lot of things. I was an only child; she had two older sisters to learn from. She was also ahead of me physically. Her breasts began developing almost a year before mine. She told me they would be sore sometimes, but that other times it could feel good to touch them. She let me touch them too. In eighth grade we both had our first periods, and we thought of ourselves as quite grown up. Sissy was already making out with boys then, and by ninth grade she was doing some petting. She'd always give me the details on my next sleepover.

It started with kissing, which Sissy was doing quite a lot of by freshman year. She said none of the boys did it right—they were all too eager and too clumsy. One night she asked if I wanted to know how it should really be done?

I definitely did want to know.

"Then close your eyes," she said.

She started by brushing her mouth across mine, so softly at first that I could barely feel it, then moved to taking my upper or lower lip in turn between hers.

"Boys always move to fast," she said.

Sissy didn't move too fast. Her slowness drove me crazy—which was the point she was making. We did a lot of slow "practice kissing" from then on. Sissy never seemed to move fast anytime. She wasn't exactly delicate—willowy was closer to it. And she moved that way, like she was responding to a breeze. I thought she was the most graceful and beautiful person who'd ever existed.

Sissy and I had to be careful in our sleepover explorations. Her older sisters usually left us to ourselves, and Mrs. Hamer only came up to enforce lights out; but the twins, Joey and Mickey, wandered up whenever they felt like it. Joey was our main problem. His dad, Otto, was scary on the outside; Joey was scary on the inside. He was just as likely to laugh when something bad happened to someone as he was to laugh at something truly funny. His sisters called him The Little Shit and, if that sounds like an affectionate nickname, it wasn't. Once, May caught him stealing out of her purse. When she told her parents, Joey lost television privileges for a week. That week May's cat disappeared. Otto and Jo said the cat must have run away. I think they must have known, somewhere down deep, that the cat hadn't run away, but the alternative was just too horrible to allow into their minds.

Joey was only eight, but he was already the most frighteningly evil person I knew. Forty years later he would prove it again—to all of us. Back then though, he did bring one benefit; he gave Sissy an excuse to ask for a latch on her door.

Once we had the latch, we could relax a little more, though I think May, Sissy's oldest sister, had an idea of what went on up on the top floor. When I'd arrive at the Hamer house, she'd yell out things like, "Sissy, your boyfriend's here," or, "Sissy, your date's at the door."

But Sissy wasn't afraid to hand it right back. Once, after May made one of her "boyfriend" comments, Sissy told her that if she didn't shut up she was going to get one of those "things" out of May's purse and take it to her dad and ask him what it was.

She was referring to condoms, of course, and Sissy already knew full well what they were for. Looking back though, I'm not sure her dad would have been all that upset. Otto and Jo always told the girls that no one should have babies until they were ready, and he did set some boundaries.

Sissy told me later that any new boy who showed up to take out one of the girls would get a visit to her dad's smokehouse. At the end of the tour Otto would pull down a hanging sausage and point out that it was contained in a casing, and that sausages should *always* have a casing around them. Then he'd chop it in two with a cleaver, hand the boy half, and tell him he wasn't ready for grandchildren.

A little crude I guess, but it did seem to work. Even if the date ended up in the backseat, boys brought Hamer girls home on time, and none of the girls ever had an unplanned pregnancy, at least not one that I know of.

In spring of our junior year, Sissy went all the way with an older boy. She gave me the details during a sleepover at her house the next night. She said it was exciting, but not very satisfying—everything happened too fast, she said, which was always her complaint about boys.

I was fascinated, but I was also crushed—I felt I'd lost her to the boy. I'm sure she read my unhappiness, and that night she kissed me even more tenderly than usual. She said I was still the most important person in her life, and that I was sexier than any boy could ever be. I remember every second. As she kissed me, she ran her finger in circles over the flannel nightgown covering my breast. Smaller and smaller circles. She took my nipple between her thumb and forefinger, just light squeezes at first, then increased the pressure until I thought I couldn't stand it any longer. Finally she ran her hand down over the outside of my nightgown until the heel of her thumb was just where it needed to be. She held it rigid, kissing me all the while, as I pushed against her hand. That was my first orgasm. She hadn't even touched my skin.

Long after I was married I still had the nightgown, buried at the bottom of a dresser drawer. Sometimes when I was alone I would put it on and think about Sissy. She'd said taking care of myself was a skill I would need even after I started having sex with boys, and probably after I got married too. She was always way ahead of me.

Eventually Sissy and I started using our mouths for things other than kissing. She was having sex with her boyfriend regularly by then, but she said he would never be able to do what I could do. I felt so powerful. Forty years later I still remember how thrilling it was to shake her whole being with just the smallest movement of my tongue. I wondered if our relationship meant we were lesbians, but Sissy said that just because we were doing things lesbians do didn't mean we were lesbians. She said she was sure she would end up as a wife and a mother, and she thought I probably would too, though she said it was possible I might be one of those people who really are in the middle— at least as far as sex was concerned.

By senior year I acquired a boyfriend myself, just not the one I had a crush on, the one who starred in my X-rated, trail-of-clothing fantasy. Unfortunately, that boy showed no interest in me. My actual boyfriend didn't treat me to any fantasies. He was a nice enough kid, but he confirmed Sissy's complaints about boys being too eager and too clumsy. He was also uncomfortable if I mentioned I was having my period. One time he told me he didn't want to know about "that stuff."

It made me so angry that I told him I pooped too. I said if he didn't believe me I could show him. My mom was a nurse, and human physiology wasn't a conversational taboo in our house.

My boyfriend did manage to overcome his disgust at my bodily functions when it came to wanting intercourse, but I found I could easily head off his pressure for a complete performance just by using my hand. Nowadays I suppose he would hope the girl would go down on him, but back then most of us considered that a step beyond intercourse. I graduated as a virgin, at least where the opposite sex was concerned.

Sissy was a good student and, because the Hamers were so well off, she had her choice of colleges. She'd talked to a summer resident, a girl who went to UC Berkeley, and Sissy liked what she heard. She applied, and after she flew out there the winter of our senior year she said she knew it was the place for her. I think she also needed separation from me. We never talked about that being a reason for her choosing such a distant school, but I'm sure it was part of her decision. That might also have been why she worked in Glacier National Park during summer vacations and spent only a week or so back here with her family. After medical school and her residency, she and her husband moved to Oregon, where she's a pediatric specialist in a Eugene hospital. I'm sure she's a good one.

My own family didn't have a lot of money but, because I was an only child, my parents were able to put together enough, along with a student loan, to send me down to the main campus of the University of Minnesota. I was still sorting out my sexuality when I arrived for my freshman year. That first fall quarter, I had a relationship with a girl who lived in my dorm. She didn't have any doubts about her orientation. She said that even as a little girl she had known where her sexual feelings were focused. She'd already come out to her parents— and to most of the rest of the world as well. She led with it, even in situations where it didn't seem to me to be necessary. I liked her, but it wasn't love. She wasn't all that much fun to be with either, always too serious. She also liked to talk dirty during sex, which I found terribly distracting. I knew what we were doing, and I didn't need a narrator.

Winter quarter I had my first male lover, a graduate teaching assistant in my freshman English class. He hinted that he'd had a lot previous experience but, looking back, I suspect it most of it was in his imagination. Whatever his real history was, the sex was less than satisfying, though at least he had a better sense of humor than the girl in my dorm. By spring quarter both the lesbian and the TA were out of my life, and I didn't mourn either relationship.

Stan came into my life at the beginning of my sophomore year. The first time I saw him, he was standing on the steps of Coffman Union, the student center, speaking to a group of a hundred or so protesters. I was on my way to class, but I stopped to listen. He had the crowd going. He was delivering his message like a hell-fire preacher, but he was talking about the war in Southeast Asia, not salvation. I thought he was probably a professor; he looked older than most of his audience—late twenties, I guessed. Dark curly hair, almost Afro curly, and it bounced in rhythm with his words. Very sexy.

After he finished speaking I went up to him and asked him some dumb question about his talk—a bold move for a woods' mouse like me. My question probably didn't even make sense, but I knew I had to meet him, and it worked; he asked if I wanted to go into the cafeteria for some coffee and talk.

I discovered he was an Iron Ranger like me, but from Hibbing, about sixty miles northwest of Big Pine. Despite his mature looks, it turned out he was only twenty, just a year older than I was. When I was watching him speak to the crowd, I'd guessed he was Italian, but it turned out his great-grandparents were Russian Jews who migrated to northern Minnesota at the start of the mining boom, late in the nineteenth century. Keller Mercantile, founded by Stan's great-grandfather, was the largest volume clothing store on the Range for almost a hundred years, up until the big warehouse operations moved in. I remember their motto from TV commercials: "Men, Women, Children, Kellers Has You Covered." I'd been there a few times with my mother.

Psych 101 went on without me that morning. During those next two hours in the cafeteria, neither of us would have noticed a moose in a sundress sitting at the next table. We took in each other's life stories in big gulps, and we were at least halfway in love by the time Stan said he had to go speak at another rally. But first he said he needed to do something. He took my hand and led me out of the coffee shop and into an empty meeting room. He closed the door then backed me up against it. He leaned against the door with one hand and put his other hand up underneath my skirt and down inside my underwear, watching my face as his finger stirred inside me. Then he put the finger in his mouth and sucked on it. He looked straight into my eyes the whole time.

I didn't know what the rest of my life would bring, but I was pretty sure I knew who I wanted to spend it with.

That first year we were together, Stan was taking mostly pre-med courses, and he probably would have ended up in medical school if one of his fraternity brothers hadn't been the restaurant reviewer for the *Minnesota Daily*, the campus paper. Stan and the reviewer were good friends, so he was often invited along on review visits. Sometimes I went along too, though Stan and I had to come up with my share of the bill because the *Daily* would only pay for his meal. There weren't as many ethnic restaurants in the Twin Cities as there are now—the explosion of Asian places that came after Vietnam was a few years off—but there was still enough exotic food to make eating an adventure. Chinese, Greek, Jewish, Indian, and Japanese, plus traditional and nouveau versions of French and Italian cuisine. For two kids from Northern Minnesota, it was a revelation.

By the end of spring quarter, Stan knew he wanted to make his living by making good food. His parents were disappointed that there wasn't going to be a Dr. Stan Keller in the family, but they finally agreed to pay for an intensive twelve-month program at a New York chef school. The downside was that Stan and I would be apart for a year. Because we'd only been together for eight months at that point, the separation seemed like a huge risk to our relationship.

Stan came home for a few days over the holidays and I made two Greyhound trips to New York but, other than that, we had to rely on letter-writing and telephone calls. Cross-country calls were expensive back then. A thirty-minute chat could cost as much as a week's worth of groceries, so long distance was mostly reserved for announcing births, deaths, and engagements. Somehow, in spite of the obstacles, our relationship survived.

Stan's parents were impressed that we hadn't wavered during the year we were apart, and I think that convinced them that I was the one for their son. Also, Stan's older brother was almost certainly gay, which meant Stan was the only likely source of grandchildren.

Three months after Stan finished chef school, we were husband and wife, and a month after that we signed a purchase agreement for the Town Talk, Big Pine's only full-service restaurant. Stan's parents were happy to finance us—they would be less than two hours away from the expected grandchildren.

Stan's mom wished our new business well, but she was most interested in seeing my midsection show signs of an occupant. Two years into our marriage, it did and everyone was ecstatic when our first daughter arrived.

It's hard to believe that was thirty-five years ago.

CHAPTER 13, MADDIE

I SHARE MY SECRET

Three days before our scheduled Saturday evening ambush of Chip, Doris called and said Ed was driving her a little buggy with his anxiety about the Friday morning Success Day reunion with Joey Hamer. She asked if I wanted to spend Thursday night and Friday in Duluth with her. Even when Stan was alive, Doris and I made occasional overnight getaways a few times a year. This one would also be an opportunity to pick up the saltwater fish for the cioppino we wanted to serve at our dinner party.

I do enjoy those trips with Doris, but the charms of Duluth are not apparent to me. As far as I'm concerned, the high point of a visit there is an actual high point—the panoramic view of the city and of Lake Superior that you get when you crest the bluff on Interstate 35 and start downhill toward Duluth Harbor. Everything after that really is down hill in my opinion. Among things Duluth is not famous for are good weather and good restaurants. In North Central Minnesota we get temperatures of minus 30 or lower most winters, so I don't ordinarily mind 50-degree-above weather. But in July or August, it seems out of place, and that can be downtown Duluth. Depending on wind direction there are days when it's 90 degrees in the neighbor-hoods up over the hill and only in the 50s downtown by the harbor. That difference can create a very dangerous situation. You'll be driving up the hill on your way out of the city, when all of a sudden you see drivers ahead of you hitting the brakes in a panic when warm air suddenly condenses on cold glass and turns their windshields opaque in just a couple of seconds. It's like being struck blind.

Duluth is also not known for its restaurants, though things have improved in recent years. On our early Duluth outings, Doris and I used to lunch at the Canton Lantern, a large Chinese place downtown, near the harbor. Their signature dish was prime rib, notable for its size, allegedly the largest slab served in Minnesota. Stan ordered it once, and I remember that it didn't quite fit on the plate. He made two more meals out of what we took home, but he said the best thing about it was quantity. In the restaurant's defense, I doubt that prime rib was a traditional offering in Canton Province. Unfortunately, that excuse didn't apply to most of the restaurant's "Chinese" dishes—the gluey stuff that passed for genuine just about everywhere in America, up until the last few decades. Then, in the seventies and eighties, Vietnamese restaurants started popping up, including a good one in Duluth. My first bowl of beef ball soup was a very happy occasion.

It was over a Vietnamese dinner on that trip that I finally shared the whole story of my relationship with Sissy Hamer. Of course Doris knew I'd been best friends with Sissy up through high school, and I might have even mentioned our "practice kissing," but I'd never confessed that we'd been full-blown lovers. I'd always worried that it might make her uncomfortable to have her best friend admit a powerful attraction to women. Foolish me. After I told her the story, Doris just smiled and said, "Tell me something I didn't know."

She said she'd always assumed Sissy and I had been more than friends—she said just watching my face when I talked about Sissy had given me away a long time ago. I felt foolish for thinking I'd been keeping a secret for all those years. I should have known better. Doris reads people better than anyone I've ever known. She says living with her mother was her real training in psychology, and that growing up with a narcissistic parent is a fairly common background for psychologists and therapists. Most often it's the mother, Doris said, just because a mother is the first person a child needs to please to get his or her own needs met. She said she spent her childhood studying her mom's needs, spoken and unspoken, then trying to give her whatever feedback she seemed to want. That analysis of subtle cues becomes a habit, Doris said, a useful one for people in her line of work. But she also says that role reversal robbed her of childhood, and that she's struggled with the resulting anger ever since.

After my "secret" was out of the way, we talked about what might come next in our late-life adventure. Doris had a lot of ideas. She doesn't do anything halfway.

CHAPTER 14, ED

BIG PINE'S FIRST FAMILY

Maddie was right. I was driving Doris nuts over Joey Hamer's Success Day appearance. I was also driving myself nuts. Why had the duty of welcoming The Little Shit back to Big Pine fallen on me?

How the Hamer family produced a Joey I don't know—maybe a chromosome broke.

In Larkin County, the name Hamer is a long-established brand, like Ford or John Deere. According to the records at the History Center, Adolph Hamer, Joey's great-grandfather, arrived here from Germany in 1878, when he was twelve years old. Germans were Minnesota's first big wave of immigrants, drawn to our area to work in the white pine forests and then to farm the land after the trees were gone.

Adolph must have been a hustler; *Register* archives refer to Hamer Logging as a going concern in 1891, and at the Center we have an 1897 photo of Adolph and his young son, Gus, standing outside a one-story white frame building with an "A Hamer & Son" sign on the false front. Hamers have been working in the Larkin County forests ever since.

In the nineteenth century, Adolph Hamer crews used muscle-powered two-man saws to drop old growth white pines for the lumber used to build homes. A hundred years later, Otto's crews used gas-

93

fueled chainsaws to chew through the second- and third-growth trees that are turned into pulp to produce newspapers and all the other disposable stuff that we blow into, wipe up with, or wrap around our babies without much thought about where it comes from or where it goes. I spent two summers on Otto crews.

With the monstrous exception of Joey, the Hamers have been good citizens who gave back to the community. Adolph helped organize the building of our first high school, the school that graduated his son. Twenty years later, son Gus and his wife led the committee that petitioned the Carnegie Foundation to build our town library. Their names are on a bronze plaque just inside the front entrance. Otto's own contribution, beyond being the town's largest private employer after the turkey plant closed, was modernizing Big Pine Fire and Ambulance, and molding it into a model for other volunteer emergency services across rural Minnesota.

In places like Larkin County those organizations do more than saves lives and property. Along with schools, rural fire departments help give people the feeling that they are living in a community and not just occupying the same geography. If you call in an emergency in the Twin Cities, professional strangers show up to rescue you; in Big Pine you'd recognize every one of the responders and hope that one of them was Otto Hamer.

By the time I joined the department, the same year I returned to Big Pine as a teacher, Otto had been the heart of Big Pine Fire and Ambulance for years. Kermit Nelson was our chief in those days; but everyone understood that, when Otto was on the scene, Kermit was pretty much irrelevant. Otto served with the Seabees in the Pacific during World War II, clearing rubble and building new airfields on islands while the fighting was still going on around him. Operating a bulldozer while being shot at probably made fires and car crashes seem a little less intimidating than they were to some of the rest of us.

Otto made suggestions in a way that made them seem like the only alternatives. He also knew how to make the "short move" in tough situations—we counted on him to figure out the quickest way to open crumpled car door, where to head off a brush fire, or how to extricate a body part from a piece of machinery.

But I was present at the incident where one of Otto's short move suggestions did go a little too far, and it was the reason he wasn't named chief until much later on. The call came in on a September evening when Irv Johnson's wife reported that he hadn't come home after fire tower duty. The towers aren't manned continuously, only when the woods are dry. It's lonely, intermittent work, and it doesn't pay a lot, so most of the towers are manned by retired guys like Irv. Their main problem is staying awake while they sit up there.

Unfortunately, the call from Irv's wife coincided with Otto's birthday celebration. He usually limited himself to an after work six pack of Grain Belt which, poured into a guy his size and with his drinking experience, didn't have a very noticeable effect. But that evening he'd already stretched the six-pack rule, and he was probably anxious to get back to the celebration.

When Irv's wife first called, Chief Larkin tried reaching Irv on the mobile radio system, hoping he had just dozed off. But Irv didn't answer. And by the time we got to the tower, we were all pretty sure that Irv was in a bad way, or likely worse. One of the guys with EMT certification scrambled up the stairway to the watch cabin. When he came back down he said it looked like Irv had just put his head on the table and gone to sleep—but that he was more than asleep.

The question then was how to get Irv's body down from the tower. The stairway was enclosed in a metal safety cage, so he wouldn't be coming down that way. Chief Nelson said we'd have to rig up a block and tackle so we could strap Irv onto a backboard and lower him down. It was already twilight, which meant we'd be at it until after dark, making the extraction more hazardous. That's when Otto pointed out that there was a faster way to the same end. It took a few seconds for the meaning of his suggestion to sink in.

Chief Nelson finally said, "Jesus H Christ, Otto, are you saying we should just pitch him off? What's he gonna look like after a forty-foot drop? Jesus H Christ."

Otto said Irv wouldn't be any deader no matter how we got him down and, as for further damage, we could pile up some pine slash in the landing zone to cushion the impact. I have to admit I could kind of see the practical sense in Otto's suggestion, but I didn't say anything. In the end we spent an hour bringing Irv down—Kerm's way.

Unfortunately, the story of Otto's suggestion somehow got back to his missus. At first she wanted Otto off the department. Of course that didn't fly—the town just wasn't willing to give the boot to the department's MVP. Then she backed off to saying that if Otto was ever made chief, she would spend the rest of her life telling everyone in northern Minnesota the story of his proposal to send her husband airborne. It wasn't until years later, after Irv's wife was reunited with Irv, that Otto got the title that went with the job he'd been doing all along.

The earlier Hamers had prospered, but Otto was the first one you could call rich—at least Larkin County rich. Most pulpwood operators just bought "stumpage," the rights to the timber on a piece of property. Otto's genius was buying the land as well, especially land bordering on lakes and rivers. By the 1960s and '70s post-war prosperity had fattened up the urban middle class to the point that many of the newly comfortable could afford a "place up north," Minnesotan for a lakeshore cabin.

When that demand arrived, Otto already owned enough lake and river frontage for a couple of hundred building lots. Almost every page of the Larkin County Platte Book had pieces with different Hamer names attached. When Otto's children turned twenty-one, they got to pick out a piece of Otto's property and have it transferred to their names. Then every few years, he'd let them select another one—which is how Joey Hamer came to be owner of Albino Point.

~

I was only vaguely aware of Joey before I graduated from high school and left for the Navy. In those days I knew him only as the baby brother of May Hamer, the most lusted-after girl in my graduating class. I also remembered that May always referred to Joey as The Little Shit. Seven years later, when I returned to Big Pine as a rookie teacher, The Little Shit and his twin sister, Mickey, were sophomores in my biology class.

Joey was a good-looking kid, though I always thought he was just a shade too pretty. Somebody once told him he looked like the actor, Tony Curtis, and after that Joey always wore his hair like Curtis—dark, greasy-looking curls.

I never did buy Curtis as a leading man.

Joey's body bugged me too. An insurance chart might say he fell into a healthy weight for his height, but that doesn't tell the whole story. He had no muscle definition. Even if he isn't an athlete, a teenage boy should have at least a hint of biceps and triceps. Those muscles should be visible just from ordinary kid activities—doing yard work or stocking shelves at a part-time job or grab-assing around with friends. Joey's upper arms were just tubes that connected his shoulders to his elbows. I hate that look in a young guy. But Joey was a shiny package: good looking, intelligent and sociable, pretty much everything parents could ask for in a son—at least if they hadn't requested a conscience.

Right from the first weeks of that first year of teaching, I brought Joey stories home to Doris. She had pegged him even before she met him. After I'd recounted a few early incidents, she dug out a text book from an abnormal psych grad school class and read me off a list of psychopathic traits. Over his three years in high school, I saw Joey demonstrate all of them. Inability to make "appropriate emotional responses" was a subtle one, but it was the thing that first brought home to me just how different from the rest of us Joey was.

I'd noticed that if someone said something funny, Joey would start to laugh about a second behind everyone else. Doris guessed he'd probably been scolded for inappropriate laughing plenty of times in his childhood, and that by high school he'd learned to cue off "normal" people to tell him what was okay to laugh about. He was like an alien doing a good, but not perfect, imitation of a human being.

"Poor object constancy" wasn't a term I wasn't familiar with, but Doris said it was just a psychology way of saying "out of sight, out of mind." For people with poor object constancy, other people only exist if they're present. Bingo. That was our boy. Joey had a girlfriend only when she was with him; if she wasn't present, that meant he didn't have a girlfriend, and he looked to dock in whatever berth was available.

Big Pine High School graduating classes are only about seventy-five kids, and consequently everyone knows everyone. By his senior year, most of Joey's female classmates knew to steer clear of him. The result was that he focused on underclass girls, freshmen and sophomores who didn't know him well and who were vulnerable to his good looks, lies, and the red Mustang convertible his parents gave him for not smoking.

One of his senior year conquests was a fifteen-year-old sophomore whose mother didn't have any trouble diagnosing the cause of her daughter's morning nausea. To make the situation even worse for Joey, the girl's symptoms were noticed only a few weeks after her fifteenth birthday—meaning she was only fourteen when Joey literally swept her off her feet.

Joey was eighteen, and potentially in very, very deep shit. His doings with the girl qualified as rape, no matter how willing she was. Otto and Jo moved fast. They made a substantial donation to a "college fund" for the girl and paid the costs of a trip to a Minneapolis clinic that specialized in zero population growth. The issue never reached the legal system. If it had, Joey's future in court would have been checking in as a sex offender instead of as an attorney.

The sole consequence for Joey was that the red Mustang disappeared from the school parking lot for a month, and he had to ride the school bus. Cool seniors didn't ride the bus; cool seniors drove to school. Joey gave everyone a lame story about needing a hard-to-get part. Later he changed to saying he didn't want to put more miles on the car before he sold it. That's another psychopath giveaway, Doris says, if you don't buy one story, they'll tell you another. They think everyone else is so stupid they won't notice that the second story contradicts the first one. I've noticed politicians do that a lot too.

Joey wasn't truly popular, but his classmates knew how dangerous it was to cross him, and they learned to stay on his good side whenever possible. I think he took that as evidence that he was genuinely liked, and that it was what led him to run for prom king in his senior year. It was a huge miscalculation on his part. Nomination was an open process, but election was by secret ballot. Even the kid who nominated Joey probably voted for someone else. The king and queen are crowned at an assembly a few days before prom. The runners up become the attendant princes and princesses. School administrators count the votes, and only the names of the king and queen are supposed to be announced, not the vote totals. Joey was not crowned prom king.

Ordinarily, he could have pretended to himself and to the world that he'd lost a squeaker. Unfortunately for Joey, someone leaked the actual vote; he'd finished last among the four candidates—last by a bunch.

Late on the night of the coronation assembly, the lights went out in Big Pine. The town administrator later explained to us that sending a single rifle slug into a big electrical transformer's fluid reservoir can turn a $100,000 piece of equipment into a twenty-five-ton hunk of scrap metal in just a few minutes.

We got a mobile unit up from the Cities in plenty of time for the dance, but the transformer assassination was never solved. Most people assumed the perpetrator was some idiot from a rival school. I had my own suspect, and thirty years later I was supposed to welcome him back to the scene of the crime.

CHAPTER 15, ED

DORIS COMES INTO MY LIFE

Doris and I met only a couple of weeks after I got out of the Navy. I was staying with my folks and cutting pulp on an Otto Hamer crew for the second time, to accumulate a little extra spending money for my upcoming freshman year at Bemidji State. On a Saturday night, I was at my cousin's wedding dance at the 80 Club, just west of town. I wasn't much for dances, but the bride was family, and my mom pushed me to at least make an appearance. When I got to the dance, I headed right for the cash bar, and that's when Maddie spotted me and waved me over to introduce me to her new best friend, beautiful Doris. I'm not that good at small talk with women anyway, and I remember being even more awkward than usual that night.

Doris seemed a little uncomfortable too, which I took as disinterest on her part. I also figured she was way out of my league. The next day though, Maddie called me and told me Doris thought I seemed like a nice guy, and that she'd like to see me again. I had a hard time believing Doris saw me that way. I'm always surprised when people like me—I've never felt all that likable—but I did want to see Doris again.

Two nights later we had a terrible dinner together at the Town Talk restaurant and then spent two hours down by the river, just walking and talking. By the end of the evening, I was already falling hard for her. I also realized how amazingly intelligent she was. She said she'd been accepted at Smith College, and that she would have gone there if her dad hadn't been diagnosed with lymphoma in the winter of her high school senior year. So instead of Smith, she stayed home and enrolled at the U of M.

By the end of her freshman year, though, her dad was in remission, and Doris felt free enough to spend the summer working at the resort with Maddie. We met there because both of us made last-minute decisions to attend the wedding dance, where I turned right instead of left as I came in the door, and Maddie saw me because she happened to be looking in the direction of the bar.

Most people don't like to acknowledge the randomness of events that change the course of their lives, but for me it's almost an obsession: *If* I hadn't stopped at Hansen's to pick up some hot dogs for my mom, the divorcing woman and I likely wouldn't have crossed paths that summer. *If* Elliot's daughter had held her water for another five minutes I wouldn't have come home early from fishing. *If* I'd turned toward the band instead of the bar at the wedding dance, my life and Doris' life would be completely different. Not to mention the non-life of our son. Even rational Doris likes to think we might have met anyway, but I know that's not true. Everything changes everything.

I think people just aren't comfortable with thoughts of life's randomness polka dancing across the surface of their minds, so they learn to weave stories that make things feel more sequential and more "intended."

Seems pretty obvious to me that blind chance is at the root of everything. Just for starters, Ed began when the "Ed" sperm won the egg run one night, beating out a hundred million or so other competitors, which meant my chance of existing was about the same as my chance of winning the lottery. And those hundred million are just one night's production. When the kid at the Dairy Queen gives you your change, the hand he extends has probably liberated enough unique microscopic tadpoles to repopulate the earth, just in the previous thirty days.

Sorry, but I am a male and a biology teacher.

Random chance or not, Doris and I must have been ready that summer. We were lovers within a week. We even had a love nest, a little house a wrestler friend from high school inherited from his grandmother. He was a deck hand on one of the ore boats that carry taconite from the Iron Range to the steel mills in Indiana and Ohio, and he was home only a few days a month. He generously let Doris and me use the house that whole summer.

During our first weeks together I could hardly believe that someone so intelligent and so beautiful had fallen in love with me. Then I began to realize that Doris didn't see herself as beautiful. Her situation was much different from Chip's. Chip just seemed oblivious to his good looks. Doris saw herself as positively unattractive. She carried herself that way too. Much of the time she walked with her head a little bit down, as if she didn't want to be noticed. She also didn't pay much attention to her clothes, and she wore truly ugly, wing-style glasses, the kind that don't look good on anyone.

But I remember a late afternoon that first summer when she wasn't wearing either her glasses or her clothes. It was one of the first times we'd made love in daylight. Afterward, Doris got out of bed to open a window to cool us off. As she stood in the window the breeze pushed the old fashioned lace curtains across her face; she looked like a bride in a veil who'd decided to forgo the wedding dress. I thought she was the most beautiful woman who'd ever lived.

I hope I told her so.

It was the best summer of my life. I was working my butt off in the pulp woods, but I had Doris to look forward to in the evenings. Almost every night, she drove to Big Pine after her shift at the resort. Sometimes we'd have dinner with my parents, and once in a while we drove down to the Heron night club, but mostly we just immersed ourselves in each other, talking and making love and planning for a life together. Mornings came early, though. We were both up by five; her job in the resort dining room started at six, and the pulp crew started work at six thirty, so we could get most of our work done in the cooler part of the day.

Society had already changed some by the time I returned from the Navy and began my second tour on an Otto crew. Change might happen in big cities and the coasts first, but it eventually seeps into places like Big Pine. Attitudes about marijuana are a good example.

When I was high school, in the 1960s, you could probably have organized a lynch party for anyone caught selling marijuana in Big Pine. But by the early 1970s, Larkin County kids were coming back from Vietnam with a taste for bud—and for some other things. After being shot at in the jungle, they weren't much intimidated by small-town cops and constables who might try to bust them for smoking an alternative substance. In turn, those cops didn't have a lot of appetite for arresting guys who'd been in a war, and who were now eligible for VFW membership. By 1975 some of the same Big Pine folks who wanted to lynch weed smokers in 1965 were lighting up themselves. My own feeling is that the anti-weed people hadn't been so much upset about dope as they were about missing the sexual revolution that seemed to go along with it. I think that was at the root of my conflict with a pulp woods coworker that summer.

My Navy service earned me some limited status with my coworkers; I was no longer The Kid. But I was still The New Guy, and that was enough to leave me open to some shit from the older hands. Mostly it was good-natured stuff, but one guy, Al, got under my skin. Al married right after high school. He had four daughters, and Mrs. Al got a little broader after each one—"two axe handles across the beam" was the unkind way Uncle Pete described her. But it wasn't the extra weight that made her unattractive—it was more a heaviness of spirit. She'd "let herself go," as my grandmother use to say about some women. I think that happens more often in rural areas than it does in cities, and I think isolation is a big part of it. Al's wife spent her days at home, half a mile from the nearest neighbor, trying to make do for a family of six on Al's income. About the only times you saw her in town were when she grocery shopped or at the Buckhorn's Friday night meat raffle.

Al and his wife were people my grandmother to referred to as "jackpine savages." I asked her once what defined someone as a jackpine savage. She said if you could see both the house and the household dump from the road, the occupants were jackpine savages.

The "right kind of people," she said, kept their old refrigerators and rusted washtubs out of sight. Al had three rusty old cars, the carcass of a school bus, and a bunch of other crap sitting in a gully about fifty yards from his house. The junk just didn't register with him. Jackpine savage.

Al liked to fill our breaks with stories about the sexual doings of "hippie girls," but as far as I knew, his experience with the new counter culture was limited to seeing clips of Haight-Ashbury on the news. He seemed to know a lot about those girls though. They couldn't get enough, he said, and that when they smoked marijuana they always wanted to "do oral."

Oral always figured big in his stories. His resentment about missing the blow job boat wasn't real hard to spot.

For the first few weeks Al called me "Rookie" and "Sailor Boy," not stuff that really bothered me. But he'd seen me around town with Doris, and his speculations about her really pissed me off. He'd say things like, "I bet she looks good all tore down," or "Are those headlights real?"

Of course the new guy in any group of working men is usually the butt of ribbing, but Al speculating on what Doris might look like naked was not okay. Things slipped out of control one day while we were eating our lunches and Al said, "I bet keeping that doe satisfied is the hardest work you ever done, ain't it, Sailor Boy?"

"No, Al," I said, "the hardest work I've ever done was getting you to let go of my dick."

For some reason that struck the rest of the crew as the absolute funniest, wittiest thing they'd ever heard on the job. I was the Don Rickles of the pulp woods.

Al, however, didn't take his turn in the barrel gracefully. He even got a little chesty with me. I was pissed enough over his comments about Doris that I wanted to beat the shit out of him. I even started after him, but a couple other guys on the crew got between us.

Then to save face, Al started huffing and puffing like he'd really been ready to fight, though I don't think anyone bought his act.

Otto must have heard about the incident—a couple days later he transferred Al to another crew. When you've got guys swinging chainsaws around, dropping trees, it's safer if they all get along. Now, looking back, I feel kind of bad about humiliating Al. He was just a guy stuck in a life that wasn't very much fun.

~

Midway through that first summer together, Doris brought me home to meet her parents. I already knew she and her mom had major issues, one being Doris's name. It was already out of fashion when Doris was born, but her mom was a big Doris Day fan, and she overruled her husband's objections. As soon as I met her mom, I also began to understand the source of Doris's distorted physical self image. I remember she criticized the way Doris was dressed the minute we came in the door. My future mother-in-law had been

Engineering Day Queen at the U of M, and she never let her daughter forget it. The picture she used on her real estate agent business cards pretty much screamed Former Queen of Something, and to me it seemed like she was still running for a title, even in her own family. Right away I felt she was competing against her own daughter for my attention.

Up until her high school junior year, Doris said, she'd been her mother's idea of the right kind of daughter—gymnastics and dance lessons in grade school and then, beginning in seventh grade, cheerleading lessons. But in her junior year, Doris refused to even try out for cheerleading. Something snapped, she said, after she read *The Grapes of Wrath*. She started volunteering at a homeless shelter near downtown Minneapolis and began buying her all her clothes at Good Will instead of at Dayton's department store. It drove her mother crazy when she refused to even try on anything she bought for her. Doris also made sure to be as outrageous as possible in front of her mother's friends. One evening at a dinner party she did a reading out of *The Grapes of Wrath* for the guests—the account of Rosasharon Joad breastfeeding the starving man.

Our Vietnam disaster was another torture opportunity. Opposition to the war was growing during Doris's high school years, but it was still mostly supported in the upper-class suburb where her family lived. Doris really did oppose the war, but her participation in protests had the extra benefit of annoying her mother. During her high school senior year, Doris regularly headed over to join the demonstrations at the main U of M campus. Sometimes she brought other demonstrators home with her, and the grungier they were, the better. Doris said she loved watching her mother twisting herself into knots, trying to be polite to them.

Most girls minimize their sexual activity to their parents. Doris went the other direction; she did have sex with a boy in her senior class, and also with a protester she met on campus, but she led her mom to believe there'd been so many that she'd lost count.

Thank God for Doris's dad. Right from the first time I met him I could tell he was her fan club. He was vice-president of Engineering at a Fortune 500 company in Minneapolis, and he loved that his youngest daughter was so bright and that she was a top student, especially in math and science classes. I'm sure he was the reason Doris kept getting all A's, even while she was rebelling and trying to drive her mom around the bend.

Her dad was a little disappointed that she didn't follow him into a technical or scientific career, but he was still completely supportive of her desire to go into psychology. He also probably felt, at least at first, that Doris might have made a better potential husband selection. A high school teacher and wrestling coach wasn't likely to provide the apple of his eye with the comfort she'd grown up in, but I know he got round to liking me. I liked him too.

Another way Doris tortured her mom was to subscribe to scandal magazines in her mom's name: *National Enquirer*, *Confidential*, the kind of reading material her mom associated with trailer parks, country western music and open-mouth gum chewers. Exactly the kind of material she would be mortified to find in her mailbox—or have some front-door visitor see in her mailbox. Doris kept it up even after she left home. We'd been married for six or seven years already when the *Weekly World News* came out. She couldn't buy her mom a subscription fast enough. Doris paid a price though; she became an addict herself. There's always a pile of that stuff under her side of the bed. The headlines are usually better than the actual stories: "Proof JFK Bugged Jackie's Bra" and "Dolphin Rapes Newlywed Couple" are a couple I remember. The bra story seemed at least remotely plausible, but I remember the writer didn't even try to describe the mechanics of the dolphin rape.

Of course Doris can't have her own subscriptions—they don't come in plain brown wrappers, and having our postmistress see them as she sorted them into our box would not be okay. Hansen's Grocery had them at the checkout, but that wasn't very anonymous either, so Doris usually picked them up at the Cub grocery store in Brainerd.

~

The main campus was a madhouse the fall I joined Doris at the U of M, and it stayed that way for the next three years. That first winter, black students took over Morrill Hall, the main administration building, for two days. Civil Rights protests and demonstrations against the war were weekly events, usually ending with arrests. Some professors announced they wouldn't fail any students—they didn't want to be responsible for a nineteen-year-old losing his deferment and then getting blown up in the jungle. Kids were also dropping acid, smoking dope, and having more sex. And they dressed a lot differently than they had a few years before.

"Foundation garments," as my mother used to call them, were definitely optional, though I had mixed feelings on that. I did enjoy seeing the freer movement of flesh under fabric—just not when it came to Doris. She has prominent nipples and, when she went braless, guys noticed.

One day I was waiting to meet her outside her class, and I heard one guy coming out say to another that "Chilly was really standing at attention today." The other guy looked back toward Doris.

After that, I pretty much begged her to start wearing bras again, or at least thicker shirts and sweaters.

During our first year on campus, I lived in an apartment with two other returning veterans, and Doris stayed with her folks. The next fall we moved in together. Her parents were a little put off at first, but I think it was easier for them that she was with a crew-cut military vet, not one of the shaggy protesters. Also, it was a new world and Doris wasn't the first daughter their social circle to shack up with her boyfriend. Still, I know her mom was relieved when Doris and I got married the year before we graduated.

When I look back, I have no doubt that the Vietnam War years were the most dramatic period of change in my lifetime. Timothy Leary's advice to "Turn On, Tune In, and Drop Out" was taken seriously by a lot of young people during those years. So was "Question Authority," though the lawbreaking wasn't just by college students.

Doris and I graduated the year of the Watergate burglary, the event that eventually drove Nixon out of the White House—and would have put his butt in jail if Ford hadn't pardoned him. It was also around then that post-mortem accounts of Jack Kennedy in full rut were becoming fair game for journalists and historians. Those scandals made it more and more difficult to pretend that men with their fingers on nuclear triggers are any less flawed than the rest of us. We've evolved to the point of creating technology that can obliterate hundreds of millions of people in minutes, but it's under the control of guys who can't keep their zippers up.

Not very persuasive evidence for Intelligent Design.

CHAPTER 16, ED

I FAIL ON SUCCESS DAY

Success Day would be the first time I'd talked to Joey since his ten-year reunion. He was just a few years out of law school, but he'd already made his first big score, and he couldn't have been happier to let us all know about it. In law school he'd worked on a case study involving Indian hunting and fishing rights. On Lake Mille Lacs, for instance, 40 percent of the walleye harvest is reserved for netting by the Mille Lacs Ojibwe band. Indian walleye netting is a bone in the throat for a lot of non-Indian sport fisherman who don't understand why it's allowed. They think the State of Minnesota should be able to determine who gets to catch how many fish within state borders. But the reality is that state and local governments must deal with the Indian tribes through negotiation, and not just by decree. It might piss off a lot of people, but Indian treaties are essentially treaties with foreign nations, and they trump state laws in many circumstances. Joey Hamer got his start by understanding that.

After passing the Bar, Joey partnered with a classmate, an enrolled member of a Wisconsin tribe. The partner was listed as 51 percent owner, qualifying the firm as a minority enterprise. Then the two of them began looking for business operations that could be carried out on reservations, but not in the rest of the state. They focused on a newly high-profile area, environmental pollution. Their first project addressed the problem of disposing of creosote-contaminated railroad ties. Joey and his partner set up a three-way project involving the railroads, the public power company, and a Minnesota tribal reservation. Their idea was to ship the contaminated ties to a reservation where they could be converted into burnable chips which would become fuel for the power company. The key was that the reservation was exempt from some of the more restrictive environmental regulations on handling the ties.

When someone asked how the project turned out, Joey said it worked out great—that they'd billed the participating companies just under a million dollars in eighteen months. Someone else asked if the project was still operating.

"Never got off the ground," Joey said, "turned out the conversion technology didn't really work."

But the billing process did work, and Joey made his first real piece of change. Now, another twenty years later, he was coming back to tell the rest of his story.

~

On the morning of Success Day, Joey and Mrs. Joey Number 3 arrived at the school in a black BMW 750, chauffeured by my surrogate son, Ned Cooley. Joey and Ned were classmates in high school, but they steered wide of each other in those days—Joey was too smart to get crossways with lethal Ned, and Ned had no interest in being one of Joey's stooges. The incident that brought them together twenty-five years later would play out in front of millions of television viewers.

The title of Joey's talk was "Positioning for Success." Ordinarily, the faculty adviser to the Entrepreneurs Club would give an introduction, including maybe a couple of endearing bullshit stories about the speaker's student years. I weaseled and assigned the introduction to the club president—anything good I said about Joey would have been a lie.

The club president introduced him, then took a seat next to Sharon, Joey's newest wife. Sharon was definitely hot, a Marilyn Monroe type, not like some of the stringy, undernourished actresses you see these days. Her presence on the stage made no sense other than as a marker of Joey's success—and I guarantee some of the boys in the audience were mentally "positioning her for success" as Joey crowed about himself from the podium.

Joey did look successful, but his physical appearance was also a little spooky—he looked too damn young, with no signs of aging or stress. Maybe it's having a conscience that ages a person. Joey was almost fifty, but you'd have guessed him at around thirty-five, tops. He still wore the same pretty-boy hair style he had in high school, dark curls on his forehead, held in place with hair gel—though apparently it's not called "hair gel" anymore.

About ten years ago, Jeanette, the woman who cuts my hair, started asking me if I wanted her to use some "product" to make my crew cut stand up better. Product? What was wrong with "gel"? Too informative? I wanted to say, "Yes, Jeanette, I'll have some 'product'— a little Velveeta and some Scotch Tape, maybe. Or do you think Lucky Charms and Super Glue would look better?"

Joey's talk covered his railroad tie project and how it set him up with the experience and the contacts he used to make his real fortune—in the PCB remediation business. Joey began by explaining to the would-be Joey's what PCBs are. Some of the audience already had an idea—at least they should have if they were listening in my biology class.

PCB stands for polychlorinated biphenyl, a chemical insulator that was used in power transformers. It was outlawed in the 1970s because of its potential for causing birth defects and cancers. For the previous fifty years, PCBs had been routinely dumped as waste into sewers and landfills.

When they were finally banned, electric utilities had a huge problem—transformer oil was almost all PCB contaminated. All that oil had to be safely disposed of, and all spill and disposal sites, no matter how old, had to be cleaned up.

Thanks to the failed railroad tie project, Joey already had the right web of connections when he recognized the PCB opportunity. He and his partner formed a new minority-owned company, then worked their contacts from the railroad tie project to get minority set-aside contracts for PCB cleanup and disposal.

"We were positioned for success," Joey told the students, "Within three years we were second largest PCB remediation company in the Midwest, minority or otherwise."

He added that his company had even done soil decontamination work on the Big Pine power substation site. He said that job made him feel good—doing something for his own hometown. Any reasonable God would have fried The Little Shit with a lightning bolt, right there on the Big Pine High School auditorium stage.

After his talk, Joey spotted me in the hall and asked me how he'd done. I told him he always amazed me—which was true. We chatted about old acquaintances for a minute or two, and then he even asked me a couple of questions. How was Doris? Was I out on White Deer for the walleye opener?

Of course Joey didn't give a shit about things like that. I figured he must have taken one of those Carnegie-type courses where guys like Joey learn to pretend they're interested in other people.

I should have let the conversation die, but instead I had to do something foolish. I asked Joey if the Big Pine PCB clean-up he mentioned in his talk was from an old spill. I said there must have been one the night somebody shot out our transformer. "I think you were a homecoming prince that year, weren't you?"

I put a little extra emphasis on "prince" and, as soon as I said it, I knew it was a mistake. In case I haven't mentioned it, I don't always know when to keep my mouth shut.

Joey looked at me like I imagine Satan looks at someone he knows he'll be seeing soon. "You know, I'd forgotten all about that."

I believe that was the moment The Little Shit decided he wasn't done punishing all of us, and that I would receive special attention.

The afternoon of Success Day, Joey held court in a workshop for members of the Entrepreneurs Club. Sharon co-hosted the session, presumably as an example of what the two female club members might aspire to if they could get genetic makeovers. The workshop didn't require my presence, so I had a couple of hours to catch up with my surrogate son, Ned Cooley.

CHAPTER 17, ED

NED COOLEY

When I first started teaching, a number of my fellow teachers were also Big Pine graduates. I once heard an education professor lecture about rural districts that hired too many of their own. He said that risked having the schools go stale, that teachers who'd grown up in the community came in with too many preformed judgments of the kids.

That might be true in some measure, but the flip side is that home-grown teachers know things about the community that could take years for someone new to understand. I came in already knowing which parents beat their kids with straps or drank too much, and whose "aunt" was really his mother. Having that information sometimes helped me see a kid like Ned Cooley as something other than a problem.

Ned was an angry fifteen-year-old the year I returned to Big Pine as a teacher and coach. Behind his back he was referred to as Chief Crazy or The Crazy Indian.

Ned's mom is an Ojibwe from the Red Cliff reservation, over in Wisconsin. Her first husband, Ned's biological father, was an Irish-American railroad brakeman. Ned's younger brother and sister show the heritage of both parents; but with Ned, his mom's genes dominated. When you look at Ned, you see an Indian.

Life changed for him when he was nine, after his father was

killed in a switching accident up near the town of Ball Club. From what I remembered, Ned was a fairly normal kid up to that point. Then two years after his dad died, his mom remarried. Town opinion was that she didn't make a good choice the second time around. Most thought that Ned's new stepfather had married her for the railroad settlement money. He was a shitty husband and a shitty father. He was also partly responsible for Ned's menacing appearance. When Ned was eleven he took a fall off his bike that opened up a two-inch gash that ran down his forehead, ending just above his left eye. His new step dad was too cheap, or too drunk, to drive him twenty miles to the doctor in Brainerd, so he had Ned's mom pull the cut closed with adhesive tape. It healed into a scar that left Ned with a look that matched his tough-guy reputation—a reputation he fully deserved.

Even as a rookie coach, the first time I saw Ned on a wrestling mat, I knew he was a talent I might never see again in my career. He was the whole package: speed, strength, and aggressiveness. As a sophomore he wrestled 145, but even at that weight he was freakishly strong. I remember in one of our first practices I was showing him a move he could use from the "up" position. When we tied up, and he clamped onto my bicep with his hand I felt like a bear trap had closed on it. Just being on the receiving end of that much raw strength terrified most kids he faced on the mat.

Sheer ability and intense anger carried Ned for the first half of his sophomore season, but he lacked self-discipline, and sometimes he'd lose it and just start brawling. By midway in the season, he'd lost three matches on disqualifications, and most of his own teammates were afraid to work with him in practice. Sometimes our heavyweight was the only kid willing to get out on the mat with him. Many of the kids I coached had to be taught to go on offense—to be more aggressive. Thanks to his home life, Ned was already a volcano of aggression.

One morning, midway through the wrestling season, I got a message that Ned's mom was in the principal's office, asking to see me. She looked like hell—big red marks on her face that were starting to turn purple. Ned was in juvenile detention up in Big Rapids, she said, and his stepfather was in the Brainerd hospital. She told me her husband had taken a belt to Ned's younger brother the night before, and that when she tried to intervene he turned it on her. She said Ned went berserk. He tore the belt away from his stepfather and went after him with it—with the buckle end. Ned's mom said she finally covered her husband with her own body, just to keep Ned from killing him.

After school that day, I drove up to Big Rapids to pick up Ned and bring him home. By the time I got up there, the weather had turned nasty. A crosswind was sweeping the snow over the road surface, turning Highway 48 into a skating pond, and visibility was less than a hundred yards. On the drive back to Big Pine we saw two jackknifed semis and at least a dozen cars in the ditch. The fifty-mile trip took us two hours. I was only ten years older than Ned, but I think it was during that ride in my pickup that I became as much his father as his wrestling coach.

The day after I brought him home, his mom had a restraining order served on her husband, while he was still in his hospital bed, and a week later a sheriff's deputy supervised as the bandaged-up asshole moved his stuff out of Ned's house for good. I don't believe he's been seen in Big Pine since. The only downside to his departure was that, back then, children of divorced parents were said to come from "broken homes." Even teachers used the phrase. *Jesus,* what lead collars to hang around kids' necks.

Now they're from "single parent" families. A whole lot better label. I used the example when Doris called a Rule on me.

Ned went on to have a good season, making it to the district finals. More importantly, he calmed down enough that his own teammates weren't afraid of him—at least not most of the time. He took state at 165 as a junior, and again at 177 as a senior—he hadn't grown any taller, but he became what coaches sometimes call "thick." The word does not imply overweight—he was only eight or nine percent body fat during the wrestling season. Ned was "thick" with muscle, and he intimidated and dominated with strength the same way the Russian Olympian, Karelin, did a few years later.

Ned's opponents made a show of trying to win, but most were probably relieved just to get pinned without any permanent damage. Some even forfeited—an unusual number of opponents came down with a twenty-four-hour flu the day they were scheduled to face Ned in a meet. I can't say I blame them.

After the incident with his step dad, Ned's only serious off-mat violence was triggered by our supremely stupid Gobbler mascot. As anyone can probably imagine, it doesn't require a genius-level teenage wit to come up with Gobbler humor. Every girl who ever attended

Big Pine High School has heard, "Hey, honey, do you gobble?" or something similar, shouted out of a car full of boys from a rival town. Football games were the worst. At least once a year you could count on some kid in the opposing stands holding up a "Gobblers Welcome Here" sign—usually with an arrow pointing straight down. The signs were automatic triggers for post-game mayhem, and I admit that I participated in my school days.

Ned would have been on the football field as a player, but he quit after his sophomore season because he couldn't stand Coach Becker. I have to agree that Becker was hard to take. He'd been my coach too, and I'd sat through at least a hundred of his inspirational team speeches. I think he'd seen *The Knute Rockne Story* too many times. His other favorite topic was the danger of "self-abuse," which always got a few guys in the audience subtly pointing at each other and doing air guitar versions of jacking off.

Ned gave up football but he always attended the games, along with a couple of his wrestling buddies. They'd sit on our side of the field, scanning with binoculars for any offensive displays in the opponent's bleachers. Then sometime before the end of the fourth quarter, they would head over to the Visitors Exit to confront the offenders. Some kids are tough in the stands; Ned was tough behind the stands. His signature move was similar to one he used in matches—grinding an opponent's face into the mat until it looked like a strawberry. Behind the stands, the grass took the place of the mat. Sometimes he'd ask the kid if he had any naked pictures of his girlfriend or his mother. If he could still talk, the kid would of course say no. "I'll send you some," Ned would say. That always got a big yuk from his accomplices. Another favorite was something like, "Did you know your mom is a great dancer? She is—she gave me a lap dance last night, and then we did the horizontal mambo. She says I do it better than your dad." More yuks.

Those incidents did illustrate the less-than-noble side of Ned's character. He would say in his defense that his targets always deserved what they got, but the fact was that he did enjoy violence.

Eventually, the father of a Big Rapids kid filed a complaint alleging the Big Pine school district wasn't maintaining a safe environment for visitors. In addition to documenting his son's injuries, the letter also referenced "obscene comments about a Mambo."

I had to drive Ned up there to meet the father and son at the police station to make amends. When we met them, I got the feeling that the guy was more upset about the Mambo stuff than about the scabs on his kid's face.

Ned droned through an apology, and I gave them a copy of a letter from our principal to the Big Rapids School District. The letter stated that, in the future, Big Pine would provide lines of parents and teachers to funnel visiting fans safely from the exits to their buses. What a pain in the ass that was.

Early in my coaching career, I'd vowed that by the time I retired, our school would dump the turkey and replace it with something better—and anything we replaced it with would be better. The opportunity came in my fifth year of teaching, when the turkey plant finally closed. The town mourned the lost jobs but having an avian slaughterhouse on one end of our main street hadn't really contributed to our advertised image of Big Pine as a woodsy "Up North" tourist destination. The plant was especially annoying on summer days, when it operated with the doors open. Grudee's Drugstore, just two blocks away, had outdoor tables where you could sit in the sun and enjoy something from the soda fountain. But if the breeze was from the west or southwest, you were like as not to have a bit of turkey feather float down onto your banana split. The noise could be pretty bad too. Domestic turkeys aren't bred for intelligence, but some of them seemed to have an idea the future was not promising and they were quite vocal on how they felt about it.

Of course kids were fascinated by the place. In the History Center we have a photo from the 1960s that shows a group of open-mouthed children standing in the doorway of the plant, looking up at an overhead conveyor line of dangling turkeys. It looks like they're watching a mass lynching. We'd all grown up with it, but many summer residents weren't comfortable with having their city-raised kids witness the traumatic first steps toward Thanksgiving dinner, and I'm sure they were happy when the plant was no more.

The plant closing was an obvious opportunity for change. Unfortunately, my first serious effort to dump our turkey went nowhere. Even most of the other teachers wanted to keep it, or were lukewarm about replacing it. We had one exploratory meeting, then nothing. It was almost twenty-five years before I tried again.

Despite his bad-boy image, Ned was a decent student. He graduated in the top quarter of his class and received multiple athletic scholarship offers, including ones from Iowa State, and the U of M, two of the top wrestling programs in the country. But more school wasn't on Ned's immediate agenda. His biological dad served with the First Marines in Korea, and Ned was determined to carry on the tradition. I knew I wouldn't be able to talk him out of it, but at least Vietnam was winding down by that spring, and we all hoped he would get through his enlistment safely.

Over the next four years, Ned checked in with Doris and me whenever he came home on leave. After his discharge he came back to Big Pine to stay with his mom while he thought about what to do with the rest of his life. His Ojibwe mom's brother was an ironworker down in the Cities, and he offered to get Ned in as an apprentice. It was an entree that a lot of young guys would have jumped at—ironworkers were the highest paid of the union construction trades.

Unfortunately, Ned had to confess to his uncle that all Indians are not fearless and sure-footed at heights, and that being even ten feet off the ground scared him shitless. Instead, he went to work on an Otto Hamer crew. On rainy days and weekends though, Ned hung around Uncle Pete's shop. Pete's business didn't justify a paid employee, but Ned was satisfied helping him for free in exchange for what he could learn. I think the two of them recognized themselves in each other. They'd both had some hard patches in childhood, and they'd both reacted by becoming brawlers in their teen years.

A few weeks into their weekend working arrangement, Pete told me he thought Ned had a lot of natural mechanical ability, and that he should capitalize on it with trade school training. Doris and I and

Ned's mom joined forces with Pete in convincing Ned to sign up for fall enrollment at Dunwoody Institute in Minneapolis. It was considered one of the best trade schools in the country, and it still has that reputation today. Our last shop teacher told me that Help Wanted ads in Los Angeles newspapers, 2,000 miles away, ask for Dunwoody graduates.

After graduation, Ned took a job with a Ford dealership in a Minneapolis suburb, eventually becoming lead mechanic and then shop foreman. He was still working there, twenty years later, when he had the fifteen minutes of fame that led to his reunion with Joey Hamer.

NED BECOMES FAMOUS

The Twins were playing the White Sox at the Metrodome in Minneapolis in a nationally televised Major League Game of the Week. Late in the game, a Sox batter sent one into the left field bleachers, right at where Ned and his girlfriend were sitting. Ned was set to haul it in when a very big guy next to him reached in front of Ned with a fielder's glove and made the unluckiest home-run catch in the history of baseball.

The TV announcer said, "Now there's a fan who'll take home a great memory."

A second later, with the camera still lingering on the fan holding the ball in the air, Ned tagged him with a left. The guy dropped like a bag of laundry, hitting his head on a seat back on the way down. The game went on, but the guy who caught the ball almost didn't. I don't know if he recovered his "great memory," but at least surgeons were able to stop the intracranial bleeding and save his life—and save Ned from a manslaughter charge.

Of course all the national media ran with the story, including a slow-motion clip of the knockout, accompanied by lots of editorial *cluck clucking* about rising fan violence. Naturally, Ned was arrested. When he was booked into Hennepin County Jail the cops asked him if he had an attorney. Ned said he didn't, but then he thought of Joey

129

Hamer, and said that's who he wanted to call. Joey explained to Ned that he wasn't a criminal lawyer, but that he knew a good one to refer him to.

Joey was right; the woman who represented Ned was good. She called me to ask if I would be a character witness for Ned when things got to the sentencing phase. Naturally I told her I would, but I wasn't really looking forward to it. I did want to help Ned—he really is a son to me—but popping someone who crossed him wasn't completely alien to his nature. The unfortunate truth is that he enjoys it. I sent the court a carefully worded letter of support that didn't contain any outright lies.

The lawyer worked out a better deal than anyone expected. She told the prosecutor that when Ned politely asked for the ball the guy responded, "Fuck off, Tonto," and that it triggered the anger he carried from being physically abused as a kid, as well as from discrimination due to his race. She also played up Ned's honorable service in the Marine Corps and his lack of an adult arrest record. The prosecutor bargained down to six months in the workhouse, and no loss of civil rights if Ned completed a two-year probation without incident. Ned would still be able to vote and own guns—though it would be more accurate to say he could start voting and keep his guns.

Because Ned's mom never had a driver's license, I drove her down to Minneapolis to visit him every couple weeks during his jail stay. Doris came along a few times, too.

Ned told us the worst thing about jail was boredom. Nobody hassled him, he said, which wasn't a surprise considering the knockout had been replayed a zillion times on the news—it even became stock footage, popping up over the next few years any time there was a news report on fan violence. Ned got a celebrity's welcome when he arrived in jail, and he was initially christened "One Punch Tonto" by a fellow inmate.

Ned said he straightened the guy out on the "Tonto" bit right away, and after that he was known as One Punch. Even the guards used the name, he said.

Neither Ned's foreman job at the car dealership, nor his girlfriend, were waiting for him when he got out of jail, but Joey Hamer was right there. The lawyer who defended Ned was expensive, more than Ned could come up with without liquidating his retirement, but Joey picked up the tab and offered Ned a way to pay him back. And that's how my boy, Ned Cooley, became personal assistant to Joseph O Hamer, Esq. Six months after he got out of jail, Ned was behind the wheel of Joey's $80,000 ride, chauffeuring Joey and Sharon up to Big Pine for Success Day.

CHAPTER 19, ED

NED'S NEW LIFE

While Joey and Sharon were doing their afternoon Success Workshop with the club members, I had a chance to catch up on Ned's new life. I asked him what exactly he did for Joey.

"Mostly just drive him around—or drive her around," Ned said, "and sometimes I sit in on business meetings."

By the time Ned joined Joey's team PCB cleanup was moving toward completion, and firms like Joey's had to sharpen their pencils to win contracts for the dwindling number of projects that remained. It was still profitable, just not exciting enough for Joey. He was already rich, but he was addicted to action, and to the fun of manipulating people into doing what he wanted—plus, he was a lawyer, a lawyer with a ton of both tribal and government contacts. It was a perfect resume for his new position as chief lobbyist for the Indian Gaming Association.

In the years following Minnesota's first high-stakes reservation bingo, down in Shakopee, Indian "gaming" became a multi-billion-dollar business. I have to admire the euphemism. "Gaming" calls to mind a healthful fresh-air activity—fauns and maidens at play on a grassy field, maybe. The reality is warehouses filled with senior citizens grinding away their Social Security in slot machines.

In an old issue of the *Larkin County Register,* I once found an article about a sheriff's raid on a "sporting house," a nineteenth-century euphemism for a whorehouse. It's all in a name, I guess. "Honey, the boys and I are going gaming for a bit, and then doing a little sporting. Don't wait up."

Reservations are still grim places in much of Indian country, even those with casino gambling, but things are a little better on some of the reservations with casinos. I'd rather the tribes were building computers or medical devices, but it's a lot easier to set up a money-making tribal gambling operation than it is to start a successful manufacturing business. Gambling income can pay for medical clinics, substance abuse resources, better schools and infrastructure, even college money for kids who manage to steer clear enough of alcohol and drugs and gangs before they graduate from high school.

Drive through the Pine Ridge or Rosebud reservations out in South Dakota sometime, places without enough surrounding population to support gambling. You don't have to leave America to see what third-world misery looks like.

Ned said his new role was to attend meetings or social events where Joey worked with whichever legislators or tribal officials he needed to get in his corner. Joey made it clear that Ned wasn't supposed to do much, other than look intimidating.

"He always works in that I'm the guy from the Twins' game. That's it. I'm never supposed to smile or say anything, but he always wants me to keep my big ugly hands on the table where people can see the scars. He likes the one on my forehead too, even though he knows I got it falling off my bike."

I have no doubt he was good in the role Joey cast him in. If intimidation was art, Ned would be Picasso.

He said Joey paid him well for what was often just babysitting Sharon and keeping her out of trouble. Beyond getting stoned almost every night, Ned said, her hobbies were shopping and working out at her club. She was an exotic dancer when Joey met her, and she was still fanatical about staying in shape.

"The workouts are fine with me," Ned said, "because I can work out too. I need it to stay sane after a day of shopping with her. She'll get pissed about something, usually about Joey, then go out and buy all kinds of shit she doesn't even want."

"Joey says I can screw her if I want to, but he expects me to tell him about it. I think he wants the information for when it comes time to divorce her. I've never done it, but sometimes she comes on to me after she's had a few drinks. Once when she was loaded, she tried to put her hand down my pants, with Joey right in the next room. She says she never had an Indian and she wants to find out what it's like. But I can't do it. Down deep she hates herself, and that turns me off. Believe it or not I got to have a positive feeling about a girl before I want to have sex with her. Sounds stupid, doesn't it?"

I said it didn't sound stupid at all. Other than his appetite for violence, there isn't much not to like about Ned.

CHAPTER 20, ED

CHIP'S BIG SURPRISE

With Success Day finally out of the way, I relaxed enough to get nervous about the next big event: our Saturday evening dinner party.

For our main course, Maddie and Doris put together a really tasty cioppino, along with an Italian salad and a garlic-buttered baguette—nice and garlicky, so we'd all be on equal footing later in the evening. The meal went just fine after we'd gotten a couple of glasses of wine into everyone—Chip being the one who probably needed them most. He was in a hell of an awkward spot, sitting at the dinner table of the friend he felt he betrayed, trying not to show how conflicted he was. Of course, at that point, he had no idea I'd witnessed his performance in the guest bedroom.

After dinner we all went into the living room. It was nearing the end of May, but spring isn't a seamless advance into summer up here, and the weather outside was chilly and rainy, giving me an excuse to build a fire. I uncorked another bottle of wine and sat down on the sofa next to Maddie, with my arm resting behind her, on top of the sofa back. Doris and Chip sat across from us, on the love seat. For a few minutes we talked about the Twins pitching problems, the long-range precipitation forecast and the possibility of another frost—the kind of edgy repartee we northern Minnesotans are known for. Then Maddie made her move.

She slid closer to me, undid the top button of her blouse, and gently pulled my hand down over her shoulder into the opening. Just like it was the most natural thing in the world.

Chip froze. I could tell he was holding his breath.

Doris turned toward him and said, "Relax, Chip, it's okay."

When he looked at me, I just nodded.

I felt the green monster stir again as I watched my wife take Chip's hand and lead him up the stairs, but this time I'd been part of the decision. I was also completely wired in anticipation of being in bed with Maddie again. The sexual newness of her was incredibly exciting, a feeling I hadn't had since Doris and I first became lovers, a lifetime earlier. Maddie and I had another glass of wine and made out for a while before heading upstairs ourselves.

After we helped each other undress, Maddie peeked around the corner into the guest room and motioned me over. She moved me in front of her to give me a better view. Doris didn't look like she was in charge this time. She was on her back, and Chip had her hands pinned above her head. The two of them were half covered by the sheet, but I could see Doris' knees move a little wider every time she pressed her feet down on the bed to raise her hips up to meet him. Her eyes were closed, and she was biting down hard on her lower lip, like she was trying not to make any noise.

When Maddie circled her arms around me from behind, I thought my legs would fail me, but we made it back to the bed.

"I've never seen anyone doing it before," Maddie said.

I told her it was only the second time for me.

Later that same evening was the first time I heard about the ideas that Doris and Maddie played with on their Duluth shopping outing.

"We were thinking four or five couples is probably the ideal number," Doris said, completely out of nowhere. "What do you two think"?

Chip stopped breathing for the second time that night.

I think I did too.

"Relax, guys," Doris said, "We were just doing a little fantasizing."

"But just for fun," Maddie added, "does anyone come to mind?"

CHAPTER 21, ED

THE NEW NORMAL

For the next few weeks, the four of us got together at our house every Saturday night—and a couple of times on weeknights when we just couldn't wait until Saturday. Doris and I bought a king-size bed the second week—her idea.

The Saturday after the bed purchase, we started off in separate bedrooms as usual, but after half an hour Maddie said maybe we should invite Chip and Doris to join us—I'm sure she and Doris cooked it up ahead of time. When they came into the room, with a single sheet wrapped around the two of them, it was way too comical to be erotic, and it took us all a while to settle in again.

By the middle of summer, the idea of expanding our secret league to four or five teams didn't seem as unrealistic as it did when Doris and Maddie first suggested it. I guess if you think about something crazy enough times, then it doesn't seem so crazy anymore. At the beginning I'd assumed we were such an aberration that our foursome might already hold all the potential libertines in Larkin County—at least all the libertine couples. Doris thought that was naive. Her guess was that there might be just as many people interested our activity as there would be for a book club, or a garden club—as long as they were very sure they wouldn't be found out. It was during that discussion that Maddie suggested naming ourselves

The Big Pine Book and Garden Club. We all agreed it had a nice, wholesome ring to it.

Of course a real book club or garden club could run a notice in the *Register* or put up a poster at the library, but we needed to identify our prospects without letting anyone else know of our existence. There's a saying that country people are both kinder and crueler than city people. The sense of it is that, in rural areas, neighbors really step up for you if they see you as an innocent victim. If your house burns down, or if you get leukemia, they're likely to be right there for you. But get hooked on alcohol or drugs, or get caught in adultery or shoplifting, anything that looks like a voluntary bad choice, and they tend to judge you pretty harshly. We had no doubt that our current activities, along with what we were planning, would put us in that second category. We tried to imagine the resulting feature stories if we were found out: "Senior Swinger Underground Rocks Mayberry," blurred face interviews on *60 Minutes*, stuff like that. Doris's secret addiction to scandal magazines made her good at coming up with titillating headlines. Those discussions about our possible exposure could bc funny, but we all knew that, if we really were discovered, it would not be at all funny, and that we'd probably have to find another town to live in. We did find a few issues easy to settle, though.

A surprisingly easy consensus was group size. Doris's and Maddie's initial instinct felt right—Chip and I agreed that four or five couples sounded most practical. We figured eight or ten people should be enough to keep things interesting and, hopefully, few enough to stay under the town's radar.

We were also unanimous in agreeing that, except for Maddie and Chip, we were looking for long-married couples who seemed to have solid relationships. Our goal wasn't to break up marriages; we wanted to enhance them. We also wanted to avoid anyone who brought unnecessary exposure risks. Heavy drinkers, for instance, might present problems. The obvious risk was that they might get to blabbing while under the influence; the less obvious risk was if they joined AA. If you confess your sins to a Twelve Step group in city of 250,000, probably no one will readily identify your fellow sinners. But in a town of 2,500, there's a risk your confessions will accidentally provide clues that allow people to identify the other participants in your "anonymous" account of your past—that eventually someone will come up with Colonel Mustard in the Study with a Knife.

It's hard to exaggerate how much our foursome changed our view of the Big Pine human landscape that summer. We couldn't look at anyone without considering their sexual possibilities. We speculated about every married couple we knew, adding and deleting names as we considered them. Reasons for including or excluding could be quirky. When I mentioned the Warrens, for instance, Doris said she'd have to overcome the memory of Ralph Warren at Steamboat Days, dancing in his John Travolta *Saturday Night Fever* outfit. Since that night, she said, she thinks of it every time she sees him. He did look pretty stupid.

Chip brought up the Twingsruds: Andy and Mary. Andy is my age, a nice-enough guy. Mary's a decade younger, definitely a looker who could hold her own against well-tended, well-off suburban women her age. Unfortunately, the Twingsruds' desirability was diminished by a memory I had of Andy on a fly-in Canada trip. He was filleting a couple of walleyes for our shore lunch while simultaneously polishing off a bag of potato chips. His fingers were slimed up enough that he didn't actually have to grab the chips, they just stuck to his fingers when he reached into the bag. Now every time I see him, I get a vision of a chip stuck to the back of his hand. Since I told the story, I'd guess Doris and Maddie and Chip probably get the same vision. Not that slime off a fish from a pristine Ontario Lake is necessarily unhealthy, but you couldn't help wondering what other personal hygiene issues Andy might be ignoring.

Maddie suggested a couple who were regular restaurant customers, and who she thought of as especially nice people. I remember Chip looked at me and we both started laughing. The woman's husband had long been a running joke between us. As it happened, I'd bowled on the same team with him a few years earlier, and during one of our first matches I noticed him taking off his bowling shoes in the middle of a game and heading toward the bar area in his socks. When I asked him where he was going he said to the men's room. He said there were always little puddles around the urinals, and he didn't want to get the soles of his bowling shoes wet— it might cause him to "stick" at the line at the end of his delivery. The even more disturbing thing was that a couple of the other guys on our team seemed to think it was a sensible idea. Maddie and Doris thought I was making it up, but Chip told them he'd witnessed it too, when his team bowled against the guy. He said he'd actually seen him standing at the urinal, mopping the floor with his socks. Another couple scratched.

The more serious hygiene issue was STDs. With the four of us, we hadn't worried about it—none of us had been with any new sex partners for the previous thirty or so years—or at least not any new partners outside our little quartet. We agreed that if we ever did find acceptable new recruits, there would have to be very frank discussions at the outset.

The speculating was fun, but it also seemed like a useless exercise—we had zero good ideas on how to safely attract new members without giving ourselves away in the process. Even with just the four of us, though, it was an exciting summer. And it wasn't just when we were all together. The Ed and Doris Olson household had a new sexual thermostat, permanently set at about 90 degrees. Some of it might have been our need to reassure ourselves that we were still okay together in this new existence, but part of it was just ratcheted up joy in each other.

Doris even revived an inside joke from our college days—my limited smoldering ability. I'm not alone in being smoldering-challenged. Most Scandinavian guys do not smolder convincingly. It seems to come more naturally to your Spanish and Mediterranean types. Bullfighters, especially, all seem to have it down. Why watching a scowling guy, pirouetting in sequin trousers and slicing live beef with a sword gets women stuck to their seats, I do not know. But it does. When Doris and I were at the U of M, one of her girlfriends went to Spain on a Junior Year Abroad program. She came back with a hot account of her fling with an honest-to-god bullfighter. In most of her pictures of him it looked to me like he was pouting or brooding about something—maybe about having to shave every two hours. In the rest he looked like he was daring you to steal his steak dinner. No smiling pictures. Zero. But all the women agreed he was about the sexiest thing ever—a champion smolderer. In the days before our sex life went south, smoldering had been a running joke between Doris and me. Now it was funny again.

Obviously our sex lives had picked up, but maybe the most gratifying change was that Doris and I touched each other more often than we had for years. If we watched TV together we didn't leave sofa space between us. She'd plop right down right next to me and pull my arm over her shoulder. If I left the house to go fishing I didn't just give her a peck on the top of her head while she kept her eyes on whatever she was doing; we kissed. Not long passionate kisses, but kisses that said we were a couple and that we liked each other. And we said, "I love you," a lot more.

I've spent a lot of time reflecting on what it was that enabled us to survive as a couple. Doris's impulsive seduction of Chip was a major rip in the fabric of our marriage, one that could have killed it, or at least left it zombified. Instead, we were able to reweave it into something stronger than it was before. I think what made the repair possible was our fundamental liking for each other. It was there even in staler times when most of the sensual and romantic elements were missing, and when "love" wasn't very close to the surface. I'm always puzzled when I see couples, especially older couples, who really don't seem to like each other, yet stay married until the end. Some of them are what Doris and I call "stereo couples," husbands and wives who talk to you at the same time as if the other one isn't even there. Life must be awful when they're alone.

There was a couple like that who lived on the next street over from us for many years. They both graduated in my class. I remember that in my senior year I'd walked past his car in the school parking lot and seen them inside with their mouths welded together, and their hands dug down into each other's jeans. They were so hot for each other, they couldn't wait long enough to drive to someplace more private. They got married right after graduation, and their first baby came along about six months later. Their kids are long grown and gone now, but the two have stayed married all these years. I just don't know why. Not long ago Doris and I saw them having dinner in the Town Talk. They didn't say a word to each other during the entire time between ordering and the arrival of their food. It wasn't just that they'd lost the match-strike lust they once had for each other. Everyone loses much of that. Familiarity plays a big part in that loss, along with money problems, job pressure, and all the other stresses and interruptions that diminish romantic intensity—like your four-year-old standing in the bedroom doorway, asking why Daddy is hurting Mommy. But for some couples everything else disappears along with the passion, and the marriage erodes down to the point that only inertia holds it together.

Why do some marriages live, and others die? Doris has a simple explanation that makes sense to me. She says that when we first become infatuated with someone, we focus on a few things we like about the person—that they're smart, funny, sexy, etc. Then we pencil in all the unknowns with what we'd like to be there. Over time, though, the person erases our pencil notes and fills in the blanks for us—usually in ink. Doris says that for some couples there are just too many ugly substitutions in important boxes. Doris and I had plenty of substitutions too, but the ink never faded on the "I like him" and "I like her" entries.

I'm very grateful for that.

CHAPTER 22, MADDIE

MARRIAGE

It was an enormous relief for me when it appeared that Doris and Ed were going to survive as a couple. Thoughts of them splitting up were nearly as painful for me as for the two of them. Coincidentally, my oldest daughter was in one of her crises with the man she lived with, the man who is the father of my granddaughter. She said she was going leave him. I always feel like I need to help her fix things, even though I know I can't. I'd often wished they were married, not just living together. It's not that I think marriage is a moral or religious necessity. I see it more as relationship insurance for those times when love gets lost so far out in the weeds that neither person can find it. Sometimes the problems are fundamental and permanent, and the relationship isn't worth saving. If that's the situation, I'm all for giving up and moving on. But sometimes there are days or weeks when hurt and anger, or the thought of someone new, make people think their relationship is irretrievable, when really it isn't.

There was a time in my own marriage when I believed there was nothing left worth hanging on to, and I couldn't find the boy I'd decided to spend my life with back when I was nineteen. I wanted out. But getting out of a marriage isn't an effortless, overnight thing. Marriage is sticky. It takes time and legal steps to dissolve a marriage, and just having to consider that process can give people time to find their way home again—assuming there really is a "home" to come back to. Over a few weeks, Stan and I did find our way back to each other, and I know now that divorce would have been a huge mistake for us. What we had was worth saving, but without the formal bond of marriage we might not have paused long enough to realize it. And of course I couldn't find the boy I met on the steps of Coffman Union that long-ago fall day—no more than he could find the girl who fell in love with him. Life changes us.

Unfortunately, both my daughter and her partner are emotionally volatile, and their fights can quickly escalate into threats of ending things. Despite those times, I thought they had a lot going for them. They'd been together for seven years at that point, and they were both loving parents to my then five-year-old granddaughter. And they laughed a lot together, too, which I think is almost as important to a couple as love or good sex. They just didn't know how to fight without putting their whole relationship at risk. Fortunately, their story does have a happy ending—or at least a happy present. A couple of weeks after their near split, they made up, and in the afterglow they went to the Minneapolis Court House and got married. My granddaughter's father is now my son-in-law.

They still fight on occasion, but now there's a buffer between fighting and leaving the relationship—marriage. I don't worry about them as much as I used to.

CHAPTER 23, MADDIE

SERENDIPITY

Halfway through that first summer, we still had no idea how we might find other like-minded Big Pine-ites. Then, one afternoon, that changed. I'd stopped into Jeanette's Beauty without an appointment, hoping to get a trim if they weren't too busy. When I walked in, there were women in both chairs and two waiting, including Sylvia Heikkela. I knew Sylvia fairly well from our mutual involvement with Food Shelf and from political doings, though we had never been morning coffee friends.

I greeted everybody and told Jeanette I wasn't too busy to wait. Then I did something that came to me out of the blue. I went over to the magazine rack and riffled through the gossip magazines. I called over to Jeanette that I was trying to find something I'd started reading the last time I was in. I said it was a scandalous article about a sex club involving older couples in some upper-crusty Connecticut neighborhood, and I said I was embarrassed to admit that I was just dirty-minded enough to want to finish reading it.

It was completely invented. I didn't think of it until five seconds before the moment I did it, but it worked. Lots of giggles and speculation from the other women. Who would the likeliest participants be in Big Pine? Maybe the Haakens? (both in their mid-nineties), more giggles. When Jeanette said she'd consider opening an orgy room at the back of the shop, one of the women said that there already was an orgy room—out at Hamer Realty. The chatter went on for a few minutes, and it propelled Jeanette into her joke-telling mode.

Jeanette is a wonderful joke teller. Stan used to say that most women couldn't tell jokes properly, but Jeanette even had a joke about that:

"Why can't women tell jokes?timing."

That afternoon she told one of her best. Most of us had heard it before, but it always makes all the women in the shop laugh.

"What's the difference between a hooker, a mistress, and a wife?" Jeanette would ask, then reel off the answers.

"Afterword, the hooker says, 'That'll be fifty bucks.'"

"Afterword, the mistress says, 'Oh darling, I hope it was as good for you as it was for me.'"

Then Jeanette would pause, look up, and scan the ceiling.

"And afterward, the wife says, 'Beige . . . I think I'll paint it beige.'"

As usual, all the women cracked up—we'd all had our "beige" moments. Betty Nelson, Chief Kermit's wife, said her husband wouldn't get the joke—which got everyone laughing even harder, and we all got into a discussion about the Meg Ryan fake orgasm scene in *When Harry Met Sally*.

The only one who didn't join in was Sylvia. I had no idea what to make of her silence, but that evening she called and invited me to her fifty-seventh birthday party, the following week. It was to be at her house, and she said there would be people there I knew, plus some of her coworkers from the hospital. She made a point of saying I should bring Chip.

Since the founding of Book and Garden, Chip and I were seen as an item. I suppose there was some gossip about it, but most people knew that Chip had cared for Ivy at home as long as he possibly could, and that Stan had been gone for almost two years.

Sylvia was a nurse at the Brainerd hospital. My mom was still employed there when Sylvia was first hired, and the two of them worked together for a year or so before Mom retired. I remember they liked each other. Sylvia grew up in Hibbing; her husband, Matt, is from Virginia, two hours northeast of Big Pine. They're both Finns—Sylvia was a Maki before she was a Heikkela. Matt has light skin and sandy hair, while Sylvia is dark-haired and olive-skinned, but what gives them both away as Finns are their roundish faces, along with high cheekbones and almond-shaped eyes. From what I know, Finns are more Central Asian than they are Scandinavian.

America might be a melting pot, but on the Iron Range it's still only partially melted. Many people up here still identify with the nationalities of their immigrant grandparents or great grandparents, and none have hung onto more traditions than the Finns. Even today, a surprising number of third- and fourth-generation Finns can still speak or understand at least some Finnish. It's not related to the Scandinavian languages, or to English, so it's hellishly hard to learn if you're not born to it. And of course English was hard to learn for the Finns. Right up through my mom's school days in the late 1940s, some kids from rural Finn households would start school without much English. They also kept their saunas and a lot of specialty foods, but their biggest impact has been political. The Finns were social activists, and some were declared socialists or communists. They led union organizing in the mines in the early twentieth century, and the result is that the Iron Range is still a union and Democratic strong-hold today.

Finns, along with Swedes and Norwegians, are also major targets of ethnic humor. "Finlander" jokes play off Finns' reputations as practical people, and a lot of jokes about them focus on their literal-minded view of the world. Stan used to tell one about two Finns, Eino and Toivo, walking on Superior Street in downtown Duluth, trying to figure out what to do for entertainment on a dead Tuesday evening. Then Eino has an inspiration: "Wait here," he tells Toivo.

Eino goes into a drugstore and comes back out with a box of tampons.

"What are we supposed to do with these?" Toivo asks him.

Eino says, "Look, it says right here on the package, we can do anything we want—riding, swimming, dancing, anything!"

That's a Finlander joke. I'm not sure it would work as well with any other nationality.

Another one of Stan's favorites was, "Did you hear that Eino and Emma froze to death? They went to the drive-in to see *Closed for the Season*."

There are hundreds more.

CHAPTER 24, MADDIE

A BIRTHDAY PARTY AND A DINNER

Sylvia's birthday party was a very sweet occasion. Along with the Big Pine guests, there were two doctors and three nurse coworkers from the hospital, as well as the hospital administrator. One of the doctors toasted her with a story about how she'd saved the life of a patient who was misdiagnosed in Emergency. Then they brought out a birthday cake decorated with the words "Happy Birthday, Sergeant Porky." I could understand the "Sergeant," just from knowing how she took charge in our volunteer work, but the "Porky" was a mystery— five-foot Sylvia weighs about 100 pounds. Tommy, one of the nurses, explained to me that Porky was short for "porcupine." "Never get her back up," he said.

I could tell they all had real affection and respect for Sylvia, and I found myself liking the people who liked her.

At one point late in the evening Sylvia and I ended up sitting together on a sofa in the downstairs family room. She leaned over and quietly asked if I'd ever found that magazine article at Jeanette's?

I said I hadn't.

"I didn't think you would," she said.

Toward the end of the evening, Matt fired up the sauna and some of us stripped down and cooked for a while before heading home. As we were leaving, Sylvia made a point of saying she and Matt would like to have me and Chip over for dinner sometime soon—maybe next week? We set a night.

~

The Heikkela home is screened from street view by the only residential berm in Larkin County. I knew the berm went up during the Reverend George Oskey's occupancy of the church-owned parsonage across the street, and that there'd been a problem between him and the Heikkelas, but I wasn't clear on the entire story until later.

Matt built the Heikkela house himself, and it has the common-sense look and feel to it that I associate with Finn homes—lots of wood, bright woven rugs on the floors, folk art, old photos and other memorabilia on the walls, all things that reflected both their families' heritage from the old country and their lives on the Iron Range.

Before dinner, I asked Sylvia about some of them. I wasn't just being polite; I love family stories—especially ones tied into Iron Range history.

She said both her family and Matt's had been involved in early union organizing in the mines, and in the living room there was a wonderful framed poster from the 1907 strike.

It read:

8 Hours for Work
8 Hours for Play
8 Hours for Sleep
and 8 Dollars a Day

Those were revolutionary demands back then. Sylvia said her great-grandfather plastered those posters all around Hibbing at a time when ten- to twelve-hour days were the rule and mining wages averaged about two dollars a day. Two of her great-grandfather's children died during that winter, she said, probably of illnesses related to malnutrition. The miners lost that strike, but they eventually won the war for unionization.

Sylvia also told us something I hadn't known—that thousands of leftist Finns, including one of her great uncles, re-emigrated in the 1920s and '30s. They went to Karelia, a Finnish ethnic area that had become part of the old Soviet Union. Karelia was supposedly a socialist paradise, but the Minnesota Finns probably should have stayed in Minnesota. It turned out they didn't get along with Stalin, so he shot most of them, including Sylvia's great uncle.

The way she told the stories didn't leave any doubt that she would have been out there freezing on the picket line herself. The more I got to know her, the better I liked her.

Matt isn't usually very talkative, but I could tell he was making a genuine effort to engage Chip—right after we arrived, he took him out to see his new hydraulic firewood splitter. He also added a couple stories about his own family's history in Iron Range politics, including that he was a shirttail relative of Gus Hall, the former head of the American communist party.

For the main course of our dinner, Sylvia served beef mojakka, a traditional Finn dish that can be either a soup or a stew, depending on the recipe, along with her own rye bread. Everyone who grows up in northern Minnesota knows what mojakka is, and there are lots of jokes about kalamojakka, the version that uses fish heads as the main meat. I've never tried it and, although I'm an adventurous eater, I will likely to go to my grave as a kalamojakka virgin.

The meal was very good, except for the Wisconsin red. Stan was a bit of wine nut and as a result I'm a little fussier than most of my friends. I think people in our part of the country should leave wine-making to Californians. For dessert we had lingonberry pie, topped with real whipped cream, and accompanied by shots of Akavit and brandy, which burned away the memory of the wine. We chatted for another half hour or so, then Sylvia said they'd fired up the sauna earlier, and were we in the mood?

People who are not sauna regulars often have misconceptions about the experience. A sauna is usually a place for some combination of quiet meditation and light socializing. The night of the birthday party had been about as noisy as sauna groups get, and even then it had been much quieter than the earlier part of the evening. Even men who swear a lot usually tone it down in the sauna. And despite the nudity, there is also not much sex in saunas—they're just too hot. Stan and I tried it once when we were first married. The problem is that when a sauna is really heated up you have to wet down the cedar bench every time your skin is going to touch a new spot. That very much discourages spontaneous movement, and the Heikkila's kept a very hot sauna.

We'd already splashed off outside once and we were back in, heating up again. There wasn't any talk at all for a few minutes. Then

Sylvia said, "Matt, I think you should take Maddie up to our room. Chip and I can stay in here a while and then we'll be down in Mikko's room."

She turned to me and Chip. "Does that sound alright to you two?" No warning. None.

She just pushed us over the guardrail and into the river.

I'd only been in bed with two men in my first fifty-eight years. Now I'd added three more in three months.

That first night, Matt seemed quite a bit more forceful than any of the others—not mean or anything like that, just forceful. It was sort of thrilling, and I felt safe enough to just go with it. He wasn't selfish—he also tried to make sure I got what I needed. He knew I hadn't come while he was inside me, and he moved himself down the bed. He was good at it—very good, for a man. And I had the sense that he wasn't just being accommodating, and that he seemed to genuinely enjoy the process of pleasing me that way. I think that's a difference that goes a long way with most women. It surely does with me. Clean fingernails are nice, too.

On the way home that night Chip and I compared notes. He mentioned that Sylvia was very strong for such a small woman, but that she seemed to get a lot of excitement from being overpowered. I thought that probably explained Matt's manhandling of me.

We got home too late to call Ed and Doris, so I got to savor the anticipation of reporting until the next morning.

CHAPTER 25, ED

GOOD NEWS, BAD NEWS

The news about the Heikkelas was exciting—dizzying almost. Maybe Oz was a real place. For sure we knew that Doris's guess about the four of us not being the only potential adventurers in Big Pine was accurate. There wasn't any certainty that things would keep moving along to include us, but it was a real possibility, not a fantasy.

Unfortunately, along with the good news, Doris and I had a new worry: Uncle Pete seemed to be coming apart. There was no mistaking his slide. I usually stopped by his place at least once a week, on Saturday afternoons, and Doris checked in with him on the phone almost every day. Halfway through our unusual summer, Doris said she was concerned about him—that he'd seemed disconnected in recent phone conversations, plus he'd begged off Sunday dinner two weeks running.

I said I'd noticed too. I told her that on my Saturday visit Pete didn't look like he was ready for an inspection—it was one of the few times I'd seen him with a two-day beard, plus the shop didn't look to have been swept in a while. I stopped in again, the next Wednesday afternoon, and right away I could tell he'd been drinking. Not that it was unusual for Pete to drink—he drank a lot, but he had a schedule. His routine was to finish up whatever work he had by around four in the afternoon, clean up the shop, then head into the VFW, sober

157

when he walked up to the bar. On that midweek visit he was almost too distracted to keep the conversation going. Beyond the effects of the booze, it seemed like the larger part of his mind was working on something else. I couldn't draw him into talking about anything, and for once he didn't inquire about how I was doing or ask for news about my son, Charlie. One of the things I'd most admired about my uncle was that, even in his eighties, he was still genuinely interested in lives of other people. A lot of people Pete's age seem to turn inward. Now Pete seemed to be headed that direction too.

I knew that a few weeks earlier he'd been down to the Cities for one of his regular checkups at VA Hospital, so I asked if he'd gotten some bad health news. He said no, nothing had changed. I finally came right out and said I could tell something was wrong, and so could Doris. That's when he told me that someone was interested in buying his property, and that he thought maybe he'd sell out and move to Florida or Arizona or Texas.

"Jesus Christ, Pete," I said, "Why the hell would you want to do that? Do you really want to spend the rest of your life playing shuffleboard with strangers?"

He tried to give me some weak bullshit about long winters being hard on him in his old age, but I knew Pete liked winter just as much as I do. For me, a hazy sunrise on a thirty-below morning, or bobcat tracks in a fresh snow, are part of what makes the world seem worthy of continuing. I can't imagine living in a place that didn't offer things like those, and I couldn't imagine Pete giving them up either.

I told him that if he had money problems Doris and I would

certainly help him, that we could even buy his place and give him lifetime estate. He said that money wasn't an issue. I wasn't sure that was true, but I figured if I sicced Doris on him she'd sniff out whatever the problem was. That's one of the things that makes her so good at her job—she keeps asking questions until she's satisfied she knows what's going on. I made Pete promise to have dinner with us the next Sunday and told him I'd be by to pick him up.

The next day Doris and I drove down to the Cities to have lunch with her mother. She'd finally sold the Edina house and moved to a fancy senior community, nearby. It was a nice setup; she had her own small apartment, but she took most of her meals in the residence dining room, and the food was surprisingly good. Doris said it was better than most of what her mother had cooked for her and her sister when they were kids. Not that she cooked much, Doris said. The deli counter at Lund's, the upscale grocery her family shopped at, provided most of the household meals.

In the dining room that afternoon, I could see that Doris's mom was still running for queen, still playing to any available male audience. There weren't enough widowers to go around, so she worked any man in the room, single or married. It drove Doris nuts to see her eighty-three-year-old mother still doing her vamp act.

Before we headed back that afternoon, we made our own Lund's visit. We always brought a cooler with us on our trips and loaded up on favorite items we can't get at home. Lund's groceries are a little spendy, especially the meat, but they sell the best quality available in just about every category, including Danish kringle. Cardamom is like catnip for me, and Lund's kringle is loaded with it. I never get all the way back home without asking Doris to break me off a couple pieces. Pete liked it as much as I do, so I always picked one up for him too.

Another unique attraction of Lund's is the women who shop there. It must have the highest percentage of hot-looking females, of all ages, of any grocery store in the country. One visit on a warm summer day would have given Willis Niemi enough inspiration for a hundred school bus performances. It's maybe not fair but, on average, well-to-do suburban women come off as better looking than less-well-off small town and rural women. Peer pressure and money probably account for the difference.

In Edina grocery stores and coffee shops and boutiques, women are in the company of other women a lot, and most of them have the money for spa and gym memberships, personal trainers, cosmetic dentistry, and cosmetic surgery, along with the right clothes and hair styles. Those advantages extend hotness expiration dates a lot further out than Al the pulp cutter's wife could have managed, even if she'd been born a natural beauty.

On the drives home from visiting her mom, Doris and I usually switch roles. I become the therapist, and she goes through her usual decompression cycle. First she complains about her mother's bad behavior, and how angry it makes her. Then she beats herself up about what a failure she is for still feeling that way. By the time we get back to Big Pine she usually has a headache and goes off to bed. When we got home that night, though, there was a phone message from the Hibbing hospital. It was about Pete. When I called them back, the desk nurse in Intensive Care was definite that we should come up that evening, not wait until morning. I was pretty sure I understood what she was saying.

Pete lost his driver's license when he was in his mid-seventies. For years the Big Pine cops and the county sheriff's deputies turned a blind eye on his shaky two-mile drive home from the VFW, but he finally got nailed by the Highway Patrol. After that he commuted on his riding lawnmower—or in winter someone would give him a ride. The lawnmower finally got him that August afternoon. He was going along a slanted shoulder, near the Reduced Speed Ahead sign just outside the Big Pine town limits, when the mower rolled, crushing much of him.

When Doris and I got up to the hospital and checked in with the charge nurse, she told us Pete was conscious, but in very bad shape, and that he needed surgery to address his internal bleeding if he was going to have any chance of surviving. She said he'd declined any pastoral visits, which wasn't a surprise to us. Pete took a dim view of religion. I remember what he said when someone told him it must have been the hand of God that saved him on Omaha Beach: "Only survivors can talk about miracles—the dead guys don't get a say." He said the miracle would have been if the German gunner aimed at a different landing craft.

The nurse also told us that Pete's lab work showed a blood alcohol content of .17, meaning Pete was solidly drunk when he rolled the mower. What the hell? What in his life had changed so much that he was getting hammered at home, even before hitting the VFW?

When we got into Intensive Care, a doctor was with Pete, gently trying to tell him he was in precarious condition, and asking did he want to have "extreme measures" used to keep him alive if things did not go well?

"Ain't that what they're payin' you for?" Pete asked.

But his voice was a just hoarse whisper, and I'm sure he knew he was at the end. Before they took him into surgery he tugged on my hand to get me down close.

"It's all nothing, Ed. I got shot, I came home and fucked around for sixty years, and now I'm dead."

Two hours later, he was right.

CHAPTER 26, ED

THE SEND-OFF

My uncle told me a number of times that he wanted to be cremated, and that he didn't want a funeral. We honored his cremation wish at a Hibbing funeral home, and I don't think anyone minded that he didn't have a funeral. In addition to smoldering, funerals are another thing Minnesotans don't shine at. New Orleans people know how to do them—clarinets and trumpets, mourners weaving past 200-year-old buildings. Scandinavian folk dancers in dirndls, bouncing past a closed turkey plant just wouldn't have the right feel. Our send-offs are more static affairs, with lots of subtle watch-checking.

But we did decide Pete's no-funeral request left enough wiggle room that the VFW could hold a brief Saturday morning memorial service at the town cemetery. In the meanwhile, Doris and I received more sympathy cards and flowers than I'd expected, including an expensive-looking arrangement of roses and carnations. Doris guessed it at a hundred bucks or more.

The card was signed Joseph O Hamer, Esq.

The memorial turnout was larger than I expected, and it was nice to see that a lot of people were going to miss Pete. Even his probation officer was there. There was no clergyman—Pete had made his views on religion pretty clear to everyone who knew him, including his VFW buddies. Instead, the Post commander spoke a nice farewell, saying that Pete had "gone on to rejoin his Omaha Beach comrades."

There was an Honor Guard of his friends from the Post, a geriatric rifle team fired off a volley, and an unseen bugler played "Taps" from somewhere off in the pines that surround the cemetery. The bugler gave me goose bumps, and it was all very moving, but I couldn't shake Pete's last words.

"It's all nothing" isn't exactly a reassuring statement on the meaning of life, especially to a person who's always had more than his usual share of existential doubt. When I was five, my mother gave birth to my temporary sister, Sarah, who arrived with a badly deformed heart. They transferred her down to University Hospital in Minneapolis in hopes the surgeons there could do something. I stayed with neighbors while my parents were down in the Cities at the hospital. The neighbors were sincere believers in the power of prayer, and every night we all prayed for Sarah. Her entire life lasted seventeen not-very-good days, all of them in a hospital. Since then, clapping for Tinkerbell hasn't been an option for me.

After the Saturday service, Ned and I drove out to Pete's place and loaded up his filing cabinets, along with some family mementos that I didn't want to risk losing to a break-in or a fire. The couple who lived across the road from Pete had been good to him over the years, inviting him over for meals and giving him rides to the VFW or to the store in bad weather. Their house has line of sight to Pete's, and they said they'd keep an eye on things until Doris and I figured out what to do with the place.

CHAPTER 27, ED

ANOTHER SURPRISE

It was a year for shocks. A week after Pete's memorial, I got a call from an attorney in Hibbing. He said Pete had left a will and that I should come see him to get things in order. I'd expected that Doris and I would get the title to Pete's three-room mansion and the forty acres. We did, but we also got something that sat me down hard— $411,000 and change. For most of the years after he came home from the army Pete had just dumped his disability checks into a savings account in a Minneapolis bank and lived off the money he took in from his shop.

I remembered a winter when Pete's furnace died. Rather than spend the money to replace it right away he heated with just his wood stove for two months. Doris and I offered to pay for a new furnace as soon as the old one stopped working, but Pete declined, saying he liked heating with wood and that he'd be able to afford a new furnace when business picked up in the spring.

Why was he so reluctant to dip into his savings? I think maybe the answer is that the savings account was his insurance against dying. It's common to hear someone say they found ten year's worth of some household item when they cleaned out an aging parent's home. Canned peaches, pepper, cleanser, shampoo. The usual explanation is that the person was failing mentally. My theory is that the hoarding is a way of buying more time. How could they die if they had sixteen jars of instant coffee left to use up? Maybe with Uncle Pete, it was the disability money. How could he die if he hadn't even started spending his little fortune?

Even though school was starting in just a couple of weeks, Doris wanted me to retire immediately—encouragement that I took as evidence she really did love me and wanted to keep me around. My dad and both my grandfathers died before they were sixty. I was already sixty-two. I was on blood pressure medication, and I'd developed an arrhythmia, both conditions being reminders that hearts do not last forever. My immediate retirement wouldn't have been hardship for us, even without our windfall from Pete. At sixty-two I could take my Social Security early, and I had enough years as a teacher, plus credit from my Navy service, to put me well over what I needed for my full pension.

Doris pointed out that our home was paid for, and that she planned to keep her job until she was sixty-five, which would give us sufficient income, even without our new riches. She also said she had plenty of ideas about useful domestic projects to occupy my extra free time, including expansion of my cooking skills beyond our barbecue grill.

Doris's arguments made sense, but the thought of retirement secretly terrified me. It wasn't that I expected to miss classroom teaching. I never considered myself to be particularly gifted in that respect. Okay, maybe, but not Minnesota Teacher of the Year material. Plus, biology can still be an uncomfortable subject in places like Big

Pine. Earlier in my career there were periodic challenges to our school board to include creationism as a viable alternative to evolution. The legal challenges ended with the 1987 Supreme Court decision, but around here the controversy didn't really go away. Teachers in a city usually see kids' parents only at PTA meetings and conferences. In Big Pine, I ran into parents every day—in Hansen's, at the post office, or just taking a walk with Doris. Those encounters could sometimes be awkward.

What do you say when a sincere parent buttonholes you in a grocery aisle and tries to convince you of the truth of biblical creation? I'm not exactly hostile to religion, but as a biology teacher I do have unavoidable conflicts with folks who deny evolution. And I admit I don't want my doctor to be someone who believes that, after three days inside a whale, Jonah emerged as anything other than whale shit.

Sex education was another prickly issue. There are a lot of people around here who believe that the only place sex should be discussed—or performed—is in the home. God and the Stork both haunted my Big Pine biology curriculum. Coaching was another matter. I knew I would miss that. I do think I was a good wrestling coach, and if I made a positive difference in kid's lives it was probably as a coach, not in the classroom.

My lifetime involvement with wrestling began when I was twelve. In those days, sports were pretty much mandatory if you wanted any status. It was possible to be cool if you weren't an athlete, but it wasn't easy. In fall we played football, the main glory sport. We did have a cross country team, but it was generally assumed the kids who ran cross country just weren't up to football. At larger schools hockey was a major winter sport, but Big Pine didn't have a high school program—hockey is expensive. For us, basketball was the winter status opportunity.

The third game of my seventh grade season was at the Hibbing middle school. Their star was a little Slovak kid who played guard, and he was deadly if left with open shots. I was an average player on offense, only an okay shooter, but I was tenacious on defense. Our coach assigned me to stay in the Slovak kid's face to try to keep his points down. I did a good job. I also ran my mouth at the kid, nonstop. After the game he came into the basement locker room as I was changing. I figured he maybe wanted to shake hands and tell me what a great defensive player I was. He only hit me once, but as I was lying on the cement floor, with rose petals flowing out my nose, I realized that minutes-long cowboy movie fights were total bullshit. If Roy Rogers got nailed first, he lost.

When I got home from Hibbing that night, my folks were intrusive enough to ask why my nostrils were plugged with bloody cotton balls. I told them the story, minus the part about my trash talking. My dad suggested I might be able to handle myself better if I went out for wrestling. He said a wrestler beats a boxer most of the time—which is true.

I quit basketball and started wrestling, and wrestling defined me for the next fifty years. There's no doubt that my life has been completely different from whatever life I might have lived without that punch in the nose.

I think crediting "fate" or outcomes that were "meant to be," are just ways of denying that randomness is at the core of everything. I wish I didn't see the world that way, but I do. If life followed a story line the way a movie script does, I would have won my state wrestling title and then gone back to Hibbing and beat the piss out of the Slovak kid. But those things didn't happen.

I'm partial of course, but I think wrestling offers the most opportunities and the most learning experiences of any sport. Unlike football or basketball, you don't have to be the biggest or fastest. A five foot seven, 135-pound high school kid, with only average natural athletic ability, just isn't going to be a star football player or basketball player. The same kid, if he's willing to work until he faints, and if he has a good coach, can become a really good wrestler. That's one of the great pleasures of coaching wrestling—a good coach makes a huge difference.

Wrestling coaches also avoid one of the problems that often comes with other sports; lobbying from parents. There are always people who think their kid should be the starting quarterback on the football team, or the starting point guard on the basketball team, and pressure from those parents can get out of hand. That's a conflict that wrestling coaches don't have to deal with. On a wrestling team, the usual arrangement is that any kid can challenge the current varsity guy in his weight class for the right to take his place. The two of them have a wrestle-off, and the winner represents the school at that weight in the next match. It's simple, and it doesn't leave much room for a parent to claim his kid was treated unfairly.

I truly believe wrestling prepares a kid for life in ways that no other high school sport can. Practices are grueling, and the pressure, anxiety, and fear before matches can be overwhelming. A wrestling match is a competition where you go out on the mat alone to face a warrior from another tribe, and one of you is going to lose. No one can help you or cover for you the way they can in team sports. And even though there is a team score, it's not just the team that loses— you lose. Sometimes the other guy is so good you know you're going to lose, but you still have to try not to get pinned—that does cost your team extra points. It's about as primal a situation as a high school kid will ever face and learning to act in that theater of fear and self-doubt is an experience that I think arms him for the future in a way almost nothing else can. There are now girls getting involved in competitive scholastic wrestling. I'm completely in favor of it. A girl who learns to assert herself on a wrestling mat is going to have a big advantage in life.

One of my favorite wrestling success stories was a kid named Kevin, a sophomore in my second year of coaching. A flash picture at a Friday night sock hop caught Kevin dancing with a girl whose effect on him became evident once the photo was developed. The lights in the high school gym were down low enough that the photographer probably hadn't noticed the bulge in Kevin's lightweight dress slacks at the time the picture was snapped, but flashbulbs are ruthless. Unfortunately for Kevin, the photo ended up on the glass front of the trophy case that sits just inside the main entrance to the school. And just so you couldn't miss the point, the anonymous poster added a marker pen arrow, pointing to Kevin's erection. Half the school saw it before a teacher took it down and the other half claimed they'd seen it. Of course every guy in school called Kevin "Boner" after that. Even his given name became a joke; kids would say things like, "I get a Kevin just watching her walk down the hall."

A cool kid might have been able to turn the situation around— maybe laugh it off by saying he was just doing a little advertising. Unfortunately, Kevin wasn't a cool kid. He was a little geeky looking and socially awkward, and the photo made him an irresistible target. An event like that can change a life, and not usually for the better, but Kevin found what he needed to get past it. A couple of weeks after the photo disaster, he came to see me and said he wanted to wrestle. I said that would be great, and I meant it—the more bodies the better. One of my practice strategies was to have a good wrestler like Ned Cooley go one-minute rounds with two or three of the backup kids, one at a time. The backups get to rest when the next backup comes in. The good wrestler learns to keep going beyond exhaustion, and the backups get experience without having a couple hundred fans watching them being manhandled.

Kevin was the worst wrestler on the team that year. In practices Ned and the others threw him around like a rag doll, but Kevin always kept coming. He was coachable and motivated, and he worked his ass off. By the end of the season, he still wasn't what you could call good, but he was a whole lot better than he'd been at the beginning. The most important change, though, was that he earned the respect of his teammates, including Ned.

Midway through Kevin's first season Ned invited him to sit at his cafeteria lunch table. That was the end of the harassment, and no one called him anything other than "Kevin" after that. By his senior year he was our guy at 154, and he won more matches than he lost. When he came back to Big Pine for his twentieth reunion he thanked me for what he felt I'd done for him. He also said that, as the sales manager for his company, he was partial to hiring guys who had wrestled during their school years. He said they weren't afraid to make cold calls, and they shrugged off rejection better than non-wrestlers.

I told him I was proud of him, and I meant it.

Kevin's story, and a few others, did sometimes give me a feeling of having done a good job, but I can't truthfully say that losing the opportunity to mold young men's characters on the wrestling mat was the only reason for my reluctance to retire.

Stab It the Rabbit also played a role.

An awareness of my own mortality has always been near the surface, and it often bubbles up in horrible dreams. Stab It the Rabbit is one of my night time tormentors. Stab It is a long toothed, seven-foot-tall jack rabbit who carries a huge butcher knife as he stalks me in the dark school parking lot. In the dreams I always park at the farthest end of the lot, and I have to walk past all the other cars and pickups, knowing that he's hiding somewhere between them, in the shadows, waiting for an opportunity to spring out and kill me. I usually wake up with the sheets drenched in sweat. Poor Doris.

And while Stab It was frightening, he was just a dream figure. After Pete died I began waking up in the middle of the night feeling vulnerable to more realistic disaster possibilities than killer rabbits. Pete was my uncle, and nephews don't die before their uncles. As long as he was alive I could tell myself it wasn't my turn yet. With Pete dead, my generational insulation was gone. Now a small blockage in an artery or a tiny rupture deep inside me could easily send me on a gasping belly flop into the waters of the Big Dark, and it wouldn't even seem untimely. People would say, "Well, his father and his grandfathers didn't even see sixty, so at least he outlived them."

And if it happened while I was fishing, they'd also probably say, "He died doing something he loved." That one always gets me. I'm pretty sure most people don't "love" gasping for breath, which is what they are likely doing at that point, and whatever pastime they were enjoying a few minutes earlier has become pretty much irrelevant.

I also doubt their last thoughts are regrets that they didn't watch enough sports on TV—or that they had too much sex—but by then it's a little late to re-prioritize.

Routine and responsibilities were what protected me from the cold plunge. My daily to-do list was the armor I donned every morning when I woke up defenseless against personal extinction. I'd think of all I had on my schedule—papers to grade, parent conferences, wrestling practices, fifth-period lunch. How could it all go on if I wasn't there to oversee things?

Of course I had to be there. And for years I'd vowed to lead Big Pine to a new mascot before I retired, but we were still represented by a fucking turkey. No way I was leaving before I accomplished that change. Retirement would strip away all those reasons that the world couldn't go on without me.

In the end, Doris agreed to my working one more year, but she insisted that I give the school notice right away. She wasn't going to give me any last-minute excuses, like the administration being unable to find a replacement.

~

With the retirement question resolved, I began going through Pete's filing cabinets to clean up any open issues—bills to be paid, equipment he was working on that needed to be returned to the owners, the kinds of obligations that don't end with death. Fortunately, my uncle was a methodical man, and every job that went through his shop was documented, including hours of labor, parts costs, and drop off and pickup dates. All his tax documents were also up to date. He'd always had his taxes done by an accountant down in Minneapolis, and now I knew why—he didn't want to explain the Interest Income line to any local tax preparer.

Most of Pete's papers were the sort of stuff I expected to find, but in one of the last drawers I went through I found a file labeled "Asshole."

There were three letters in the file, all from Joey Hamer, and all concerned Pete's property. The earliest was dated in mid-June, just a couple of weeks after Joey's Success Day appearance. In that letter Joey expressed interest in buying Pete's place, but the tone was casual, as if the purchase was just a possibility that had crossed Joey's mind. The second letter was an actual offer: $75,000 plus the costs of moving Pete's small house and shop to a nearby ten-acre piece Joey already owned.

Judging from that proposal, Joey wanted the place bad. I estimated that between the cash, the moving expenses, and the new site, Joey was offering close to double what the property was worth. I'm sure Joey thought the deal would be irresistible, though if he'd had any understanding of human emotions he might have anticipated how difficult it might be to extract an eighty-six-year-old man from a piece of land he'd owned for sixty years.

We all sometimes lose sight of the fact that other people's lives are as real and important to them as our own lives are to us, but I don't think Joey even recognized that other people existed, other than as tokens to be moved around on his board. And of course he also had no idea about Pete's $400,000 savings account. From what I could tell, Pete never bothered to respond to either of the first two letters.

The last letter was completely mystifying. The date showed it was sent a week after Pete's last trip to the Cities and his visit to the VA hospital. Accompanying the letter was a contract outlining the terms of sale, at a price of $60,000. In the letter Joey refers to "the attached agreement, per our recent telephone conversation." *What the hell?*

Pete was going to sell after all? And at a price $15,000 lower than Joey offered two months earlier? Also, there was no mention of relocating Pete's house. None of it made sense, but it seemed that Pete really had agreed to a deal—Joey wouldn't have sent the letter out of the clear blue sky.

I'd already figured out the real reason Joey wanted Pete's place: revenge. Revenge on the town for his homecoming prince humiliation, revenge on me for taunting him about it, thirty years later.

Albino Point itself wasn't a building site—not enough set-back from the water to meet legal requirements for building. But owning Pete's property would have given Joey a prominent building site on the hill above the Point, and I had no doubt that he intended putting up something that would dominate the view from any spot on the lake. If a white doe ever returned to the Point, any photo of her would have a monument to Joey in the background.

Not to mention that Joey's estranged sisters would be reminded of The Little Shit every time they looked out their windows; likewise, anyone out on the water in a boat—me, for instance.

If Pete hadn't rolled the mower, Joey would have had what he wanted.

What I couldn't understand was why Pete had agreed to the deal. Doris couldn't make sense of it either, though she was sure the pending sale was connected to the deterioration in Pete's grooming, and his symptoms of depression and anxiety in the weeks before he died. Her first guess was the same as mine—that Pete had received bad news at his last VA checkup.

Pete had denied it, and the VA follow-up letter I found in Pete's files confirmed his denial. After Pete's final visit, his doctor sent him a summary that described him as an "86-year-old man in overall good health."

What the hell?

The only other possibility we could think of was money worries, but we'd already discovered that wasn't a problem.

Nothing made sense.

CHAPTER 28, ED

THE SNAKE RATTLES

A couple of weeks after Pete's memorial, I heard from Joey. He first contacted me by letter—not Joseph O Hamer, Esq. stationary, just a personal note that started with, "Hi Coach."

That pissed me off before I'd even read the rest of it. As a point of etiquette, Joey had not earned the right to call me "Coach." I should have been "Coach Olson" to him—or "Ed," or "Mr. Olson," anything but just "Coach." Only if a kid has wrestled for me does he have the right to use the familiar, single-word title. Fifty-year-old former students still observe the distinction. I've already said it, but I really hated The Little Shit.

The note led off with some insincere bullshit about what a great guy Pete was, then Joey got around to the point. He said he'd had a deal with Pete to buy his place, and that he was still interested in completing the purchase, "to bring the land back into the Hamer family."

Sentimental Joey. He added that he knew Pete would have wanted to have the agreement "honored" after his passing. When I didn't respond right away he followed up with a phone call. I told him I appreciated his interest in reuniting Pete's land with the Hamer holdings, but I said Doris and I felt the same way about keeping it in the Olson family. Then, just to piss him off, I said I might be interested in doing something in the other direction—buying the Point from him. *Stupid, stupid.* I think I've mentioned that I sometimes don't know when to keep my mouth shut. Joey said he had another call coming in, and that we should talk again.

Three weeks after I tweaked him about the reverse buyout, Joey fired his broadside; he applied for a building permit variance. The building site was Albino Point. I found out about the application from one of our county commissioners, a former teacher at the high school. She said I wouldn't believe the structure he was proposing. Albino point is only about 100-feet wide at the shoreline and tapers down to nothing, about 200 feet out in the lake. In the platte book, the outline looks like a skinny T-bone steak, with the "T" being the narrow strip of shoreline running north and south, and the "steak" being the point. Although the owner is listed as J. O. Hamer, no one ever gave much thought to it because the Point has no building site that would comply with setback regulations. It's all too close to the water—at least that's what we all assumed until Joey dropped his building permit application on us.

The Big Pine Register published an artist's conception of what the point would look like with Joey's "home" sitting on it—above it, really. The proposed structure was supported by eight-foot columns, anchored in the granite. The architect's description called for solar heat, composting toilets, and super insulation, all supposedly the latest in environmentally friendly living. Doris said it looked like a lunch box on stilts. I thought it was more like the tripod alien things I remembered from a *War of the Worlds* comic book.

It might as well have been a statue of Joey with his pants down, mooning out across the lake at all of us. The commissioner couldn't figure out why Joey thought he could get away with something so outrageous. But I knew why.

Joey did think he could get away with it. Disfiguring our county symbol would be the perfect revenge on everyone who'd crossed him: the classmates who shamed him with princehood, his sisters who didn't speak to him, and of course me, Idiot Ed Olson.

Word of the proposed project spread like news of a presidential assassination. Double takes don't just happen on TV shows—Doris actually did one when I first told her about Joey's project. "He wants to do what?"

I think that was a common reaction around town. Albino Point was our Taj Mahal, and Joey was proposing to build a McDonald's at the entrance. It was the transformer strategy again—punish the whole town. If we could have done it over again, Joey would have been elected prom king in a walk.

When the application was turned down, Joey's appeal arrived almost by return mail. I'm sure he'd anticipated the denial, and he'd prepared his response well ahead of time. The county attorney said Joey's appeal was all bullshit that wouldn't get anywhere in court, but he said what worried him was a newspaper article Joey included with his paperwork.

Along with the stack of legal arguments, Joey included a copy of a *Minneapolis Tribune* feature story about an illegal brick boathouse on a suburban lake. The rich fuck who built it had gone ahead despite local ordinances that specifically prohibited building any permanent structure on the water. The suits and counter suits had been running for years, the article went on, but the town finally gave up trying to get rid of the boathouse; they just couldn't afford the legal costs of fighting it. Joey's warning shot couldn't have been any clearer—he had more money than we did, and he was willing to spend it to get what he wanted.

CHAPTER 29, MADDIE

ANOTHER HEIKKELA SURPRISE

Our second evening the Heikkelas' came less than a week after the first. Sylvia called me in the afternoon and asked if Chip and I felt like coming over for a drink later that evening. When we arrived she had a tray of cheese and crackers ready, a bottle of red, and she said there were frosted beer mugs if anybody wanted one. We all started with a bump of Akavit. That night, again, it was completely clear that Sylvia was the conductor of our quartet. After we'd socialized for half an hour she looked at me and said, "Matt really loved fucking you on Saturday. We shouldn't make him wait much longer."

Now I've always been a little iffy about that word when used in its literal sense, but the quiet, matter-of-fact way Sylvia spoke it made me want to get Matt into bed that minute. Just like the first night, we went to our separate rooms. Sylvia didn't seem to have a need for any nearer grouping. The closest she came to it was a couple weeks later as Matt and I were heading upstairs: "One of these nights" she said, "I might have to poke my head in the door and see what you're doing that makes my husband so happy."

I said that would be fine, but she didn't seem in any hurry. She seemed content with private replays of the scene Chip had mentioned after their first night together.

We were having a wonderful time with our new companions, and it wasn't just the sex. It turned out they were glorious fun to hang out with, and just plain funny, especially as a duo, playing off each other. When we weren't in separate bedrooms, we spent much of the rest of the time laughing. In fact, we were having so much fun that both Chip and I were a little reluctant to risk breaking the spell by bringing up Ed and Doris, and Book and Garden.

It was on our fifth trip to their house that I decided it was time. We'd fallen into a pattern—first a couple of drinks and then, after the main event, we'd reassemble in front of the family room fireplace for a nightcap and some laughs.

That night in the family room, I screwed up my courage and asked them if they'd ever considered meeting any other couples. I remember them looking at each other, smiling.

"We were going to ask you the same thing," Matt said.

That was one response I hadn't anticipated, but at least I recovered enough to stay on offense.

"Too bad," I said, "but we asked you first."

Matt told the story. He said he and Anne had been in a similar relationship with another couple for several years—Jim and Anne Foster.

If he'd said George and Barbara Bush, I wouldn't have been much more surprised. Matt said the couples started becoming friends at the time of the Heikkilas' battle with their new across-the-street neighbor, Reverend George Oskey. The minister who'd preceded Oskey was considered quite a nice guy, and he was on good terms with the Heikkelas, despite their atheism. Oskey, however, was not a nice guy.

"He stopped over the first week he moved into the parsonage, and of course my little cobra had to go out of her way to piss him off," Matt said.

"I didn't go out of my way," Sylvia said, "I just have a thing about assholes."

"Things kind of escalated," Matt said, "when Oskey asked her how she could be so sure God didn't exist. Syl told him that if God did exist, she would have put men's dicks on their chins. Not a good start. The trouble started right away."

"The *trouble*," Sylvia said, "was that he was an asshole."

Matt said that after the confrontation with Sylvia, Oskey began complaining that his family was forced to witness nude frolicking outside the Heikkela sauna. Jim Foster was still police chief at the time, and he visited Oskey in response to the complaint.

Jim said the Heikkela's privacy fence blocked any view of the sauna from Oskey's living room, and even from the second-floor bedrooms, but the reverend told him that wasn't where the problem was. Matt said Oskey took Jim up to the dormer window in the attic storeroom. From there, Jim told the Heikkelas, standing at full height, he could see the top third of the sauna door, meaning an offensive bare breast sighting was possible. Jim also reported there was a step stool next to the window, presumably to allow Mrs. Oskey and the children to be offended as well.

"When Jim said Oskey might have been able to see my boobs

from fifty yards away," Sylvia said, "my wonderful husband told him Oskey must have the world's best eyesight. He told Jim he could barely see 'those little fried eggs' from the other side of the bed."

She raised her middle finger toward Matt.

"But maybe that's when Jim got interested in seeing them," Matt said. "Look at the positive side, Sweetheart."

"The Oskeys didn't notice anything attached to you, did they?" Sylvia asked. "Apparently that would have taken even better eyesight."

"I like to make it easy for her," Matt said, "makes her feel clever."

Within a week of Oskey's complaint, Matt had the first nine-yard truckload of black dirt delivered. A week later, Big Pine's only berm was up, sodded, and topped by a row of close-set junipers. Matt said Oskey would have had to add two more floors to the parsonage if he wanted to see anything of the Heikkela sauna or Heikkela anatomy. I must say Finns know how to get things done.

Matt said a result of the kerfuffle was that the Heikkelas and the Carlsons developed a couple's friendship that went on for almost a decade. He said it stopped being an ordinary friendship on New Year's Eve, three years earlier, when the four of them went out to dinner, then returned to the resort to greet the New Year. At midnight they each kissed their spouses, then switched partners. The kissing went on for a while, and Matt said it soon crossed the line from kissing to earnest making out.

"We'd done some flirting over the years," Matt said, "But that night felt a little different. I looked over at Jim. He just shrugged and said, 'Why not?' I was going to check it out with Syl, but before I could ask her, she threw Jim over her shoulder and headed up the stairs."

"You are a true asshole, Matt," Sylvia said, "and a liar on top of it. How is it possible I've stayed with you for thirty-two years?"

"Because you're crazy about me?" Matt said.

"I must've forgot that part," Sylvia said.

They told us that during the first two years of their foursome they had to be exceedingly discreet because both couples still had teenagers at home. The Fosters' twin daughters and the Heikkelas' youngest son were only juniors in high school when everything started, and the conclusion of the New Year's Eve celebration had been possible only because the girls and Mikko had been out west on a class ski trip. Matt said the consequences of having the relationship found out by their teenage children were too overwhelming to contemplate.

Sylvia rolled her eyes and mimed shooting herself in the head. "We thought that might have cost us a tiny bit of moral authority," she said.

At the beginning, the couples managed about half-a-dozen rendezvous' a year, mostly on overnight trips to Duluth, or down to the Cities for Twins or Vikings games. After they became empty nesters, Matt said, things were a little more relaxed.

Then it was our turn.

I told them about Ed and Doris, though not about the specific event that started everything—I didn't think that was a necessary part of the story. The Heikkelas seemed just as surprised about our partners as we were about theirs. They knew both Ed and Doris, of course. Everyone in Big Pine knows everyone else, at least on a nodding basis. Ed was the better-known quantity because he'd coached their son, Mikko, in wrestling.

Fortunately, both Matt and Sylvia seemed open to the possibility of the Olsons as potential partners, and Chip and I were okay with the possibility of the Fosters. In fact, Chip was more than okay with the idea of the Fosters. He told me later that he'd always thought Anne was a very hot-looking "big" woman.

We ended the evening by agreeing the best way to start would be to see if everyone wanted to get together for an evening out—with the understanding that it would be a non-sexual occasion. On the way home that night, Chip said we had to remember to tell Ed and Doris the story about Sylvia carrying Jim Foster up the stairs.

CHAPTER 30, ED

CONSIDERING THE FOSTERS

Chip and Maddie told us about the Heikkelas right from the first night, but the news of the Foster/Heikkela foursome pretty well knocked us flat. Doris and I had a lot of spontaneous, can-you-believe-it moments—the kind of moments when all you can do is shake your head and laugh. Maybe like the reaction you'd have if the neighbor's golden retriever came over and played "Love Me Tender" on a harmonica. How to react, other than shake your head and laugh? We were in a world we couldn't have guessed at a year earlier.

The Fosters had, of course, come up in our possible member fantasies—we'd considered just about every couple in town and pegged Jim and Anne as desirable, but unlikely. Too wholesome maybe. I didn't know Anne all that well, but I thought I had a pretty good measure of Jim. After he moved up here from the Twin Cities to take the police chief job, he sometimes joined us on the annual, all male, fly-in fishing trip to Ontario. On those occasions, even with no women around, he hardly ever swore or initiated any randy conversations. We all drank more than we would have at home but, unlike some of the guys, Jim never got completely shit-faced or out of control. He was fun to BS with too; he had lots of stories from his years as a cop, both in Minneapolis and as the Big Pine chief.

There was one Big Pine incident that I think sums up Jim's credentials as a human being. It also led to his resignation from his job.

Jim was on duty the night Eldon Fernstrom went a little nuts and manhandled his wife, Nina. It happened a day or two after Eldon returned from his fall elk hunting trip to Montana. He'd mislaid his car keys, and in the course of looking for them he checked the sofa to see if they'd slipped down between the cushions. He didn't find the keys, but he did find a pack of Camel Filters. Neither Eldon nor Nina smoked, but Merl Hansen, Nina's employer at Hansen's Grocery, did smoke—Camel Filters. Merl was also a known philanderer. His first wife divorced him, naming the woman who held the cashier job before Nina as corespondent.

Whatever the truth was, Eldon was convinced Nina was fooling around. They had words, fueled by booze, and that's when Eldon pushed her and she fell onto their coffee table and broke it. Nina wasn't hurt, but she was angry enough to call the sheriff's emergency number—we didn't have 911 back then. After she made the call, Eldon told her he was going out to spend the night in his deer shack, forty miles north of Big Pine. He also told her he'd shoot anyone who came after him.

Because the Fernstroms lived inside the town limits, the sheriff radioed Jim to get over to their house and deal with the situation. Jim listened to Nina's story and then did maybe the smartest thing any law enforcement officer has ever done. He told Nina he didn't see any point in chasing after her armed, drunk husband in the woods at night. He figured Eldon would sober up by morning, come back from his shack, or from wherever he was camped out, and that he could take him into custody then.

But Nina had already reconsidered the notion of having Eldon arrested. She told Jim that, except for that night, there had never been any physical rough stuff in thirty years of marriage and that her landing on the coffee table had been more of an accident than an assault. She said she honestly wasn't the least bit afraid of her husband. Jim said if that was the case, and if she really did feel safe, she should leave a note telling Eldon they could work things out if he promised to go to counseling, and maybe AA, and also telling him that she would keep calling the house to make sure he made it home safely. Then Jim called Anne and told her he was bringing Nina home for the night.

Hungover Eldon was back home to answer Nina's phone call at six-thirty the next morning—no manhunt, no hovering *Channel 4 News* helicopter, no shootout. That should have been the end of it, but the sheriff got wadded up about Jim not pursuing Eldon that same night—to protect the public from danger, the sheriff said. The investigation went nowhere, but it soured Jim on the job for good. A few months later he resigned, and he and Anne bought Carlson's Lodge.

Apparently the Fernstroms resolved the Camel Filter issue—not long ago there was notice in the *Register*, announcing their fortieth wedding anniversary. If they didn't invite Jim to the party, they should have.

By that first fall, things looked promising for B&G. We had our current fun with Maddie and Chip, and now the possibility of adding the Fosters and the Heikkelas. But it was also a sweet and sour time— Doris and I we were still mourning Pete, and we still had no clues about the source of his misery in the last weeks of life. *Why would he sell to Joey?*

I couldn't get my mind off it.

CHAPTER 31, ED

THE NEXT STEP

Maddie and Sylvia coordinated arrangements for a four-couple date at the Heron on the last Saturday night before the late-November deer season. The Heron is a dinner and dance club on the north end of Lake Mille Lacs. Every other Saturday they have an oldies cover band. It's a good draw for a lot of us in the over-fifty crowd, though I'm always surprised how many young people show up too.

I think sixties' and seventies' music has endured better than most of the recent crap will. Not long ago I saw a great bumper sticker in the Heron parking lot:

"It's Not that I'm Old, Your Music Really Does Suck."

Pretty well sums up my feelings.

I was looking forward to the evening, but with some amount of terror about the dancing. I'm a reasonably well-coordinated guy, but I always freeze up on the dance floor—another Scandinavian male handicap maybe. Most of us truly don't want to be the center of attention. Luckily, I got a little reassurance the Sunday before our outing when *60 Minutes* reran a funny piece on the tango craze in Finland. The segment shows a bunch of middle-aged Finns doing their version of tango in what looks like a school gym. The couples don't exactly glide across the floor—more like a march, and their expressions have all the fire of people thinking about getting their cat neutered. Doris said I might get lucky—the Heikkelas were Finns, and maybe they'd be just as dance impaired as I am.

60 Minutes is one of the few programs Doris and I can watch together. She likes some of the drama series and movies, but those don't usually work for me. She can get emotionally involved in what's going on where, most of the time I just see a bunch of people in front of a camera. Instead of getting all tense when some onscreen character is hanging off a cliff, I wonder how they made it look like he's hanging off a cliff. I get especially pissed in driving scenes where actors take their eyes off the road for five or ten seconds at a time to talk to the passenger.

I'll say something like "Keep your eyes on the road, asshole," and then Doris will get mad at me for breaking the mood. I also hate when a character makes some illogical move—like when a woman watches an escaped slasher story on the ten o'clock news, then decides to check out the creaking noises coming from her attic. I don't just think *why did she do that?* I'll say something out loud like, "Whoever wrote this is a fucking idiot!"

I've been that way since I was a kid. Doris says I have no ability to suspend disbelief. If she really gets into something she's watching, she doesn't even want me in the room. She says it kills the story for her because she knows I'm probably not buying in to whatever is happening on the screen. I'm not a very fun husband.

But there are a few upsides to my suspension of disbelief disability. Since my visit to the Thai comedienne, I've understood that professional sex won't work for me—that I need at least some unfeigned enthusiasm from my partner. But I know that isn't the case for all men.

Years ago, I was at a wrestling coaches' clinic at the U of M, and one night a couple of the other coaches wanted to go to a "gentleman's club" just off Hennepin Avenue in downtown Minneapolis. They said it was the best one in the city. I learned later it was the club where Sharon danced, and where she met Joey.

The dancers were very fit and attractive, and they had great body control—I would for sure classify them as athletes. After they danced on stage they worked the audience for lap dances. For twenty bucks they'd swoop their thongs back and forth over a guy's crotch. The bigger money came from private dances, which cost something like a hundred and fifty bucks for twenty minutes in a side room. One of the guys I was with went for that.

I didn't understand it—coaches don't make that much money. Was the private lap dance a hundred-forty-two dollars better than jerking off to an eight-dollar, in-room porno at the hotel? I guess for him it was.

Something that did impress me, though, was how good the women were at acting like they were really turned on by the customers. I think that illusion is the thing guys give them money for. Maybe it's not all that different from donating to a politician who convinces you that his or her real reward is making life better for you.

CHAPTER 32, ED

THE HERON

On the night of our Heron date, Chip and Maddie rode with me and Doris. We were all wound a little tight during the drive. Doris went into her chirp voice, and Chip tried to launch some forced conversation about the upcoming Vikings/Packers game. Our nervousness was understandable. How could we not be nervous? We were about to meet with people we'd known for years to see if they wanted to have sex with us. I'm sure they felt the same way. The possibility of rejection was scary as hell.

Luckily, the Heron was busy. At dinner we could hardly hear one another over the crowd noise, which made it easier to avoid saying anything meaningful—we couldn't very well shout about the subject that brought us together. Dancing was the icebreaker. Like I said, I don't dance very well, but it was a chance to get close to the women without seeming like a lecher.

When I had a slow dance with Anne, she must have picked up how tense I was, because she put her mouth up close to my ear and said, "Don't worry, Ed, I've always thought you were a good guy."

Right away I had the same feeling I'd had four decades earlier, when May Hamer asked me to drive her someplace where we could be alone—that maybe something really, really good was going to happen.

On the drive home Maddie asked what everyone thought about how the night had gone. Chip said he knew what he thought, and he hoped the Fosters and the Heikkelas thought the same thing. I felt the same way, but I said I couldn't quite read Sylvia.

Maddie said not to worry. Nobody could read Sylvia, she said.

And practical Doris pointed out that Sylvia wouldn't have been there if she wasn't already 90 percent in. Then we all decided that the evening's "no sex" agreement only covered the Fosters and Heikkelas, and that it was early enough to continue the evening at our house.

It turned out everyone passed the first cut with everyone else. The day after the Heron outing, Anne Foster called us and offered to host a get together after they closed up the Lodge at the end of deer season. Three weeks seemed like a long time to wait, but there was nothing for it. In Larkin County, deer season trumps everything.

CHAPTER 33, ED

DEER SEASON

Minnesota issues almost 500,000 deer hunting licenses every year. To put that into perspective, it's about a quarter of all the adult males in the state (90 percent of licenses are issued to men). The only requirements for getting licensed are that you have thirty bucks and that you haven't committed any violent felonies—or at least none that resulted in convictions. For ten days much of the state is occupied by a half-million-man army with no command structure, and with unlimited access to booze. Larkin County gets about 25,000 of them, which is a bunch considering we have only 16,000 permanent residents.

There are good reasons for hunters to come here. The area could have been designed as deer country—an ideal mixed habitat of forest, farm fields, wetlands, and taverns. The miracle of deer season is that there are so few human casualties. The entire state averages less than twenty hunting-related gunshot wounds a year, and most years only three or four are fatal. The low mortality rate is most likely because a shooter who mistakes you for a deer is probably too loaded to make an accurate kill shot.

Like most Big Pine boys, I began hunting early. I got a single-shot .22 for my tenth birthday, and a .410 shotgun when I turned twelve. Back then we thought nothing of bringing our guns to school if we planned to hunt at the end of the day. It wasn't at all unusual to see a kid with a cased shotgun or rifle, standing at a school bus stop. We just stored them in our lockers until last bell. I shot my first buck when I was thirteen, and since then I've been out in the woods every year, except during my Navy service. Nowadays though, I don't have quite the same enthusiasm for hunting. When I was younger I was always disappointed if I didn't come home with something; now, I'm usually happy either way. I just don't have quite as much appetite as I once did for turning a live animal into a dead one. It's even affected my fishing; I quit using minnows as bait because it just didn't feel quite fair to sacrifice a small fish just to catch a bigger one that I probably wasn't going to keep anyway. I still use night crawlers and leeches though—my reverence for life hasn't reached that far down the ladder yet. And to be honest, I still use minnows once in a great while—but only if the walleyes aren't biting on anything else.

I know a few other older guys who've gotten less interested in hunting, or even given it up altogether. Maybe it's the end of our own lives coming into view that makes killing other animals a less-attractive activity than it was when we were young and immortal. I think part of what's changed for me is that I don't see animals as completely separate from us quite the way I once did. Now it feels more like we're all on a Mobius Strip together—ahead of each other in some ways, behind in others. Makes it harder for me to shoot them—though I still do.

And up here, even if you don't hunt, you're going to kill animals on occasion. If you drive a car regularly, it can't be helped. Township roads have trees and brush crowding within a few of feet of the gravel or the blacktop, and sometimes you don't have enough time to react when a rabbit or a deer darts out. I understand there are shelters in the Cities where people can take injured animals as small as squirrels, but up here an injury means the end. All you can do is try to make sure it's a quick end. If I hit an animal, even a rabbit, or if I even think I might have hit one, I always stop and look for it to make sure it's dead. If it isn't, I club it with the tire iron I keep under the front seat of my pickup. It's painful to finish them off like that, but there's no excuse for leaving an animal writhing for half an hour before it dies. In nature, a rabbit's life usually ends fast; he's eating something green and delicious, he's startled, jaws crunch, it's over.

We should show them the same mercy.

~

That first year of Book and Garden, I got my buck on the morning of Opening Day and; for the rest of deer season I helped out behind the bar at the Buckhorn. A cousin on my mom's side owns the place, and it's become kind of a tradition that I show up to lend a hand after I've gotten my deer. He's always happy when I score early; the tavern is a lunatic asylum for those ten days and he needs all the help he can get.

I don't know who said, "There are no grownups," but if you doubt the truth of that statement you need to visit the Buckhorn during deer hunting. Our guests are mostly men, they're away from home, they carry weapons, and they drink a lot. What could possibly go wrong?

For ten days I watch attorneys dancing around with deer testicles impaled on sticks, bankers curled up on the tavern floor trying to light their own farts, and all sorts of supposed adults acting like drunken eighth graders. I can't think of a single positive human characteristic that is accentuated. We even have race issues. After Vietnam, the Twin Cities became home to a large population of immigrants from Southeast Asia, and a considerable number of them are avid hunters. You hear a lot of ugly comments, and a few years ago there was a racial confrontation over in Wisconsin that ended with three guys shot dead. I think if space aliens visited Minnesota during deer season they might vaporize our entire planet, just to make sure we didn't infect other places in the universe.

Testosterone levels do seem to go up in tandem with blood-alcohol percentages, so most local women avoid area night spots during hunting, either voluntarily, or under pressure from husbands and fathers. The Dew Drop Inn, out on Highway 49, brings in a crew of strippers, and I understand they do very well, especially those who do some private catering after closing time. And though there aren't many amateur targets of opportunity around here during those ten days, there are a few; the Hamer sisters always have fun. Even as they closed in on their sixties, May and Jessie weren't buying any of their own drinks during hunting season—and when Mickey was between husbands she drove up from the city for her share. The three of them would sit at the bar with a bunch of complimentary shots lined up in front of them, laughing and flirting and swapping dirty jokes with the hunters, many of them far younger than any of the seven ex-husbands the sisters have rung up between them.

I don't think the hunters' success rate was very high with any of the Hamers, but May and Jessie handed out a lot of Hamer Realty business cards. After Otto died, they both got licensed. Initially it was just to save money on the sale of their family properties, but May eventually got a broker's license, and Hamer Realty became the dominant local firm. Despite the juicy tales about their personal lives, both May and Jessie have excellent business reputations.

For local merchants, the deer season is a moneymaker—any business that sells booze or food is busy. The Buckhorn does two months of business in ten days, and Maddie says the restaurant does three to four times its normal daily volume. She says they'd do more yet if they could get people to eat faster. That first year of Book and Garden, she was still helping out the young couple who'd bought the restaurant, and she called me opening weekend to relay that Joey and another guy had come in with two young women, neither one of whom was Mrs. Joey.

At first, I was surprised The Little Shit had the nerve to make an appearance after his Albino Point building permit request became public knowledge. But then I realized he was just being Joey, grinding our noses in it.

Ned came up for a couple days too, just to visit his mom, not to hunt. He said he lost his enthusiasm for deer hunting because of his mom's worthless second husband. Whenever the family was short of meat, any time of year, he would send Ned out to find some venison. His step dad knew the law would go easier on a kid than on an adult if a game warden happened onto the scene. I suppose that's true, but it's not much of a parenting philosophy. Ned also said that within a twenty-five-mile radius of Big Pine, there were probably a dozen guys he'd beat the snot out of in earlier years, and a few more who thought he might have fooled around with their wives or girlfriends. He figured that raised the odds that a stray rifle shot would make him an "accidental" hunting fatality. Made sense to me.

Ned didn't just stay out of the woods, though. He and a couple buddies spent their deer seasons down in the Cities, doing their own hunting at Widow's Balls.

A Widow's Ball is a city bar or nightclub event that caters to hunters' abandoned wives while their husbands are getting loaded up here in the woods and chasing the Hamer sisters around Big Pine as if they were the year's Miss Minnesota finalists. A resentful wife, sitting at a bar in Minneapolis, feeling more resentful with each drink and knowing her husband was 150 miles away for the next week? A darkly handsome young Indian guy with an intriguing scar sits down next to her? What could possibly go wrong? Ned always said the scar was his greatest asset in those situations. I doubt he mentions falling off his bike.

Before Ned headed back to the city, we had him and his mom over for dinner. Ned told us that recently he'd been spending almost all his time watching after Sharon, and that Joey wasn't bringing him along to meetings the way he had in the first months after Ned got out of jail. I assumed it was because it was because of the Albino Point situation. Joey obviously knew Ned and I were close, and it made sense that that he would keep Ned out of the loop, to prevent anything getting back to me. At the dinner I didn't admit I thought the initial reason for Joey's insane project went back to Success Day, when I taunted the little prick by mentioning the homecoming election and the transformer incident. I was too embarrassed to let either Doris or Ned know how stupid I'd been. As Pogo said, "We have met the enemy, and he is us."

Ned said Joey did have a hard on for me over my opposition to the Albino point project, but he thought there was something else involved in his being shut out of Joey's plans. He said he started being left at home with Sharon soon after Joey became a regular in back-room poker games at the state capitol. Ned said he'd looked on at the first couple games. The first night he watched he saw Joey fold "the nuts," in a Hold'em game—meaning Joey had the two best-possible down cards, and was a lock to win the pot if he stayed in. Ned said Joey was obviously losing by intention, but he couldn't understand why. Most of the other players were legislators who were already friends of Indian gambling. Joey's losses looked like payoffs for services rendered, but Ned said that didn't make sense. He said the tribes were already rewarding those legislators by way of campaign contributions, trips to gambling conferences in the Caribbean, and other not-quite-illegal means. Indian gaming was doing great without breaking any laws, and Ned said he couldn't imagine the tribes would risk getting caught in a blatant cash bribery situation. He thought there had to be another angle, one he hadn't figured out yet.

Although I didn't yet know the purpose of the payoffs, I had to admire The Little Shit's ingenuity. Private poker games are vaguely legal in Minnesota as long as no one is "raking" the pot—meaning taking a percentage or an hourly fee from the players. Getting caught handing a legislator an envelope full of cash would be worth five years of state bed-and-board for both of them. Lose the same amount to the same legislator in a private card game?

"Gosh, Your Honor, it's embarrassing, but I'm just a really bad judge of poker hands."

CHAPTER 34, ED

OPENING NIGHT ~ FOUR COUPLES

Deer season finally ended, and the Saturday night get-together was at hand at last. Doris and I both had opening night jitters, but hers were worse than mine. She must have tried on every outfit in her closet that afternoon, and she wanted my feedback on all of them. Men and women definitely assess their appearances in very different ways. When most guys look in the mirror we squint a little and try to take in the whole picture from the most attractive angle. Ever hear a guy ask, "Honey, do you think this sweater makes my stomach look big?"

I doubt those words have ever been spoken by a man. Men just suck it in before they look in the mirror and then don't breathe out until after they look away. But women look at themselves carefully, one area at a time, and they always find things they don't like. Then they want you to look at those things too. It's like they want to convince you they're unattractive.

Doris has a habit of sizing herself up in the mirror right before she comes to bed. Sometimes she puts her thumbs behind her jaw and pulls the skin upward to make her double chin disappear. Then she'll ask me if I think she should get a face lift. Not exactly the Dance of the Seven Veils.

Foster's Lodge was Carlson's Resort for about thirty years. Anne and Jim bought it after the second-generation Carlson boy and his wife split up. It's a beautiful site, and the lodge and the cabins are situated in a way that shows the original builder had some respect for the land. There are pines and other mature trees standing between the cabins, and also between the cabins and the lake. There's also a barrier of native plants and shrubs along the shoreline. Nothing pisses me off more than seeing a lake place with a suburban type lawn running all the way down to the shore, and no vegetation barrier to stop the runoff. You just know the property owners are fertilizing and pesticiding the hell out of everything, and that the phosphates and other chemicals drain into the lake every time it rains. If people need to look at a nice lawn they should move next to a golf course.

The main lodge and the cabins had deteriorated along with the previous owner's marriage, but Jim said the rundown condition was the only reason he and Anne could afford to buy the place and, even then, it was a big stretch financially. They updated and remodeled a little each year, including an impressive renovation of the main lodge, adding family living quarters on the back side, central air, and a glass-walled hot tub room overlooking the lake. They did a nice job of making the changes without destroying the original character of the place.

The lodge itself is built to a design quite common in Northern Minnesota resorts; a great room, two stories high, bordered on three sides by a balcony that overlooks a big stone fireplace. I've been in three or four similar ones. Foster's has six guest rooms off the balconies, though they're usually occupied only when the cabins are completely booked, like during the fishing opener and deer season. The knotty pine walls of the great room are hung with mounted animal heads, two-man saws, old black-and white-photos of people with stringers of way too many fish and other old-timey stuff that helps people feel like they're "Up North," despite the central air and microwave popcorn. It seems to work.

Our invitation was for 9:00 p.m. Doris and I arrived, stylishly late, around 9:01. The Heikkelas got there the same time we did, and we were all still saying hello at the front door when Maddie and Chip pulled up. Inside, the place couldn't have looked any more inviting. If you were going to shoot a north woods romance movie, it was the perfect setting. Three of the half-dozen leather couches were arranged in semicircle in front of the stone fireplace, close enough to the fire that the cushions were warm to the touch. It took a while for our eyes to adjust when we first came in. The only light in the room, other than the fire, was the low-wattage yellow glow from an old-fashioned fringed lamp in a far corner, the kind of lamp my grandmother had in her living room.

Jim offered drinks, and nobody turned him down. Matt hadn't taken any chances—he brought a fifth of Akavit, "just for a toast," he said, and we all had a couple toasts right away. There's a reason people drink; it works. While we were calming ourselves with wine and beer and Akavit, Anne went into the back and came out with an armful of new white terrycloth robes. The robes were all Large or Extra Large, Anne said, except for one Medium for Sylvia. "There are changing rooms off the hot tub," she said, "and showers, if you want one later."

By "later" of course she meant *after.*

Jesus, I thought, we were really doing it. We all grabbed our robes and headed into the changing rooms.

It was only about six steps from the changing room back to the great room, but I didn't get that far before Sylvia Heikkela intercepted me. She showed me a little paper with my name on one side and hers on the other.

"It's decided" she said. "You're with me."

She led me back past the fireplace and up the stairs to one of the balcony bedrooms. When we were inside, she left the door cracked a little and whispered, "Wait."

A minute or so later, Matt and Doris passed by and went into the next bedroom. After she quietly clicked the door shut, Sylvia whispered, "Matt's going to fuck your wife now."

A candle burning on the dresser made for oversized shadows on the wall as we shucked off our robes and got into bed. The room was chilly, but the cold made it all the sweeter under the comforter. Sylvia didn't waste any time. As she kissed me, she slid her hand down between us.

"Doris is probably holding him like this right now. Think about it, Ed. That turns you on, doesn't it?" she said, "And he probably has his hand here already," she said, drawing my hand down between her legs.

"Matt works fast," she said, "He'll be inside her as soon as he can. Maybe he already is. He can be a little rough, but I think Doris is liking it. What do you think, Ed? Is she liking it?"

A minute later she pulled me over on top of her. "You should fuck me now, Ed, just like Matt is fucking Doris. Just don't expect me to come. You're not getting that."

The little Finn witch surely knew how to stir the pot. Right away I realized I was too excited to last more than a few minutes, but Sylvia still beat me to it. As she started to orgasm, she slid her hand back down between us and hooked a finger around me. It was so intense I strained a muscle in my back when I came. *Uff da*.

A few minutes later, I was still waiting for her to rave about how terrific I was, when I realized she was asleep. She woke up when we heard Doris's muffled pillow scream on the other side of the wall. Of course I knew exactly what was happening. I hadn't made a ten-minute recovery since I was about nineteen, but no erection-enhancing drug could ever compete with sights—or sounds—of Book and Garden.

The night of that first gathering, Doris and I got home a little after one. In bed, we started to talk about the evening. I said I knew she'd had an exciting time with Matt—I could still see the remains of her "fever rash" above her night gown. The rash is a rosy splotch that covers the front of her chest when she's running a temperature, or after intense lovemaking.

I asked her how she felt about the evening.

"It was exciting, Ed. Should I worry about that? I didn't know Matt that well and I was still all over him, doing things I've only done with you," she said.

"You're not counting Chip?" I asked.

"Alright, Mr. Accuracy, things I've only done with you and Chip. Anyway, I felt like I was betraying you all over again, even though I knew you and Sylvia were in the next room."

"But you got over it?"

"I got way over it. Did it turn you on knowing I was on the other side of the wall with Matt?"

I told her it was still turning me on, and I proved it by making the sheet jump a little.

"You better get over here," she said. "I'll sleep better if my husband is the last man who takes advantage of my innocence tonight."

"The husband who loves you," I added.

CHAPTER 35, MADDIE

ANNE SETS THE STAGE

For the ten days of deer season, I worked ten-hour shifts at the restaurant. My contractual half-time obligation to the kids who bought the place was over, but I'd been through the deer season frenzy many times, and I knew how much they needed and appreciated my help. The hunters usually tip quite generously too. My view of them isn't as jaundiced as Ed's, but then he sees them while they're drinking, and I see them while they're eating. I think most of them are decent guys, though there are always a few who try my patience. Those few used to get to Stan too. The only time I ever saw him get physical with anyone, ever, was when a hunter didn't just give my butt a pat— he grabbed it like he was trying to tear off a chunk of it. Stan shoved him over, chair and all, and ordered the whole party out. The violence of it was a little shocking, but later I told Stan that I felt like a maiden defended by her knight—though I suppose there weren't many Jewish knights.

Because I was so occupied at the restaurant, I hadn't had time to get nervous until the day of the big event at Fosters', but I made up for it. After I ate breakfast that morning, my tummy told me that was it for the day. That afternoon I think I tried on every sweater and slacks combination in my closet. A little silly when I was really more worried about what I would look like after I took them off. The idea of that was very scary. I think I'm fairly comfortable with my body, at least for a woman my age, and I'd gotten used to being seen by the Olsons and the Heikkelas, but there would be two new sets of eyes at the Lodge, and they would be looking at me as something other than a casual sauna partner.

Getting naked with one new person can be uncomfortable, even for a twenty-year-old woman with a perfect body. I was a fifty-eight-year-old woman, with a fifty-eight-year-old body, about to get naked with seven people. God, I was nervous. Fully dressed, we can camouflage with wardrobe tricks; sturdier bras and shaping underwear to improve our silhouettes, scarves and high-collared blouses to hide our necks, makeup to fill in the wrinkles and conceal discolorations, and flashy accessories all around the perimeter to diffuse the focus of those beholding us. Naked is naked. Naked is butt dimples, stretch marks, and belly fat, plus all the depressing effects of our main enemy—gravity.

The drinks and the low light were helpful on that first night, but the robes were close to a miracle. Once we all had them on everyone was more at ease. In the women's changing room off the hot tub area, Anne had put out a cut glass sugar bowl with four little scrolls in it. They were rolled up like party favors, each tied with a red ribbon. It wasn't a lottery, though—each scroll had one of our names on the outside and the name of our male partner on the inside. Anne handed one to each of the women. When I unrolled mine it read, "Jim."

The robes helped, but I was still very nervous. After everyone had else paired off and disappeared, Jim and I were left alone in front of the fire. Of the men, he was the one I knew least well, and I told him so. He said that he would be happy to just sit and talk, and that it would be okay with him if that was as far as we got.

He told me about meeting Anne after both their first marriages ended. I'd known they'd both been married before, but I didn't know that Anne was living with a woman lover when she and Jim met. He said that hadn't bothered him—that Anne was the most sensual woman he'd ever known, and he wasn't surprised that her interests and her appeal extended to women as well as to men. Moving to Big Pine was a big adjustment for both them, he said, but he'd never regretted the choice. He also had no regrets about quitting the chief job—it was sometimes rewarding, he said, but there were too many situations where he had to deal with people's uglier sides. He told me he would have given up police work even sooner if he and Anne had stayed in the Cities. All in all, he said, life up here had been wonderful for them and for their twin daughters. I liked the girls very much—in high school they'd both worked part time at the restaurant after the Lodge closed for the season.

The more we talked, the more I realized why everyone seemed to like him so much. I asked him if he wanted to kiss me. He did, and it was a good kiss. I said maybe we should go upstairs after all. Before we went into the bedroom, I remember looking down over the railing at the empty great room and the fire. It looked like a Christmas card. By the time we came back down everyone else was already soaking in the hot tub.

CHAPTER 36, ED

THE FIRST MONTH

We'd all been nervous before that first lodge event, and I think some of that carried through the next three gatherings, leading up to Christmas. What differed between the men and the women was the source of the nervousness. Both Doris and Maddie seemed most worried about how they'd look in the altogether (in fact, they both look just fine). I think the men were more anxious about possible performance failure, something most guys our age experience on occasion—and of course the Catch-22 is that worrying about it makes it more likely to happen. Fortunately I think everyone got over their stage fright, and we muddled through to our holiday break without any major physiological or psychological disasters.

Our son, Charlie, his wife, and our two granddaughters flew in to spend the holiday with us. Because Charlie is out of the country a lot, Christmas is really the only time of year we can count on seeing them. He tells people he works for the State Department, and that's what his business card says, but he's really with the CIA. He goes out of his way to tell Doris his work isn't dangerous, which makes her worry even more. Charlie's wife, Amanda, is a diplomat's daughter who works for the State Department herself.

Doris is always nervous before they come; she loves seeing Charlie and the girls, but she's never really bonded with Amanda. Not that there's tension between them, it's more like distance. Doris thinks Amanda sees us as uninteresting. I tell her we are uninteresting, but that we get to enjoy seeing Charlie and our granddaughters anyway.

I love my son, but our relationship has been complicated. I'd always foolishly assumed that a son would be a younger version of me—just without the flaws. Not so. Charlie and I are very different. For starters, he decided on basketball instead of wrestling. In one way that was understandable, given that his father was the wrestling coach, but I think it also reflected his instinct to be a "team player," not a loner like me. He did like fishing, but he didn't love it the way I do. He was more interested in technology than in nature. When I took him to see the first *Star Wars* movie, he couldn't talk about anything else for weeks afterward. I think we made the trip to Brainerd Theater at least three more times during its run. Fortunately, he inherited is mother's intelligence—he scored 1510 on his SATs, and he went on to graduate from the University of Wisconsin with honors. I'm very proud of him, but I've never felt like we made the complete father/son connection that I'd imagined, and I know he always felt closer to Doris than to me. The truth is that I felt more like a father to Ned Cooley than to my own son. That's hard to accept.

The first evening of their Christmas visit that year, Charlie made a joking comment about our new king-size bed, asking if we needed the extra space because we weren't getting along. I said we never knew when guests might pop in.

"Who would like some more eggnog?" Doris asked.

In bed that night she informed me that I would not be making further cute remarks related to beds, or sex, or anything that could conceivably, under any circumstances, be connected to those subjects.

The visits are always too short. We wished they lived closer, so we could be real grandparents to the girls, not just strangers whose laps they're forced to sit on a couple times a year. It's tough, especially for Doris. She has off-and-on crying spells for days after they leave.

CHAPTER 37, ED

CHIP . . . AGAIN

Two days after Christmas, Chip called and said he needed to talk to me alone. He isn't given to urgency, so I figured it was probably important. We couldn't talk at his house, he said, because his daughter and her kids were up from the Cities for an after-Christmas visit. He said he'd rather it be just between the two of us and asked me to meet him at the Buckhorn. When I got there, he was in the furthest back booth, already with an empty shot glass and a near empty bottle of beer in front of him—I'd almost never seen him drink straight shots, other than a ceremonial Akavit at the start of a B&G gathering. He ordered another round for himself and one for me, and by the time he finished his story, we'd finished off two more rounds of shots and beers.

On Christmas Eve, Chip said, he'd been out to Cal and Carolyn Peterson's for dinner. The Petersons are childless, and they had no out of town visitors for the holiday. I knew that Cal and Carolyn made a point of having Chip over frequently after Ivy was gone, much the same as we did with Maddie. The Petersons and the Brakkmans had often socialized as couples, but the close relationship was the one between Chip and Cal, and it centered around muskies.

Chip grew up with muskie fishing, but Cal came to it pretty much by accident, the result of a life-changing moment at a dental school classmate's family cabin, a few miles north of Big Pine. Cal and his friend were casting the shore for bass when, right next to the boat, a big muskie exploded at Cal's lure, just as he was about to lift it out of the water for his next cast. I can tell you from personal experience that a four-foot muskie, launching up toward you from nowhere and close enough to splash water on you, makes for an electric moment. I've had muskies follow my baits many times, and I've hooked a quite few and landed some, even though I never wanted to. Cal didn't hook that fish, but he was hooked on muskie fishing, and that's when he began thinking about Big Pine as the place to set up his dental practice. Now there are people around here eating corn off the cob who might otherwise be passing on it; and our homecoming queens flash toothy smiles as they wave from the float—all thanks to a random electrical impulse in a fish's brain. Everything changes everything.

Like me, Chip had been an early patient of our new dentist, and once Cal discovered Chip's muskie bonafides their friendship was inevitable. Muskie fishing is probably freshwater fishing's closest equivalent to big game hunting, and it's best done with a partner. For many muskie guys, it's the only kind of fishing they want to do—I'd qualify it as more of an addiction than a hobby. The sheriff could be dragging a lake for a body, and if muskie fishermen thought there might be a fish in the area they'd be casting right over the grappling hook.

If you've never seen a muskie, just imagine a beefier barracuda. Mature ones run thirty to fifty pounds in our area. That's a big animal to try to handle by yourself: think even thirty pounds of contracting muscle attached to a jaw full of very sharp teeth, thrashing to avoid the net and then flopping around frantically while you try to retrieve your lure from its mouth. Years ago, many fishermen used gaffs or clubs or even .22 pistols on them, to kill them before bringing them into the boat. Nowadays the idea is to take some pictures and then get them back into the water, alive and uninjured, so another fisherman can have the same experience. A successful catch and release is almost necessarily a two-person activity, and Cal and Chip had been partners on the water for three decades.

It's a kind of fishing that isn't nonstop action. Muskies train fishermen the same way humans train dogs—through intermittent reinforcement. If you never reward dogs for a behavior, they don't learn; if you reward them every time, they get bored. Intermittent rewards work best. But for a lot of us the rewards from muskie fishing are way too intermittent—it averages out to somewhere around fifty hours of fishing per fish boated. Another downside for me is that muskies aren't much of a table fish. The family of the girl with the conch necklace would likely have been thrilled to trap a spawning muskie in the shallows, but in recent years almost no one eats them. Smaller fish are tastier, and also less likely to be contaminated with mercury, PCBs, and other toxins that accumulate in the flesh as a fish grows older and larger.

Thousands of hours on the water as fishing partners gave Cal and Chip a lot of time to talk, and Chip had always said how impressed he was by how much Cal knew about the world. Cal didn't just know a little about many subjects, Chip said, Cal knew a *lot* about many subjects. I already knew from our work together at the History Center that when he became interested in something he really went into it. Doris is like that too. But Chip said that despite all the hours on the water together, mining into each other's lives, sex wasn't a very frequent topic—at least not as personal history. Chip's sense was that the Petersons were happy together, but more interested in their hobbies and avocations that they were in sex. Naturally they'd come up in our speculations about possible B&G membership—just about every couple in town had come up—but we'd accepted Chip's opinion that they were not likely possibilities. That was before Christmas Eve.

Chip said the Christmas Eve dinner was accompanied by a lot of alcohol. He also said the Petersons drank more than people might guess, even on non-holiday evenings. When they went down to the Cities for Gopher basketball games or professional conferences, they always stopped at a liquor store near the U that had a big variety of single malts and a good wine selection.

Carolyn liked martinis, as many as three in a social evening, Chip said. That didn't necessarily make her an alcoholic, but it did surprise me, given her reputation as a fitness buff. She'd played basketball at the U, a guard on one of the first Gopher women's teams. Up here she teaches third grade at Big Pine Elementary, but she's also an unpaid assistant coach for the Lady Gobblers. I've watched her at their practices, and I think she could still make our team. She's really stayed in shape—even in her middle fifties she still ran Grandma's Marathon in Duluth every spring, finishing right around four hours. Doris and I would see her passing our house on winter training runs, puffing clouds of condensation out the mouth opening of her balaclava. She has a nice smooth stride that doesn't waste energy on up and down motion. If you just watched the upper half of her, it was like she was on wheels. Ten below zero was her cutoff: anything above that and she'd be out there, eating up the miles.

On Christmas Eve, they were already feeling no pain, Chip said, when Cal lit up an after-dinner joint. Chip wasn't much for that, but he said that night he took a couple of drags himself. Then Cal put on some mood music and encouraged Chip to dance with Carolyn. As they danced, Chip said, Carolyn told a story about her and Cal being walked in on by his college roommate. After the roommate left, Carolyn said, Cal told her that he might like to watch her with another man sometime. It had never happened, but Carolyn told Chip she knew Cal would still like that. Chip said she talked about it in a matter-of-fact way, with her husband sitting in his recliner, just a few feet away.

When she finished the story, Carolyn sat him down on the sofa and knelt down on the carpet in front of him. Chip said he'd started getting an erection while she was telling the story, and that it made it hard for her to maneuver it out of his jeans once he was on the sofa. When she finally had Chip in her mouth, Cal said, "Thank you, Honey, thank you."

Chip said they spent the rest of the night, and deep into Christmas morning fucking Carolyn, both separately and together. He also said Cal seemed to enjoy the watching as much as the doing. By the time Chip finished his Christmas tale, I'd pretty much shed the idea that I knew anything whatever about my fellow citizens. Mr. Boy Scout had been seduced by another Big Pine matron, this time with the encouragement of her onlooking husband. *Jesus.*

We'd already scheduled a New Year's dinner at the Heron, and we planned to return to Foster's Lodge for midnight festivities. I made some phone calls. Should we invite the Petersons? Were we ready to "out" ourselves?

Chip said that in the early hours of Christmas morning he told the Petersons they weren't the first Big Pine-ites to take advantage of him. He said they were surprised, and also interested. He hadn't gone into specifics, he said, but given the Petersons knew how frequently he and Maddie hung out with me and Doris, there wasn't much doubt they would assume we were involved. Security was always a concern, but Doris pointed out that the Christmas Eve event with Chip meant the Petersons were just as vulnerable as we were, and it didn't seem likely they would betray any secrets.

In the end everyone agreed we should invite them to Heron, then just see how things developed. Not a very carefully planned agenda, but no one had any better ideas.

CHAPTER 38, MADDIE

THE PETERSONS

If you'd asked me, even before B&G, to name the most interesting married couple in Larkin County, I'd have said Cal and Carolyn Peterson. I started going to Cal as soon as he set up his Big Pine practice. I remember being surprised at how big he was. He looked more like a professional football lineman or an oversized butcher, than a dentist. In a bloody apron he'd fit right in behind a meat counter. It's a wonder he can do such delicate work with those wide fingers. And not just dentistry. His passion is sculpture, and his dental office doubles as a gallery where he rotates pieces in and out from his home studio. I very much like his work. He won a blue ribbon at the Minnesota State Fair for one of my favorites; a head and upper torso of a Neanderthal-looking man peering out from behind a tree trunk. He looks like he's fascinated by something but isn't sure he wants to be seen.

When I first started seeing Cal in his office, I'd ask him a couple of questions about himself before he started to work on me. A dental patient's conversation is usually limited to sounds made in the back of the throat, so dentists get pretty good at monologues. After my first few visits, I had a pretty good history.

He didn't just look like a football player; he'd been an all-conference tackle in high school, and he said he was heavily recruited by major football colleges. But he also said he didn't enjoy the game enough to play in college, and that his family was well off enough that he wasn't tempted by the athletic scholarships. He'd been hooked on clay modeling ever since making ashtrays and dinosaurs in kindergarten, and even in grade school he'd asked his parents to send him to summer art programs. After high school he enrolled at the U of M, intending to major in studio art. His parents weren't thrilled. They saw art as a nice hobby, not a career choice, and at the end of Cal's freshman year they had a heart-to-heart with him about his future. His parents told him that if he'd pick a "real" profession, they'd finance all the required education and give him whatever financial help he needed to get started on a career. His father made the dentistry suggestion and pointed out that it required some of the same talents Cal brought to sculpture—good hands and the ability to visualize in three dimensions—and that dentistry usually paid a lot better than sculpture.

Cal said he'd already figured out that supporting himself in art would likely mean being a high school art teacher, something that didn't at all appeal to him. He and Carolyn were already together by then, after meeting in a pottery class, and she voted for dentistry, along with Cal's parents. So despite it being his dad's suggestion, Cal switched to a pre-dental curriculum.

Beyond being dental patients, Stan and I knew the Petersons mostly as regular customers at the restaurant. Stan was always impressed by how knowledgeably Cal talked about food. We also sometimes saw them at Gobbler basketball games and other community doings, and we'd been in each other's houses a few times, though the occasions were community organization meetings, not social dinner visits. I think most everyone liked them, but they didn't socialize much. And because they never had children, they hadn't been drawn into the kind of default friendships that parents develop with other parents, just because they happen to have kids around the same ages. I never knew if they were childless by choice or by physiology, but Carolyn certainly had nurturing impulses that flowed over onto her third graders. Both my daughters remember her as their favorite teacher, and they each keep in touch with her. Carolyn's very reserved with adults, though. Before Book and Garden, I don't recall her ever talking about anything very personal.

Dentistry pays well, and so does not having kids. Cal and Carolyn live in an architect designed, Prairie school-style home on Whiskey Creek. There's an attached studio, complete with skylights, where Cal does his sculpture and where Carolyn has her potter's wheel. It's a beautiful house that blends in with the wooded landscape it sits in, and they own enough frontage on both sides of the creek that no one can build anything that would intrude on their privacy. One of my first thoughts when I heard about Chip's Christmas Eve was that the Peterson place would be a wonderful spot for B&G gatherings.

Our last-minute New Year's invitation turned out wonderfully well. By the time we left the Heron, it already seemed certain the Petersons were going to be the newest members of our little society. The Lodge part of the evening was successful too. The atmosphere was more boisterous than usual, but it was a New Year's Eve cele-bration. If you put us in togas instead of robes and replaced the unfortunate mounted animal heads with pornographic wall frescoes, like the ones Stan and I saw in Pompeii, we could probably have passed for decadent Roman partiers.

Cal and Carolyn didn't add any new partners on that first visit. After the traditional New Year's midnight kissing, when people began to separate themselves for intimate activities, the two of them and Chip went off to one of the balcony bedrooms together, then joined us in the hot tub later on. I don't think any of the rest of us felt slighted; it seemed like they were saying they were "in," but to give them a little time. It didn't take very long.

A few weeks later, I had an encounter with Cal that left me with an appreciation of just how "large" he was in every area. The only time I'd seen a male member that size was on one of the Pompeii frescoes, and there I assumed some artistic license had been exercised.

That New Year's Eve was the culmination of the unlikeliest year of my life, and I think all the other B&Gers would say the same. What four of us had fantasized about in May was real life just eight months later, and what was most amazing was how easily it all came about. We'd really just stumbled into it. Even my story about the imaginary magazine article had been a spur of the moment improvisation, and that was about the only thing you could say was intentional. The rest just sort of happened.

CHAPTER 39, ED

THE FIRST WINTER

Doris and I and Chip and Maddie had gotten used to being together in a "natural" state, but when we went to four couples, and then to five, there was a period where everyone was extra careful not to look like we were checking out other people's bodies. For most of our social time together we were in our robes, but the hot tub area was challenging for the first few weeks. We were all careful about not letting our eyes wander below each other's neck levels, which made it kind of like we were having staring contests. Gawking avoidance is a learned discipline, not an instinctive one. I doubt Stone Age people were shy about checking out members of the opposite sex, but 50,000 years later it's considered bad manners.

Before Doris and I were married, I wasn't always discreet enough in the way I looked at other women. I remember a college party where one of the other female guests was wearing a blouse that she'd forgotten to button up all the way—she was maybe distracted by a phone call or something while she was getting dressed. Whatever the reason, the blouse hung open in that way where you're waiting for the person to move or shift position, so you can see a little further in. Stupid, I know, but it's an instinctive guy thing.

I was checking on the situation as Doris was waving at a friend on the other side of the room. She wasn't even turned in my direction when she said, "Why don't you take a picture, Ed? It'll last longer."

Since then I've developed a technique that seems to work a little better; instead of fixing my gaze, I move my whole head, allowing my field of vision to sweep across the object of interest, like I'm taking a panoramic photo. The trick is not to hesitate as your eyes pass over the target. It doesn't always work, though. Many years ago, I had a lapse at school that still haunts me. It was one of my earliest unpleasant encounters with Joey Hamer, and I could blame only myself.

I was standing in the doorway of my classroom, between periods, when one of our cheerleaders walked by in a crowd of other students. For just a brief moment my eyes rested on her rear end. During the school day I did my best to avoid such occurrences, but the ancient lizard portion of a guy's brain can sometimes trigger an autonomic response to a stimulus before the more recently evolved frontal lobe can override it. That morning the override wasn't fast enough. When I regained control and lifted my eyes, there was Joey Hamer, grinning at me. He said, "Pretty nice, eh?"

What was I supposed to do?—say, "No, Joey, I know my eyes were pointed at her ass for a couple seconds, but I wasn't actually seeing it?"

I couldn't deny it without admitting it. I had no place to go, so I said something lame about not knowing what he was talking about and told him to keep moving. But he'd caught me, and he knew I knew he'd caught me. I was angrier at myself for giving him the opening than I was at The Little Shit for taking advantage of it.

The whole incident lasted about ten seconds, and I'm still pissed at myself half a lifetime later.

Of course, Book and Garden visual discipline was impossible to maintain forever. After the first few weeks we were all a little freer about taking in the sights. Men were not the only gawkers—especially when we first added the Petersons. I've been in a lot of men's locker rooms, but I haven't seen many guys who Cal wouldn't have bragging rights on. It wasn't a regular topic of conversation between me and Doris, but it did come up one night as we were getting dressed for a Saturday gathering.

Doris was posing in front of our full-length mirror, looking at her bare legs from various angles—her usual flaw-hunting behavior. She said that standing next to Carolyn Peterson made her feel "stumpy."

It is undeniable that Carolyn has nice legs. In fact, she has an all-around-amazing body for a woman her age. Genetics might be part of it, but I'm sure the work she does to stay in four-hour marathon shape also helps. But Doris's legs aren't stumpy; they're just a little shorter than she'd like. I reminded her that Elizabeth Taylor didn't like her own legs either—a long time ago I saw the headline "Liz Hides Her Legs" on one of the magazines Doris keeps under the bed. I also said I had my own reasons for not wanting to compare body parts with the Petersons.

I could see the light bulb coming on, but she played it straight.

"Whatever are you talking about?" she asked.

She couldn't quite carry it off, though. A few seconds later she started laughing, and she said, "Size doesn't really matter, Ed."

It would have been okay if she'd left it there, but then she said, "At least not *that* much," and laughed so hard at her own brilliant stand-up bit that she had to sit down on the bed.

Doris, the comedienne.

~

A sex scandal was a hot topic that new year, though fortunately Book and Garden wasn't the subject. Just days after we filled out our roster with the addition of the Petersons, Clinton's impeachment began. That disaster not only reinforced the reality that "There are no grownups," it also underscored a corollary, which is: "There are no great men."

The truth is, there's a deer season idiot lurking somewhere inside all of us, including inside presidents and CEOs and religious leaders. Powerful men often seem to have risky impulses, usually sexual ones—and too often they act on them. I'm sure that being surrounded by people who worship your ass, or think you're their ticket up, or who just want to be able to say they were in your bed, probably makes it easy to do whatever the hell you feel like doing. Clinton wasn't the first American president to take advantage of that.

We want to believe that people with great power and responsibility, such as having their fingers on nuclear triggers, are wiser and more stable than the rest of us, and that we can trust them to act in restrained and rational ways. If we didn't pretend that was the case, we'd all be in an even worse state of anxiety than we are about the future of civilization. That's why the most important skill presidents and other leaders have is their ability to convince us that they really are grownups. especially when you realize the insane risks they sometimes take in pursuit of sex.

Present-day historians and journalists are less reluctant to take note of "great man" flaws than they were fifty or a hundred years ago, a change in press etiquette that makes it more and more difficult to have confidence in the stability of our leaders. My late-life history addiction, and the way history writing has changed, leaves me a less-than-Mount Rushmore view of "great men." We now know, for instance, that from the beginning of American history roughly half our presidents have been confirmed adulterers, often while they were in office. President Harding's only biological child was a result of his adulterous relationship; FDR managed to betray Eleanor despite his mobility challenges, Eisenhower spent plenty of World War II nights belly to belly with his female jeep driver, and the word on LBJ was that he'd "fuck a brush pile if he thought there might be a female snake in it."

There isn't much dispute, though, that JFK was the champion of the riskiest presidential philandering. When you think about him trying to steer us away from extinction during the Cuban Missile Crisis, it isn't exactly reassuring to know he was the same guy who smoked dope in a White House bed with two hookers, and that he shared a girlfriend with the head of the Mafia. Jack and brother Bobby were also Marilyn Monroe's lovers, the only question being if she entertained them serially or simultaneously (a claim made in several of Doris's informative magazines). By comparison, Clinton's sneaky Oval Office blow jobs seem about as shocking as jaywalking.

Not that politicians have a monopoly on sexual misbehavior; religious leaders might be even worse. How do you recite Mass and sermonize against homosexuality, then assault the altar boy after the service? And it's not just Christians. In my youth there was the saintly Maharishi Mahesh Yogi, a man cleansed of all worldly desire. He attracted a lot of disciples among the rich and famous, including the Beatles—though they didn't sit at his feet for very long. In fact, they un-discipled themselves and headed home in a major huff after they discovered Mr. Yogi was trying to anoint their female companions with his transcendental love scepter.

We don't even have to look far from Big Pine to find a Great Man philanderer. Charles Lindbergh grew up about an hour from our town. His Great Man status started crumbling early as a result of his crush on Hitler, but it was his polygamous approach to marriage that probably led him to exile himself and die in seclusion in Hawaii. Turned out he had three other families in addition to the six kids he had with Anne Morrow. Two of the families were with German sisters that his secretary pimped to him. It was generous of her, considering she had two children by Lindbergh herself. "Lucky Lindy" was actually kind of a jerk.

CHAPTER 40, MADDIE

B&G ETIQUETTE

Those first months of the new year, B&G convened at either Fosters'
or Petersons' almost every Saturday night. We had no *Senior Sex Group
Dynamics* manual to guide us, so we had to figure out our own set of
rules. Health concerns were at the top of our list. The ages of the
women meant there wasn't any chance of pregnancy, but we were
obviously still vulnerable to STDs. Sylvia had some alarming
information about the rising incidence of the diseases in retirement
communities and nursing homes. She said she intended to complete
her life without being a statistic, and added that she would
disembowel anyone responsible for making her one. She said she
wasn't trying to lay down any moral rules but, instead, she proposed
that any B&Ger who had sex with anyone outside our group was
honor bound to abstain from group activities until they had a clean
bill of health. It was agreed to unanimously.

For cold and flu viruses though, B&G was a Petri dish, and
we've canceled a few meetings for lack of a quorum. Also, early on in
our adventure, I had a urinary tract infection. My gynecologist said
UTIs are a common experience for women who resume having sex
after a long layoff. She said it more like a question. I think she was
inviting me to talk about it, but I just smiled and nodded. Then she
said that whoever it might be was "a lucky guy."

She's been my doctor for a long time and I trust her, but I wasn't quite ready to tell her there were four lucky guys—five, after the Petersons joined us.

One lesson we learned early on was the necessity of keeping conversation light and avoiding potentially controversial topics, similar to the sauna tradition. The wisdom of that came home when Cal Peterson made an offhand comment about unions that brought Sylvia's quills up. The two of them got uncomfortably pissy with each other before Anne intervened and calmed them down.

In the end Sylvia said she forgave Cal; she said she'd forgotten that one of the requirements for getting a dental license was swearing lifetime allegiance to the Republican Party. Cal was equally gracious; he said he knew that Finn parents read their kids the *Communist Manifesto* at bedtime, and that Sylvia's views were probably not entirely her own fault. He also added that he was more of a libertarian than a Republican. We did get the party back on track, but we'd learned a lesson, and I don't recall any contentious political discussions since that one.

Avoiding risky conversational topics was not the only thing we were careful about. Almost nothing about our early meetings was haphazard. Anne had made very thoughtful preparations for that first four-couple evening at the Lodge, and I know we women were especially grateful, especially for the lighting. When Chip and I walked in the door that night I'd almost stumbled over an ottoman because my eyes hadn't had time to adjust. I didn't complain, and I doubt sixty-year-old women ever complain about low light at a social event—certainly not one where getting out of their clothes is on the agenda. I remember my mother's response on an occasion when my father had complimented her on looking good on her fiftieth birthday.

"I can get by at dusk, with the light behind me," Mom said.

Even young people try to get their dates out of the tavern before the lights come on at closing.

Forgiving lighting was a feature of that first evening—and every one since—but that was only part of Anne's careful staging. I've already mentioned the effect of the robes, but she'd also thought through all the other elements—the fire, the music, the arrangement of the sofas, and the romantic candles in the bedrooms. All perfect touches. The scrolls naming our partners on that first occasion also helped reduce the opening night uncertainty and anxiety. Pairing me with her husband, Jim, seemed strange at first, given that he was a man I'd spent little time with before B&G, but she knew what she was doing, and it couldn't have worked out any better.

As time went on, things became a little more free-form. We always began with changing into our robes and half an hour or so of socializing, usually accompanied by some alcohol, but we did a lot of informal experimenting in the course of figuring out what was going to work for everyone. It turned out that most of the sex took place in private, even when there were more than two people participating, but there were also some opportunities just to be an audience. If a bedroom door was open, it was understood that anyone was free to look in—though joining in required an invitation

Once in a while people became quite intimate in the lodge great room, though usually with at least some robe camouflage. Most often though, only the preliminaries took place in front of the whole group. For most of us there was slow dancing, maybe with hands inside robes, or some kissing and underwater touching in the hot tub. For the X-rated activities, it was usually off to more private space. Sylvia was the only one who didn't bother much with mating dances; she usually just picked out her target and led him off to a bedroom.

The newness of the situation was exciting, but it was also sensually disorienting at first, at least it was for me. I think for others too, especially the women. After thirty years with one partner, we all had new bodies to learn. Everyone touches and reacts to being touched differently. It wasn't so much new positions or techniques as it was how different those things felt when you were with someone new, someone whose skin had a new scent, someone whose mouth had an unfamiliar taste—not necessarily unpleasant, just new and different. Different sequences too—I sometimes found myself thinking *Wait, this isn't what's supposed to come next.* Your partner could respond to something in a completely different way than the person you'd been with for decades. For instance, when I was first married, I'd read that some men had sensitive nipples and liked having them touched and kissed and sucked on, but when I tried it with Stan I got almost no reaction. He didn't dislike it; it just didn't do anything for him. Jim Foster turned out to be at the other end of the spectrum—he loved being played with that way.

I think the male B&Gers adapted to new partners a little more readily than the women did. I read an article in *Cosmo* or some other woman's magazine about adultery and female orgasm. The gist of it was that women stepping outside their main relationships found excitement, but often didn't orgasm as regularly with the adultery partner as they did with their spouse. The point was that practice and familiarity are big factors. It makes sense to me. I was never unfaithful during my marriage (though I once came close) but there was a change over the first couple of years as Stan learned my body. The romantic element declined a bit, as I think it inevitably does, but after a year or so I almost always had orgasms with him. When I first began having sex with the men of Book and Garden, it was exciting and new again, but it took a while before we were efficient together—efficient for me, I mean. Men have it a lot easier. I doubt that a book titled *Achieving the Male Orgasm* would answer any existing need.

I suppose we could be described as "swingers," but for me the word had always called up images of sexual free-for-alls, with everyone rutting like rabbits with everyone else and bouncing from one partner to another every few minutes. That was not us. Over time, everyone was eventually intimate with every member of the opposite sex, but certainly not at every gathering. And there were pairings and threesomes that occurred with much different frequency than others. Cal and Sylvia's first encounter, for instance, turned out to be their last. My own favorites were Jim and Ed, who also happened to be the two men I felt emotionally closest to. I don't think that was a coincidence.

There were also nights when some members of the group didn't participate in anything except socializing. After our first few meetings it felt more and more comfortable to sit things out if you felt like it. Then too, some were interested in more variety than others. Anne, for instance, was up for just about anything—and anyone. If someone seemed to be isolated, Anne was usually willing to offer some kind of companionship. She was the efficient plump spider who maintained our web and made sure everyone stayed connected. And when small tears occurred, like the spat between Cal and Sylvia, she was right there to patch them. She also led us into a range of sensual experience, both sexual and nonsexual. In her commune days, she'd learned several types of massage, and we all received the benefits of that. Group massage was an instant hit. I'd never before experienced the delicious sensation of having two or three pairs of hands kneading me. It was so wonderful that we agreed that a few minutes of it was the one (and only) thing a person automatically got if they asked for it. On most nights a couple of us took advantage of that.

Anne had an especially wonderful gift for head and neck massage. The first time she did it for me was on a night when I was having an anxiety attack at the Lodge. The anxiety was, as usual, about my oldest daughter. She'd called that afternoon to tell me she'd lost her job when her company was sold. She was very distraught. I always feel like I need to fix things for her, even though I know I usually can't. Somehow Anne picked up on my worried state of mind. She came up behind me as I was sitting on one of the leather sofas and began working her fingers around my scalp. Then she moved to my temples and my jaw and told me to relax and focus on my breathing. It was magical—within a few minutes I was able to see my daughter's situation as something beyond my control, and I felt calm and centered and ready to enjoy the evening.

Anne said she'd used the same technique to deal with her own daughters' hormonal thunderstorms during adolescence. It didn't always work perfectly, she said, but usually it was enough to deescalate things down to rain-shower level. I hope those girls know how lucky they were.

CHAPTER 41, ED

ME AND SYLVIA

Maddie's mention of favorite partners applied to me and Sylvia. Like Anne, Sylvia was inclusive, but she and I did make a special connection. For starters, we just plain liked each other. I also trusted her right away, probably because she was so wonderfully damn blunt. If she said it, she meant it, even though it might not be very diplomatic. We were also a good sexual match, and I think that was a residual benefit of my wrestling background. Arranging someone's body in the position you want them in is something that comes naturally after years of competitive wrestling. In sexual situations you do it without even thinking about it. I'm not talking about doing things against a woman's will but, once the event has been agreed to, wrestlers are pretty good at guiding the action. I think that's why Sylvia sometimes went out of her way let me know that she liked me in bed. Of course I knew she always got off with the other men too, but a former wrestler might have been a little more fun to struggle against. Maybe now that high school girls are getting into wrestling there will eventually be guys who find themselves being configured the way their partners want them.

Another particular joy of sex with Sylvia was timing. From my admittedly limited experience I'm going to say that simultaneous orgasms happen most often in movies and novels. In real life, people generally take turns. But Sylvia always went off on a predictable schedule and having her body detonating underneath me would carry me along at the same time, even when she didn't do her little reaching down between us trick. I've never asked any of the other men, but I bet they all had the same experience with her. I think she made all of us feel like thoroughbreds at stud.

Sylvia also had an anatomical gift, one she enlightened me on about halfway through that first winter. We'd been together many times by then, and one night, as we relaxed in the aftermath, I said something about how reliably orgasmic she was, and that it was too bad all women couldn't have that. Without saying anything, she stretched out straight and flat, took me by the wrist and placed my palm on her breastbone. She slid my hand straight down over her belly until it went up over the furry rise at the bottom.

"There," she said, "that's my secret."

She said she knew from her hospital experience that her whole apparatus was set a little higher and further forward than on most women. She said her mother recognized it and early on discouraged her from wearing flat-front skirts that would emphasize her pubic mound. The result of being built that way, Sylvia said, was that her most sensitive bit almost always matched up nicely with a man's pubic bone in missionary-position sex. That was why she always entwined her legs with mine as soon as I was inside and held herself so tightly up against me that I usually couldn't slide in and out more than an inch or so. If I tried to draw out further, her light body just lifted off the bed. That way she kept things rubbing together just the way she liked. She said our dentist was the only man in the group who was a problem. Sylvia was short, and her interior was apparently short as well. The first and only time she and Cal tried to have sex, she couldn't use her reliable technique because Cal bumped against her cervix. Very painful, she said. With the rest of us she had no problem.

"Five or ten minutes of basic missionary position and I pin a medal on 'em," she said. "Then I go to sleep,"

I told her I'd noticed the sequence.

"It used to drive Matt crazy," Sylvia said. "He says going to sleep is the man's role. Apparently, women are supposed to want to talk afterward. Talk about what? My feelings? My feelings are that I want to go to sleep."

"You do know how to make a guy feel special," I said.

"Don't be a needy asshole," she said.

She wasn't much for pillow talk.

Sylvia usually knew exactly where her evenings were heading, but for most of us the early portion of a group night usually included a few drinks, some dancing, and other preliminaries. Dancing worked as a nice transition into other things—sometimes even for the observers.

One occasion that's burned into my memory began as I was sitting on a sofa, talking with Anne, while Doris and Jim Foster were dancing a few feet away—really just swaying back and forth in front of the fire, kissing as they moved to the music. Then Matt Heikkela joined them, massaging Doris's shoulders from behind until she turned to kiss him too. They were both whispering to her. I couldn't hear what they were saying, but she was arching up on tiptoes, and I could see she was getting very turned on. After a few minutes they each took her by a hand and led her up the stairs. Later, Doris told me she thought her knees would buckle before she made it to the top.

Watching them also had an immediate effect on me and Anne. "That was wonderful," Anne said, "I think you and I should have some fun with it."

Desire is contagious. One of my all-time favorite cartoons has a middle-aged policeman taking off his uniform coat in his bedroom. Smoke and flames are coming out his nose and ears as he looks down at his middle-aged wife. She's under the covers, with her hair in curlers and a "not again" expression on her face. The caption is her saying, "Oh God, you've been out patrolling Lover's Lane, haven't you?" Something like that anyway.

The point is that he's all stoked up from his official voyeur duties. I think most B&Gers would recognize that effect. But there was also a seeming paradox in my reaction to seeing Doris with both Matt and Jim: Somehow the scene was less threatening than it was if she was with only one of them. It took me a while to figure out why, but now I think I understand. No matter how enthusiastically Doris might respond to the attentions of two lovers, I didn't feel diminished by comparison—I couldn't be expected to compete with two, so I was free to relax in the erotic idea of it. It was when she was with only one that I felt the most twinges, especially early on. When someone else strikes a fresh high note in your spouse, a note that maybe you haven't played recently, it's hard not to feel compared.

During our first weeks, I think we all had some of those uncomfortable moments. It can be a little shocking, especially for guys. Most of us have been conditioned by our spouses to think we're dynamite in bed. There's a saying that all guys think they're good in three departments—fishing, driving, and sex. But how do they measure that last one? They go by what their girlfriends or wives tell them. And does any woman ever tell a man he's crummy at sex, compared to her last boyfriend or her previous husband? Not unless she's super angry, and not even then if she has any sense. You might be the lamest lover on the planet; but if you're her only partner, what does she have to gain by giving you a candid negative assessment? Of course she's going to say you're wonderful, even the best. The consequence of women's self-interest is that most guys really do think they're terrific in the sack, and B&G could be a direct threat to that confidence. It was the first time most of us had been in a situation where it was almost impossible not to feel "compared" as lovers. Fortunately, all of us seemed to get past it. Repetition alone certainly took some of the sharp edge off those feelings, but I think everyone also did their best to be considerate about their spouses' feelings—it wasn't as if Doris ever said, "I wish you could do that the way Matt does it."

And I completely agree with Maddie about Wonderful Anne being central to our success. She was an expert at making things fun and making the rest of us feel more comfortable and relaxed. By just about any standard, Anne was obese—at least fifty pounds over "ideal weight," maybe more. But, if anything, the extra weight made her all the more sensual. You could tell she was completely comfortable with her body, and I'm sure that made everyone else more comfortable with their bodies, especially the women. And, *Jesus*, she was really good at sex, both as a participant and as a teacher. When we were together she'd take me through doing something in a way that she liked then suggest I might want to try it that way with Doris. She was so comfortable with everything that she made the rest of us comfortable too. We all reaped the benefits. A good example was Doris's new expertise at fellatio—not that anyone uses that term to describe it.

"Want fellatio?" and "Want a blow job?" are both welcome questions, but I'll venture the second one gets the fastest and most intense biological response, just about every time. Sometimes correct terminology doesn't carry the same punch.

Anyway, whatever the label, my wonderful wife had never been unwilling; she just didn't really get the hang of it. It was a little knot in our love life that we'd never really talked about, but it wasn't all that important, so I'd sort of played down my interest in having her do it.

Then, that first winter of B&G, things changed, thanks entirely to our resident sex goddess. I started receiving treats at home, sometimes completely spontaneous ones while we were watching television together. She was doing it differently too—differently in a really nice way that I recognized from my encounters with Anne at B&G gatherings. I'd noticed Anne peeking up, studying my reactions in those situations. Having her looking directly into my eyes was a huge turn on for me. Now Doris was doing the same thing, and I could tell she was having some fun with it. She was also a whole bunch better at making it feel wonderful.

Eventually she admitted that our kindly den mother had arranged private tutoring for her in one of the Lodge bedrooms, using Jim as a mannequin. Anne started the lesson by putting a condom on him, using only her mouth. Then she had Doris do the same but, with Doris, Jim took her hand and put her index finger in his mouth. He sucked on her finger with his tongue, showing her just exactly what he wanted her to do it him, and also telling her moment by moment what felt the best. After ten minutes he gave her an "A" for the course.

The finger idea was so simple and so obvious, I can't believe it isn't in chapter one of every sex manual—but I'd never heard of it. Fifteen minutes of instruction and Doris moved up to professional courtesan level. I was grateful to the Fosters, but I never mentioned it. "Hey, Jim, I really appreciate you working with my wife on her blow job issues," would have sounded too strange, even in our new world.

But tricks and techniques weren't the most significant changes. What really changed was the way I saw Doris. She was no longer just Doris, my wife, and the mother of our son—she was Sexual Doris, wanted by other men in the most basic way and capable of responding to them in that same way. After thirty years of marriage, that was a jolt. My guess is that everyone in the group experienced some heightened awareness of their spouse's sexuality, and that it added a new dimension to their relationship beyond B&G gatherings.

CHAPTER 42, MADDIE

SOMETHING NEW

Reading Ed's reaction to Doris in a threesome brought home to me how differently we'd all experienced sex in our lives. Before B&G I'd never been in a sexual situation other than with a single partner; and my feelings about the kind of threesomes I'd been offered, threesomes with one man and two women, were not positive. I always thought of them as performances for the benefit of men. The girl in my freshman dorm warned me not to tell men about my bisexuality. She said her bisexual girlfriends all told her that when their male lovers found out, the first thing they wanted was a threesome, preferably one that included sex between the two women.

What is it about men and lesbian sex? I don't think most women get all worked up by the thought of two men having sex together but, for some men, woman/woman sex is the erotic Holy Grail. They also seem to assume that a bisexual woman will automatically be up for inviting another woman into bed with her boyfriend or husband. I discovered my dorm partner was right when my first male lover, the English TA, found out my previous lover had been female. Right away he tried to get me to set up a threesome with another woman. The night he brought it up I said that would be great, but that first I wanted a threesome where he and another guy had sex while I watched and rated their performance. Then I got dressed and left.

When Stan and I first became lovers, I didn't tell him about my relationships with Sissy and the girl in the dorm, but as time went on I decided I'd feel better if I was candid, especially about my first love, Sissy. To say he found it interesting is an understatement. Just like with the teaching assistant, I could see his threesome gear engaging, and he began making obvious little test comments to see if I might be interested. I felt he was trying to change me from his lover into a performer, and it was one of the first times I was truly angry with him, and more than a little disgusted.

Now I regret landing on him quite so hard. I'm still not a fan of lesbian shows for men, but after B&G was underway, I had some very exciting moments that involved more than one partner, including some where I was one of two women with a man. I don't often have orgasms in those situations—it's too distracting. It's much easier when I'm focused on one person, but there have been a few exceptions. One of the more intense sexual experiences of my life was a threesome that first winter of B&G. It began with a conversation between me and Carolyn in the hot tub at Fosters'.

Of the women, Carolyn seemed to have had the least-fulfilling sex life before B&G, at least in terms of being orgasmic, and that night in the hot tub she told me she blamed her mom's attitudes about sex for much of her problem. When she was very young, she told me, her mom kept a bottle of vodka behind their basement washing machine. Her mom told Carolyn it was medicine that helped her get ready for "certain things." Carolyn said it wasn't hard to decipher her mom's lack of enthusiasm for the physical side of marriage. She also remembered her mom screaming at Carolyn's older sister, calling her a "slut" when she discovered her daughter was having sex with her boyfriend. I felt bad for Carolyn. I'm no expert on sexual psychology but I'm quite sure things like the bottle hidden in a dark basement, and having her sister labeled as a slut by her own mom, wasn't a very good start toward giving a little girl positive feelings about sex.

Carolyn said she'd managed to overcome her mother's legacy to the point that she could often enjoy sex, but that her main reward was that Cal enjoyed it and that it made her feel close to him. She did have battery powered orgasms, she said, but none otherwise. She said she came closest when she was with Chip, or one of the other men, and knew Cal was watching. We'd all assumed the idea of Cal watching had been his fantasy, but Carolyn confessed it was hers as well. That set me thinking, and before we ended that evening I talked to Cal and Carolyn about an idea. They liked it.

At our next Saturday gathering, right after we changed into our robes, Cal and Carolyn headed up to one of the balcony bedrooms. A few minutes later, Matt and I followed. The only light in the room was the candle on the bed table. Carolyn's hands and feet were tied to the bed frame with strips of cloth, and she was wearing a black sleep mask. The restraints weren't just symbolic—Cal had tied her snugly enough that she could tell she wasn't going anywhere without permission.

As Cal sat in the chair across the room, I motioned to Matt to lift up Carolyn's hips so I could tuck two pillows under her. Then I lay down on her left side and put my arm under her head, and Matt moved to a kneeling position between her legs. I began kissing her and touching her breasts while Matt ran his hands up and down over the tops of her thighs, moving a little higher up each time, until his thumbs almost touched. By then she had to know it was a woman kissing her, but she didn't seem to mind (I hadn't mentioned the gender of the third person when I described the plan). I whispered to her that Cal was watching.

After a couple of minutes, I nodded at Matt. As he pushed into her, I clamped my right hand over her mouth. I could feel her go rigid. She strained against the ties, as if she really was trying to get loose, then relaxed—at least as much as could relax while being muzzled and impaled at the same time. I had my free hand between them, and for the next few minutes I ran it up and down Carolyn's belly, coming a little closer to the connection with Matt each time.

I could feel both of them twisting, trying to urge my fingers further down. I held off until I thought they were ready then moved my hand all the way down to where they wanted it. I spread my fingers just enough for Matt to keep sliding between them, and I pressed down on Carolyn. They both went off almost immediately. Having my hand sandwiched between their sweaty bodies as they came was indescribably exciting. The memory still turns me on.

When I took my hand off Carolyn's mouth she gasped like she was having as asthma attack, sucking in huge gulps of air. When she had her breath back, she said, "Untie me."

As soon as she was free, she rolled toward me and reached down between us. When I raised my leg over hers, so she could get her fingers up inside me as far as possible, Matt grabbed my calf and held it pinned in that position until Carolyn could tell I was finished. Probably everyone in the lodge could tell I was finished—I guess I was embarrassingly noisy by the end. I know everyone can remember a few peak B&G moments. That was one of mine.

Later, Carolyn said her first rush was when the pillows went under her hips. And she said that the restraints, and my hand over her mouth, somehow helped her let go of whatever it was that stopped her short so often before. She said it was also the first time she'd felt the inside of another woman, and I could tell she was a little embarrassed for having done that.

I told her I was very glad she'd taken the opportunity, but not to worry, that it didn't mean she had to call herself a lesbian. Both Petersons warbled about how wonderfully insightful I'd been, and I was very pleased with the way things turned out. I just never confessed that I set it up because the idea also turned *me* on.

That threesome was something of a turning point. It offered a choice of roles—dominant, submissive, and audience—and over time most of us, men and women, tried all three. Anne was especially good at all of them, and she also introduced some new variations on restraining the "victim." It was very sexy and very fun, even without a spontaneous second act like the one I had with Carolyn.

Doris was right after all. I did have some talent as a "catalyst."

CHAPTER 43, ED

B&G GOES ON VACATION

I don't have much sympathy for Minnesotans who complain about Minnesota winters—moving vans have been around for a long time. And besides, winter isn't really that long—maybe five months with snow on the ground and three more with occasional frosts. But I'll concede that the later months between the Christmas holidays and open water on the lakes can be progressively challenging, especially March. Unless you're into snowmobiling or ice fishing, you spend a lot of time indoors, and indoors up here is usually more confining than indoors in a city; our houses are generally smaller than city houses, and attractions like malls and movie theaters and health clubs are further away.

By March, cabin fever can set in, sometimes even for me. On cloudy March days, color film is a waste up here. Just about everything is some shade of gray, and the roads are all bordered by ridges of "snirt," the ugly blend of snow and dirt and road salt excreted by snowplows. Snirt gets people down. It also drives a lot of Minnesotans to book impulse vacations.

The Petersons were regular winter vacationers, and their favorite destination was St. John, in the American Virgin Islands. They'd been there a half-dozen times, and that first winter of B&G they suggested we do a group trip there over the school spring break. One of Cal's dental school classmates owned two rentals on the island. Cal and Carolyn had stayed only in the smaller one, but they had seen the larger one and said it was spectacular. They promised we would love it. When it turned out that we could all make the trip, we booked the place.

Getting to St. John is a multi-part journey. We flew into to St. Thomas, taxied across the whole length of that island, took the ferry to St. John, then rented jeeps for the twenty miles between the port and our villa on the far end of the island. It's a challenging drive. There are a dozen places where a mile of shoulderless road takes you from beach level to skyscraper height and back down again. When you crest the hills, the blacktop drops away in front of you like the downhill on a roller coaster.

As we went over the first hill, Doris gave out a couple "Oh shits," closed her eyes and tried to press her feet through the floor boards. But the destination was worth the effort.

Doris and I went to Florida once and, except for the palm trees, Florida suburbs looked a lot like Minnesota suburbs. Franchises have pretty well homogenized the whole damn country. St. John didn't look like anywhere most of us had ever been.

Our villa was wedged into a steep hillside, 150 feet or so above Haulover Bay. We'd seen the photos, but they didn't convey the suck-in-your-breath reality. Just watching the rest of us take in the view must have been fun for Cal and Carolyn. They hadn't exaggerated. At either end of the compound, there was a two-level bedroom and bath building. The beds were all kings, a nice amenity, given the nature of our group. In between was a forty-foot-long living room/cooking/lounging area, and behind the buildings were an outdoor swimming pool and a ground-level hot tub set in a narrow tropical landscaped yard that butted up to the hillside. On the ocean side an eighty-foot-long deck ran in front of all three buildings. From the deck we had a panoramic view of the whole horseshoe-shaped bay, the surrounding steep green hills, and a scattering of sailboats and motor yachts, so far below us they looked like toys in the water. It was like stepping into a travel poster.

That first evening we all just relaxed and drank in the surroundings. It had been a long day of travel, and we all felt a little ragged. We looked it, too. Eighteen-year-olds look good even when they're tired, but tired shows on sixty-year-olds.

Other than taking in the view from the deck, the only thing most of us did that first night was relax in the hot tub and the pool. I did wear my bathing suit. I'm a little phobic about swimming nude, and being a fisherman probably adds to it. I've spent enough of time dragging bait through the water that I'm just not keen on trolling my own lure when I think there could be something cruising underneath me.

I know it's irrational to worry about that in a swimming pool, or even in a lake, but that doesn't mean the feeling completely disappears. Matt's got it worse than I do. Said he read about piranhas when he was a kid and he can't shake the thought of them. I understand.

CHAPTER 44, MADDIE

A GOOD TIME

I love Minnesota too, but Ed is right; March is not our best month. It can be depressingly dingy. St. John was the opposite of dingy. There was color everywhere—the ocean, the sky, the vegetation, and the people. The villa was a perfect accommodation for our group, but it was the setting that had us speechless. Sitting on the deck was like being on an open-air observation platform of a blimp hovering over Eden. Even indoors was like being outdoors. On the sides facing the ocean, all three buildings had floor-to-ceiling hinged glass windows that went up and down like garage doors. Other than during a couple of windy rain squalls, we left them up all the daylight hours.

Things went even better than we'd hoped. We had time to just hang out in the sun, play games, and do the things any other group of sociable older couples might do on vacation with friends. One morning we went on a guided snorkeling tour of a reef. I'd never done that before, and I loved it. I thought I'd be afraid of something biting me, but it was so beautiful underwater, seeing the fish and the coral and the turtles, that I forgot my fear.

Another day we took a tour of historic sites, but mostly we just lounged around the villa, or in the pool, reading or playing board games or just talking. Talking was the best part. Things turned another direction as the sun started sinking, but even then there was an especially nice languid quality to everything.

Sleeping arrangements were something I'd been apprehensive about before the trip. Chip and I were the only people in the group who weren't part of a couple who lived together. We'd spent time in bed together, but not as sleeping partners. I was a little concerned about how things would work, especially since we had just enough beds to accommodate our group.

In some ways sleeping with someone new is more personal than having sex with someone new, and most everyone preferred retiring with their regular partners at the end of our evenings. Fortunately, the Petersons were the exception. They both let Chip know he was welcome to spend the entire night with them. The arrangement was fine with me. Even when Stan was alive, I often went to another bedroom because he twitched and snored so much. For sleep, I like having a bed to myself.

Chip's situation with the Petersons was evolving into something I'd never seen before. There was obviously a strong sexual connection, but in other ways they treated him almost like a favorite son home from college for summer vacation. It sounds a little weird when I describe it that way, but it was actually very sweet. When I watched the three of them together, it seemed to me that both Cal and Carolyn worked at making sure Chip was happy, and I think they did make him happy.

I noticed changes in him after Cal and Carolyn joined us; he became more outgoing than before, more inclined to let loose and be silly. By the end of B&G's first year, the three of them seemed like members of a family, just not a kind of family I'd ever known. When Cal began to talk about buying a place on St. John and spending February and March there after they retired, we all expected that Chip would be down there too.

CHAPTER 45, ED

THE CHANGES WE'VE SEEN

It was a terrific six days, and Eeyore stayed out of sight the entire time. Doris never once had to call The Rule. I was even able to wall off my most of my anxiety about The Little Shit's assault on Albino Point, and the grim end of Uncle Pete's life. The weather was wonderful. There were a few rain showers, but they were wonderful too. We watched them roll in from the west, sweep across the water, and move on. There were only a few other houses on the green hills above the bay, and those were mostly situated so they weren't easily visible from one to another. We felt we had our own private piece of the Caribbean. Beautiful as it was though, I agree with Maddie that all the hours of conversation were the best part of the trip. I think that being so far from home, and in a place so wonderfully relaxing, encouraged us to take a more aerial view of our personal and family histories, and of the changed world that brought us to our unusual present.

We talked a lot about how much attitudes about sex had changed during our lifetimes. We'd all come of age right around the beginning of the "sexual revolution," in the sixties and seventies, though in smaller towns like ours it probably lagged a couple years behind upscale suburbs like the one Doris grew up in.

Anne was the only group member who was a full-fledged

participant in the counterculture, but we'd all witnessed the changes in the ways young people dealt with sex—and the language they used. My dad said that when he was in school he never once heard a girl say "fuck." By the time I was in high school, some girls did use the word, though only a few could reel it off without seeming self-conscious. When May Hamer told a kid to "fuck off," it flowed naturally, but with most girls it seemed like they were trying too hard. But by the time I returned to Big Pine as a teacher, the word was common in many girls' vocabularies, and these days I wouldn't be surprised to hear a Girl Scout complain about how "fucking hard" she had to work to get her citizenship badge.

In just the seven years between my own high school graduation and my first year of teaching, there was a noticeable increase in the number of kids who were having sex, not just talking about it. In my senior class, there were only a handful of kids I was sure had "done it." Most, like me, graduated as virgins.

If you didn't count Maddie, the only B&G members who lost their virginity in high school were Cal, Doris, and Anne, and all three of them went to big high schools down in the Twin Cities. By the end of my first year as a teacher, though, I was aware of quite a few Big Pine students who were having sex, and there were certainly some I didn't know about. That fits with statistics I've seen that show high school virginity rates gradually declining from the 1960s through the 1990s, then leveling off at around 50 percent.

The even more surprising changes were in student attitudes about oral sex, and about masturbation. Oral sex, as Maddie pointed out, was considered by most kids in our time as an intimacy beyond intercourse. Cal, Anne, and Maddie were the only B&Gers who'd given or received oral sex in high school. Cal said there were only a handful of girls in his class who were known providers. He said he'd been a recipient, but that he'd never returned the favor. In my case, I only fantasized about being a recipient, and the thought of reciprocating was intimidating. I wasn't turned off by the idea, I was just afraid I wouldn't know how to do it right. It was the divorcing woman I met in Hansen's Grocery who finally coached me through it.

Statistics do show a dramatic increase in the frequency of oral sex among teenagers, and Doris says her counseling career confirmed that. She said it became more common to have girls acknowledge it without much embarrassment, and that they did consider it a lesser intimacy than intercourse. That's a huge change from my own student years. Al the pulp cutter, my nemesis back when I first worked for Otto, really had been born too soon. Oral sex hasn't become the equivalent of good-night kisses, but it happens a lot more often than it did in Al's day.

Attitudes about masturbation have also changed, at least among boys. One night on St. John, Cal told us a funny story about masturbating to a *Playboy* centerfold, thinking his parents weren't home, then seeing in his dresser mirror the image of his dad standing behind him in the bedroom doorway. They never discussed the incident, he said, but he remembered how mortified he felt. That might still be a little embarrassing to a kid today, but by the end of my teaching career most boys acknowledged masturbation without shame.

A healthier attitude, in my opinion.

Statistics show that roughly 90 percent of men do gratify themselves, at least occasionally. Apparently the rest become coaches or preachers or youth group leaders. In my own school days, most of those authority figures were relentless enemies of "self-abuse."

Becker, my high school football coach, preached against it almost daily, saying it would sap the strength we needed to win championships. He also said it would erode our characters, weaken our eyesight, deform our penises, and cause all sorts of unspecified problems after we married. After we went on to a one win, seven-loss record in my senior year, Becker must have concluded that my teammates and I were starching our sheets pretty much nightly, and that our penises were probably already too misshapen to be of any use to our future wives—wives we'd be struggling to even see through our inch-thick glasses.

Back then Willis Niemi told me the leader of his church youth group suggested resisting temptation by wearing mittens to bed. Judging by Willis's performances on the bus he could probably have gotten himself off just by imagining the art teacher was wearing the mittens.

If you asked him, though, Willis would tell you he never masturbated. But then he'd give you his sleepy smile and say, "but sometimes I like to wash it really-fast,"

Unlike Willis, some boys did try to seriously deny they ever masturbated. Not surprising I guess, considering the shameful nonsense that was attached to the practice. Most deniers were lying, of course, and Willis had a clever little trick that sometimes caught one of them out. He would start in as if he was telling a joke, saying, "So this kid was in the bathtub jerking off, right? And . . . well, you know what cum looks like in bathwater, right?"

Of course the target would nod and say yes, at which point everyone listening would burst out laughing at how Willis had trapped him. I really loved Willis.

I also remember a particularly cruel trick that a group of boys would play on a gullible kid. At a party, or maybe in someone's basement, all the guys in on the joke would start talking about masturbating and admitting they did it. Then one of them would suggest a "rabbit race," which involved turning off all the lights and masturbating until someone "won."

When the room was as dark as they could make it, the boys would make jacking off noises until the target joyfully announced he'd crossed the finish line. Of course when the lights were turned on, the "winner" realized he'd just earned enough humiliation to last the rest of his life.

By the time I retired, though, boys were less likely to feel like secret sinners, and might even talk about having to "squeeze one out" after a frustrating date. Big change.

~

Even before St. John, I think all of us had created personal rationalizations for our participation in B&G, but on our vacation we explored them as a group. I suppose we were trying to make the fun we were having seem like a well-thought-out response to life. But there are some pretty good arguments that B&G *was* a rational response to life, even if we didn't come up with them until after the fact. To me, the most obvious barrier to some late-life freedom is that present-day seniors are expected to live by rules of sexual behavior that were laid down at a time when there were damn few seniors. If Western morality was formulated in biblical times, 2,000 years ago, then it was defined for a population where average life expectancy was late thirties—which roughly spans the years of reproducing and raising our young to a state of physical independence. For that lifespan, there are good arguments that sexual monogamy makes biological sense. Human young are unusually helpless, and they need parental protection for a longer time than the young of most other mammals. In a completely monogamous relationship, men know which kids are their own, and likely care for them and the mothers more diligently than they might if we didn't know which ones were "theirs." Because of those advantages to our offspring, it does make sense that evolution would have favored genes that encouraged monogamy during our child-raising years.

But after that? For 99 percent of human history, there wasn't any "after that" for most people. Even when my great-grandfather was born, late in the nineteenth century, life expectancy was only late forties—or just over fifty, if you take infant mortality into account. Now most of us have more than thirty years ahead of us after we carry out our biological orders—meaningless years, from Mother Nature's perspective. As far as she's concerned, we're just excess biomass once we've raised our young. So, what does it matter what we do with our non-reproductive sexuality? Seems to me that it's unreasonable to use first-century morality, laid down by people who lived only into their thirties, to hobble present-day seniors who live into their eighties.

Actually, "unreasonable" doesn't quite cover it. It's more like stupid. What better, safer time to branch out sexually? If that sounds like a rationalization, it is. But it's a pretty good one, and I think everyone in our little group would tell you they're glad they bought into it.

Of course none of those rationalizations work if you accept that a Supreme Being holds us to those first-century moral rules. Then you have the problem of religious conscience, not to mention the fear of being toasted like a marshmallow for all eternity. But that wasn't an issue for most of us. Chip still attended church, but he seemed to have somehow reconciled his B&G activities with scripture—with the Song of Solomon maybe.

Doris and I and Maddie grew up in families where religion and church attendance was not a big part of our lives. Until I was about ten, my parents would drop me off at Redeemer Lutheran for Sunday school, but I think that was only so they could have a couple of hours alone on Sunday mornings—they never stayed for the service. When I finally announced that I didn't want to go any longer, they didn't try to convince me otherwise.

Jim Foster was confirmed as a Catholic, but that was the end of his religious life. Anne Foster said her parents described themselves "spiritual," but she said she never really understood what that meant. She said she wasn't sure her parents did either.

The Heikkela's were atheists, and Sylvia was what you'd have to call a "militant" atheist. She was especially proud that present-day Finland has the highest percentage of declared atheists in Europe—well over half the population, she says.

I know I've mentioned a few biology-related run-ins with local believers, but I honestly have no problem with religion, just so long as people don't take it seriously and start trying to apply it to their actual lives. Then it can get in the way. A good local example was Mike Martinson, Big Pine's crackerjack auto mechanic, who fell under Reverend Oskey's spell for a couple of years. In fact, Mike got on fire for the Lord so intensely it almost cost him his business. Not long after Oskey ignited him, I went in to get a slow leak in my right front fixed; it took Mike fifteen minutes just to get the tire off. He'd spin off a lug nut then spend three or four minutes educating me on some finer point of the End Times. He even showed me how to lower the hoist myself, in case my pickup was still on it when he was raptured—though he said if I had trouble figuring it out, Helen, his wife, could help me.

Apparently, Mike didn't think she would be ascending with him. Helen sat behind the counter and ran the business end of things, but she was also within earshot of the mechanic's bay. The day I had the tire problem, she finally yelled out that if I wanted it fixed "before midnight," I should probably relocate to the Customer Lounge—the stuffed chair and pedestal ashtray next to the Lion's Club gumball machine across from her desk.

Fortunately, after Oskey rotated on to a congregation in North

Dakota, Mike's fervor abated somewhat and business picked back up. Everything in moderation, as the Greek guy said.

CHAPTER 46, ED

MISSING HISTORY

Doris accidentally started a long-running St. John conversation when she joked about how horrified her mother would be if she knew about B&G. She said she was tempted to tell her, just to punish her for the cheerleading lessons, and for naming her Doris. But then Cal asked her how she knew that her mother didn't have her own history, maybe just as far outside the lines as Doris's. Doris said if he knew her mom, he'd know what a crazy idea that was.

I think she was probably right, though when Cal pressed her she admitted she didn't have much hard information about her parents' love lives, either before or during their marriage. I told the story of finding the letters in the garage. That started a group potluck where everyone chipped in what they knew about their own family sexual histories. There wasn't much. Beyond stories about accidentally walking in on their parents, or hearing the creaking of a bed frame, no one had a lot of information.

Carolyn said that when she was an adolescent she went through a period where she fantasized that she and her three brothers were adopted—she just couldn't imagine her mom going through the whole disgusting sequence of having sex and giving birth that many times.

I think she felt better when she found out the rest of us, even liberated Anne, weren't keen on thinking about the details of our parent's sex lives either—at least not in our childhoods.

Anne came from the family most open to discussing sex. She said her mom talked freely to her about any sexual topic, and she remembered candid mother-daughter conversations about oral sex, anal sex, and other things most parents would be squirmy about discussing with their kids. But she said her mother never made specific references to her own sex life with Anne's father, and Anne said that was fine with her.

I think there are sound biological reasons why parents, even parents like Anne's, don't usually talk to their children about their own sex lives, and why most children wouldn't want that information. "Your mom and I saw a great movie last night" is a lot different than, "Your mom and I had great sex last night."

That second statement sounds so strange it would almost make you want to call in Child Protection. I think we're hard wired by evolution to have that reaction. Being put off by thoughts of our parents as sexual beings reduces the likelihood of inbreeding—incest—and the consequent genetic risks to our species. Animal mothers often abandon their offspring, or even drive them away as they approach sexual maturity, but human family members stay connected, and that makes our aversion to seeing our parents as sexual an understandable development.

I once overheard one of my wrestlers advising a teammate on how to deal with his reluctant girlfriend: "Next time, tell her *her* mother did it," he said. A 100 percent accurate statement of course, but probably the worst seduction advice ever offered—roughly equivalent to showing her a film of a difficult birth, I'd think.

Unfortunately, that natural aversion to passing on sexual history also robs us of lots of other family information, not just sexual information. Most parents don't talk much to their kids about their previous relationships, because that might imply they were sexually active before they met one another. So when they're gone we lose more than just the story about their love lives with each other—we lose information about other people who influenced their lives. All that history dies with the person, the Etch-A-Sketch gets a shake, and everything restarts with a blank sheet.

The result of that missing history is that each new generation makes decisions about relationships without many guidelines from the past. Maybe one of your grandparents had an affair, but their marriage continued. How did they work that out? That could be useful information to their descendants, but chances are they'll never hear about it. Did your grandfather get a girl pregnant in high school? Was it your grandmother? How was it resolved? How did he feel about it?

The way family history works—or doesn't work—means you will never get the possible benefit of lessons from those long-ago happenings. We all end up feeling like relationship pioneers, when really there's all kinds of historical information. We just can't get at it.

Writing down our own stories and the story of B&G will maybe get a more complete version of our lives to generations beyond our own—not necessarily to our kids, but at least to people further down the family line. I think people who would be uncomfortable knowing the intimate details of their parents' relationships probably wouldn't be at all squeamish reading about their great grandparents' relationships. In fact, I bet they'll be fascinated.

~

None of us in B&G had any information about the love lives of our own long-gone relatives, but during our St. John stay we did plenty of speculating on the subject. Nineteenth century Big Pine-ites obviously did have sex in their lives, but how did it play out, especially in the one-room log houses and sod houses of earliest settlers?

Their entire living space was maybe fifteen by twenty feet. That's about half the size of a present-day efficiency apartment. That single room was bedroom, kitchen, nursery and, at least in sub-zero weather, the bathroom for all the occupants. Sexual privacy would have been near impossible, especially in winter when you couldn't send the kids outside to protect them from primal scene trauma. The only camouflage would have been the blankets covering you, and maybe one hung up as a room divider. It's hard to imagine people thrashed around a lot, or got into any positions where they weren't lined up in the same direction.

Our consensus was that marital sex, at least for people with kids, was probably a quieter business in those days. Maybe less frequent too. Or maybe not—there couldn't have been many other recreation choices, especially after dark.

Female B&G members tended to have bleaker guesses about pioneer sex than did the men—especially about sex in the winter months. Most of the women thought hygiene would have been a major factor. Carolyn said she'd read that the reason female tango dancers looked away into the distance was to get their noses as far away as possible from the aroma of their gaucho partners, and she thought people in nineteenth-century Big Pine probably did the same thing during sex.

Nurse Sylvia, who'd dealt with more bodily emissions than any of us, said she could imagine what a nightmare it was to deal with the consequences of stomach flu and explosive diarrhea in a one room house in winter, when the "bathroom" consisted of a chamber pot and a wash basin. It would have been terrible just to have her husband or a couple of kids sick, Sylvia said, but there would surely have been times when the wife was in the same condition with them. Sylvia's guess was that most of a pioneer woman's fantasies were about unlimited hot water, not sex.

Anne saw things a little differently. She thought personal hygiene might not have been quite the deterrent that Sylvia and Carolyn imagined. She made the sensible point that in nineteenth-century Minnesota, especially in winter, everyone would have had much different standards when it came to their partners' hygiene, and that while some odors of close living might have been unpleasant, they probably weren't quite the turn-off they might be for us. She said the time she spent in communal living taught her that people can get used to infrequent bathing, and still manage to work a lot of sex into their lives.

Of course, people did adjust to the hygiene practices of their times—it's not as if they had options—but when you read about cultures with lots of nudity and sexual variety, they do seem to have bathing as a common element. In ancient Rome everyone used the public baths, even poor people. In nineteenth-century Big Pine almost no one would have had many, if any, baths during winter months. By spring you could probably sprout radishes on some parts of people's bodies. Carolyn thought that alone would have been enough to make our female ancestors major boosters of brothels, and she guessed they would contribute their egg money if their husbands were short of the going price.

Whether or not nineteenth-century Big Pine husbands and wives had the same interest in sex, or participated in it as frequently as later twentieth century couples is hard to know, but we do know for sure that there were women in the business of satisfying men's itches. In the archives of the *Register,* I'd found a few sly references to doings at Marsh Crossing, where there was obviously a brothel of some kind. The lack of sexual detail in a nineteenth-century newspaper story isn't surprising, but I do wish someone had written a frank account in a journal or a diary. That the place existed wasn't exactly shocking, especially considering the presence of a couple thousand lumberjacks in area logging camps.

It's not knowing the specifics that's frustrating. What exactly was on the menu? Did the women service their customers naked? Was oral sex as popular as it is now? How about a threesome? A spanking? How much did specific activities cost? Were the customers mostly single men, or did local husbands also patronize the place? All that information is gone forever.

One factor that might have favored commercial sex, and maybe even arrangements similar to ours, was that plain old garden-variety adultery must have been tough to arrange in those days, even for people who had the inclination and sufficient energy left after a day of farm work. Farms of all types were smaller in those days, which meant farmers would usually be within a few hundred yards of their cabins. When the wife wasn't working indoors she was probably in the field or the barn, right beside her husband. Where was the opportunity for either of them? And even if you had a willing adultery partner, just a mile away, how would either of you let the other know the coast was clear? You couldn't phone ahead of time. For sure people can be resourceful when it comes to creating sexual opportunities, but it didn't seem to us that undiscovered adultery would been all that easy to accomplish for married Big Pine-ites, a hundred years ago. Anne thought that made it more likely there had been some agreed-to spouse exchanging, and maybe even some earlier versions of B&G. Our dentist thought so too, and he had some interesting theories to back that up.

Cal is a very smart guy and, like Doris, when he gets interested in something he goes all in. His speculations on the possibility of earlier groups like B&G were partly based on his hobbyist interest in the history of alcohol and nineteenth century patent medicines, both subjects he dug into after learning a little about them in dental school. His collection of bitters and other early medicine bottles is on permanent loan to the History Center, and the collection keeps growing when local people find items turned up by plowing or digging foundations and bring them to Cal to find out something about them.

Cal said most people today don't realize just how much alcohol and drug use there was in earlier America. Per capita alcohol consumption, for instance, was much greater than it is today, he said. Many of our pioneer ancestors drank homemade hard cider at breakfast, more cider and beer or wine at dinner, and maybe added some corn whiskey in the evening. The whiskey was often from their own stills—farmers made it for their own consumption, but also because it was a way to monetize corn without having to ship it in bulk. And alcohol wasn't the only available high. Cal said people who might have claimed to be teetotalers could easily get just as buzzed as the drinkers, and maybe more so if they used some of the popular patent medicines and tonics.

Those were usually some form of opium, heroin, or cocaine, suspended in an alcohol solution, he said. Even non-alcoholic Coca-Cola used coca leaf extract in its nineteenth-century formula. And the patent medicines with hard drugs weren't just for adults; the most popular "soothing syrups" for cranky babies contained opium. I smoked opium once, in Thailand, then spent the next four hours lying on a bed, completely happy to just study my toes. I can easily imagine it was very popular solution for frazzled mothers, trying to care for colicky babies in snowbound sod houses or cabins—popular with both the mothers and the babies, probably.

Cal's guess was that all the alcohol and all the patent medicines probably did help send some of our ancestors off in directions they might not have gone sober. He said to imagine a couple of well-lubricated farmers sitting against a tree in the evening, sharing a jug, and maybe a bottle of cough medicine or tonic:

"I know I'm a little drunk, Tom, so don't take offense. I just always wanted to tell you what a fine-looking woman your wife is."

"No offense taken, Virgil, and you know, I'm glad you brought it up, because I've always wanted to tell you the same thing about your missus ... Say ... I know it sounds a little crazy, but did you ever think ... ?"

Or maybe it was their wives who had the notion. Either way, how would we ever know if it happened? The newspapers of the time wouldn't have touched the subject, and the people involved wouldn't have been likely to include it in journals or diaries. Even today, the stories of people's sexual relationships usually end when the people do. The Etch a Sketch phenomenon again, and everything starts over without any reference points from the previous generation.

By the end of our stay on St. John, I think all of us were at least open to the idea that we might not have been the first married Big Pine-ites to explore non-exclusive sex lives.

Our last night on the island was especially fun, thanks again to Anne. We were all relaxing on the deck, in the dark, when she suggested we should each share one of our favorite sex fantasies. Of course, by that time most of us had acted out at least a few with other members of the group, but there were still plenty of good ones to be told.

In the years after we lost our sexual edge, Doris and I both used our imaginations to create the illusion of desire—we were a lot more candid with each other after Book and Garden became part of our lives. Doris shared one of her favorites, one she'd already told me about—her abduction by a small band of South American revolutionaries. I know she's gotten a lot of mileage out of it. It is pretty good—I almost feel I know Rafael, their leader: dark hair, mustache, and a devastating smolder. At first he kept Doris for himself, but then he generously began using her as a reward for the man he thought had fought most bravely in the last raid. Sometimes he couldn't decide between two men.

I told about my imagined post-plague adventure with Billy Wiederholt's mom, and it turned out that both Cal and Chip had their own adolescent last-man-servicing-hot-harem fantasies. Must be a common one. In Chip's version, his minister dad brings him along to drive the bus on a girls' choir tour. As they go through a long mountain tunnel a burst of radiation wipes the rest of mankind. The excitement causes Chip's dad to have a heart attack, but with his dying breath he tells Chip that biblical rules don't apply in the situation, and that it's Chip's Christian duty to make sure humanity survives.

I also told the group about my fantasies that grew out of a real experience that hadn't ended well—my disastrous night with the girl I met at the Steamboat Days dance. In my fantasies I do get her jeans off without humiliating myself, and I have half a dozen wonderful imagined conclusions. In the long run I've gotten more sexual pleasure out of the incident than if I'd been able to hold myself back that night on the blanket.

All in all, it was a great trip.

CHAPTER 47, ED

DISASTER

Two days after we got home from our vacation, I got a Sunday morning call from Ned. He said he needed to see me right away, and that he was heading up from the Cities. He also said that he wanted to talk to me, alone. I told him Doris would be leaving for grocery shopping in Hibbing after lunch, and that he could come to the house. Three hours later he was at the door, with a video tape in hand.

Ned said he'd been minding Sharon for the weekend while Joey was at an Indian gaming conference in Arizona. On Sunday afternoon a DHL driver came to the door. After she signed for the package, Sharon told Ned he could go back to the carriage house.

"That was fine with me," Ned said, "The NCAA tournament was on."

But he said it was lucky that she called him back on the intercom, saying she had something to show him. When he got back in the house, Sharon sat him down in front of the TV. "She said she had some home movies, featuring people I knew," Ned said. "When she started the tape, I saw right away that some of the people were you and your wife and Jim Foster and his wife, and Doc Peterson. Mrs. J said the place was St. John," he said. "You weren't wearing clothes."

It was like one of those demolition scenes on the news—

someone pushes a plunger and five seconds later the building is just rubble and a cloud of dust. The ultimate disaster. I didn't know what to say other than to tell Ned I was sorry he had to see it.

Ned said, "I'm really sorry, Coach. You know I didn't want to see it. But if she hadn't showed it to me, you'd have been screwed for sure."

I said I was pretty sure we were already screwed.

"Maybe not," he said. "I think it might be okay."

After they watched the video, Ned said Sharon laid the whole story on him. Joey was looking for a way, any way, he could pressure us off our opposition to his Albino Point plans—me and Jim Foster in particular, probably because we were the perceived leaders of the opposition. Somehow Joey'd gotten wind of our planned St. John trip. That the ten of us were going down there together was no great secret. Among other things, we'd all had to let people know how to reach us in an emergency. But obviously some of our planned activities were a secret. Did Joey already know something? Ned said he didn't think so. Sharon told him Joey wasn't after anything specific, that he just hoped he might catch us smoking dope, or drunk, or sunbathing in the nude, anything he could use for leverage. He'd paid three thousand bucks, plus travel expenses, to send a private investigator down from Miami for two days, just on speculation. Unfortunately, he hit the jackpot.

Ned said he watched the first few minutes and then asked Sharon to turn it off, that he didn't want to see it. I believed him, but I said the real disaster was going to be Joey seeing it.

"I don't think he will," Ned said. "And if he doesn't, you can thank Sharon."

Ned said that after she turned off the video, she reacted in a way he hadn't expected. She said her husband was the single worst human being on the planet, and that she couldn't believe he was willing to ruin a bunch of people's lives just to get his way on a building permit for a house he was building out of spite. She said she was sick of living with someone who screwed over so many people, and that Joey made her feel like a prostitute on his payroll. A few weeks earlier, she told Ned, she'd found a valentine in the pocket of one of Joey's suit coats when it came back from "the sewing slut"—Ned said that was Sharon's name for the Russian seamstress Joey used for all his alterations. The valentine was homemade, a puffy cloth red heart with black threads woven into it.

Sharon said the pubic hair valentine was the end for her. Unknown to Joey, she'd already contacted a divorce attorney and she was gathering as much dirt and financial information as possible before serving papers. She'd also rented an apartment on the river. One of her former coworkers acted as the lease holder, which meant Sharon could live there anonymously. Whatever the court outcome, she said, she wouldn't be starting out completely broke. She'd always made liberal use of the household credit cards, but starting early on she'd also squirreled away much of her $4,000 monthly cash allowance, just in case. She told Ned her rainy-day fund was close to a hundred grand.

"Then she said I could take the video and get rid of it," Ned said. "I asked her what she was going to tell Joey. I mean he was expecting the tape, and the Miami guy had already called and told him what was on it—and she'd signed for the delivery. I said Joey'd go crazy if it wasn't there when he got back from Arizona."

Sharon told him she had it covered. She showed him the mailer and how she'd opened it with a steam and a razor blade. She said she opened and resealed a lot of Joey's mail, and that was how she found that the seamstress wasn't Joey's only detour off into the bushes.

"Then I found out how really smart she is," Ned said. "She sent me off to Best Buy to get another tape—same brand. She put the new tape in the envelope and resealed it. She said how much fun it was going to be to see Joey watching a blank tape, waiting for the action."

"If the guy in Miami made a copy of the tape, that's bad news," Ned said, "but Sharon thinks it's probably the only one. It was rush rush to get it here, and she doubts the guy took time to duplicate it. We'll know pretty quick. I told her how much I appreciated all she was doing, and I asked if she still wanted to find out what it was like with an Indian. Turned out she did."

Thank You, God, for creating Ned Cooley. If Ned's guess that there was no other copy of the tape was correct, we'd just dodged a bullet—dodged a nuclear missile, really.

I told Ned I hoped I'd be able to pay him back some day. He said I'd paid him back a long time ago. I didn't hug him, but it was close. Ned said he had to get back down to the Cities to meet Joey's return flight from Phoenix, but that he'd call me as soon as he knew anything more.

CHAPTER 48, ED

THE TAPE

That evening, Doris I screwed up our courage and popped the tape into our VCR. There was about twenty minutes of footage, all taken in twilight or at night, which was understandable—during daylight almost all of us wore bathing suits, or shorts, just like any other group of older vacationers. When the sun went down we switched to robes, and spent our pool and hot tub time in our birthday suits. The date stamp on the video showed it was taken on the evening of our third day on St. John. Unfortunately, there's enough light from the lanterns in the pool area to make everyone identifiable.

In the first thirty seconds, Doris and I are with the Fosters at the shallow end of the pool. I could tell the video was shot from somewhere on the hill between the villa and the main road above. Jim and Doris are kissing. She has one arm around Jim's neck and the other arm is angled down into the water toward him. Anne and I are kissing too, not quite as intensely as Jim and Doris, but the fact we're kissing naked doesn't leave much doubt about the relationship. Those first few minutes are all of people at the pool.

Cal is just lying in a chaise, but there are two separate zoom close-ups of his substantial personal equipment. I thought it might be an indication of the camera guy's own orientation. Matt and Sylvia are seated at a table, sipping on drinks. The rest of the video is mostly people walking to and from the buildings, though near the end there's a minute of Matt and Carolyn in the hot tub. She's straddled across him. Because it's so dark, you can't really see much, but the rhythmic way they're moving didn't leave any doubt about their point of connection. It would have made a nice scene in an "R" movie.

Overall, Joey would have plenty enough to drive people out of employment and social acceptability in Northern Minnesota. But I have to say it was well done, especially when you consider it was shot by someone hiding in the dark on a nearly vertical hillside—the side of a cliff almost.

At the beginning B&G had seemed like an insanely crazy risk, but by the time of the St. John trip it was just a regular part of our lives. The video tape was the baby alien bursting out of the astronaut's chest, putting our activities back into the "insanely crazy risk" category.

Doris was as close to hysterical as I'd ever seen her. Inside, I was plenty worried too, but I did my best to fake my way through it and calm her down. If there was no backup copy of the tape, I told her, then Joey had no proof. I also said there was no point in getting everyone else in a panic before we knew if a backup existed. Neither of us slept much that night.

~

We got lucky. Saint Ned called back the next morning. Sharon had told him that Joey went wild when he saw the tape was blank. He called the Miami guy and started yelling at him, but Sharon said the guy fired right back at Joey and said he'd watched part of the tape before he sent it, and that it showed what he said it showed. Joey even offered him an additional three grand, but the guy stuck to his story—which happened to be the truth.

I doubt that people who live near a volcano spend much time worrying until the thing starts rumbling, but at that point they probably can't think of anything else. Joey's sleuthing was the rumble that brought home to us that the risk had been there all the time. Thanks to Sharon and Ned, we'd been saved from immediate disaster, but we knew we weren't safe. The Little Shit didn't have any solid proof of B&G's existence, but he probably didn't think the private detective made up the story about the tape's contents. Now that he was on to us, there was no doubt he'd be clawing at the ground anywhere he thought he could scratch up hard information to destroy us. We had to suspend our activities until we figured out what to do.

A week after the tape scare, both Jim Foster and I received letters from a swinger group, thanking us for our interest and telling us how to proceed. We didn't have any doubt who made the inquiries on our behalf, and he was sending a shot across our bow. Of course we didn't respond to the letters, but a few days later I got a call from a woman asking for personal information about me and Doris. I told her I had no idea what she was referring to, and hung up. Then I left a message at the number on the swinger letter, saying that someone had called us and that we were going to take whatever legal steps we could. I got a call back from a sincere-sounding guy who said he was the organizer of the group. He said it wasn't the first time someone had applied for membership in someone else's name, and that he would take us off the mailing list. But he also said that no one in his group had contacted us. He was sure of that, he said, because all inquiries came directly to him, and he was the only one who had seen the one that was supposedly from us. He was emphatic about it, and I believed him.

I decided to return fire; I made a late evening call to Joey's office number, knowing I'd probably get a recording. I left a message telling him that we were being harassed by a swinger group, receiving unwanted letters and phone calls from them, and that I wanted to go after whoever was behind it. I said I knew that wasn't his area of law, but could he point us to an attorney that did handle that kind of thing?

He didn't call me back. Not ever.

CHAPTER 49, MADDIE

IN LOVE

The news about Joey's investigation was very scary. The videotaping was as upsetting to me as the threat of exposure. It felt like such a personal violation. I'm thankful that I've never been raped, but I think my reaction to being unwillingly filmed gave me a small insight into how violated rape victims must feel. It's been years now, but I still sometimes wonder if someone is hiding nearby, taking pictures. There was a silver lining to the crisis, though: Anne. That head-and-neck massage she gave me when I was so worried about my daughter was a tipping point.

Anne was the only other female B&G member who'd had previous sexual relationships with women, and that first winter we began to have very warm feelings for each other. Both of us felt, though, that group meetings weren't really the place to explore the possibilities. We didn't think anyone would necessarily disapprove, but the kind of intimacy we were considering would be too time consuming and too exclusive for group evenings. When panic over the video put B&G on hold, the two of us decided to get together in the interim.

Our first "date" was a dinner at my house. I don't often use the fireplace when I'm alone, and I liked having an excuse. I cooked for her, my own version of bouillabaisse. We split a bottle of Pinot and exchanged our stories, starting with my love affair with Sissy.

Anne had a lot of relationships before she married Jim. She was, by far, the most experienced—and open to experience—of all of us. Her first marriage was an "open" one that hadn't worked out. After her divorce she'd spent a year with a woman lover at a commune in New Mexico, then the two of them returned to Minnesota and started another experimental living group in southeast Minneapolis, near the U of M. There were quite a few alternative lifestyle communities in those days, even in relatively staid Minneapolis.

Anne said that both times she'd been involved in group living, things started out well but quickly went downhill. Men caused most of the problems, she said. They talked a good game, but too many of them weren't interested in any sharing beyond sharing their bodies with all the women. Sharing the toilet cleaning, or bringing in money from outside jobs were often not high on their priority lists. The Minneapolis community took in the brother of one of the women members, and a week later he ran off with the treasury, almost two thousand dollars. Anne called the police, and that was how she met Jim.

She said that when she'd started seeing him she appreciated how different he was from the men she was used to. The first time she went to his apartment it was so tidy that she wrongly assumed he had a cleaning service. Then she watched him cook their dinner.

"All that, plus he knew how to make me laugh and he was a lot of fun in bed. Two weeks after we met I knew I wanted to have kids with him, and I wanted to start right away—I was thirty two."

Her mention of Jim making her laugh struck a chord. Stan had a good sense of humor, and so did the male Book and Garden members—even Chip and Ed, once you tuned in to Scandinavian wavelengths. When I asked her about the transition to married monogamy, she said it was an adjustment for both of them.

"Cops get a lot of opportunities too," she said, "There really is something to the uniform thing. But we both believed that raising kids is best done in a monogamous two-parent marriage. We came within a couple of years of getting that done, and if those evil Heikkelas hadn't been such good kissers we probably would have made it."

Chip and Ed were right about Anne's sex appeal, and I'm not sure she would have been as appealing without the extra few dozen pounds. Stan's mom used to refer to women like Anne as *zaftig*. In Yiddish it means something like "plump and juicy." Chip said that the first time he saw Anne naked he felt like he should whistle and applaud. Her wonderful huge breasts hung a little lower than they probably had twenty or thirty years earlier, but she was indeed a sight. If you needed an actress to play Mother Earth in a nude musical, Anne probably wouldn't even have to audition her singing voice— she'd be cast the minute she took off her clothes.

We didn't hurry through the food or the wine—we had the luxury of time, the whole night if we wanted it. After dinner she came around to the back of my chair and kissed her way around the top of my head. She worked her fingers on my temples and the back of my neck, the way she had the night I was worried about my daughter.

"Ready to relax a little?" she asked.

When my fireplace is going, the thermostat doesn't switch on, so my bedroom was chilly enough that we spent our first few minutes under the covers just warming each other with our hands. There's a lot of Anne to warm up. I was a little at sea about where to go next.

Anne took care of that by asking if it would be all right for her to take the lead for a while? *Yes, please.*

She propped herself on her elbow so that her face was above mine. She kissed me everywhere she could reach—my forehead, my eyes, my mouth, my neck, my breasts. When she discovered how sensitive my nipples were she pushed them up between her fingers and rubbed back and forth over them with lips and her tongue and made little scrapes of her teeth across them. Then she sucked on them. If she'd kept on with it long enough, I think I would have come from that alone.

When she finally moved down, she took her time there too. When she could feel I was about to go over the top, she eased off and whispered, "Not yet."

No one has ever listened to my body that closely, not even Sissy or Stan. Anne brought me up to the very edge three or four times before the end. I'd never experienced an orgasm that rolled on so long. I've had some good sex with men, first with Stan, and later in B&G: Jim and Ed especially. I also had a sweet introduction to sex with Sissy, but it wasn't until those nights with Anne, while everything else was on hold, that I fully understood what my body was capable of. For a woman soon to turn sixty, that was a very wonderful discovery.

Sissy was probably right in her prediction about me being in the middle. For me, sexual joy hasn't depended on my lover's gender or anatomy. If I had to come up with differences between my male and female lovers, I guess it would be women's soft mouths, and their ability to listen to my body. But love itself has turned out to be the real aphrodisiac. I loved Sissy, I loved Stan, and now I was at least half in love with Anne.

Falling in love was a risk I think we'd all considered. I don't remember any group discussions on the subject, but Doris and I had talked about it privately. She had her own emotions to keep in check. She said her feelings for Matt Heikkela were very strong, and she thought that Ed and Sylvia had the same issue.

I thought I'd seen the same thing. It was subtle, but it was there.

I think everyone assumed "love" would be disaster. Anne was the only B&G member who had previously lived a life in which openly having multiple sex partners was the norm.

For the rest of us, it was new territory. And for us, at least for the most part, sex had been on a continuum of falling in love and getting married. In B&G the goal was having sex with people you liked, but did not want to fall in love with.

As teenagers we probably do "fall" into love, but as we move into adulthood most people are able to exercise at least some control, and love becomes more a thing we step into. For instance, I have very warm feelings toward Ed. I find him physically attractive and I think he's a good human being. In another life I could easily fall in love with him. But that just isn't an option. He's married to my lifetime best friend, and it would be inexcusable for me to allow myself to "step" into love with him.

Jim Foster was the other man in the group who had the potential to invade my heart but, with both Jim and Ed, I was able to enjoy their company and still keep boundaries in place. Not falling in love with them was a choice I could make, and I made it. But now there was Anne.

During the weeks B&G was in limbo, Anne and I got together several more times. We usually spent the whole night together, enjoying the rich feeling of having all the time we needed. Sometimes we spent the first hour in bed just kissing and saying how much we loved being together. When we moved to something else, our bodies were always ready. I'd almost never come more than once in an evening with anyone, but with Anne I knew the first one wasn't necessarily the last. Two or three hours would pass in a blink. It might be ten o'clock when we got into bed, then one in the morning the next time I looked at the clock. And it didn't end when we parted.

When Anne is aroused, she gives off a musk that would make her a fortune if she could put it in an atomizer and sell it as an aphrodisiac. Dear God, it turned me on. I'd never experienced anything quite like it. It penetrated the layers of my skin so deeply that a soapy shower didn't remove it. Two days after we'd been together I could cup my hands over my mouth and nose and still catch Essence of Anne. Usually I loved that persistent reminder, but on one occasion it gave me an awful scare. My daughter, her husband and my granddaughter came up from the cities for a visit on a day after I'd spent the previous night with Anne. I didn't remember they were coming until about an hour before they were due, and I was completely panicked. I always hug and kiss them when they arrive, and I was sure my daughter and son-in-law would know immediately where Grandma's face had been recently. I finally solved the problem by spreading Mentholatum around my mouth and nose, telling them I had a cold and they shouldn't get too close.

~

Our forced time out also coincided with our group's first serious medical problem: Sylvia's breast cancer.

She'd received her diagnosis a few days before the trip, but she hadn't said anything about it to the rest of us. She scheduled the surgery for the week after we returned. Only Matt knew. The news did explain something I'd noticed on St. John; the two of them had seemed more openly affectionate than usual. I'd never doubted they loved each other, but much of the time they used each other as comic foils, and the barbs could be quite sharp. On the trip, they'd been noticeably softer toward each other, and I'm sure the knowledge of her cancer was the reason.

The surgery was an apparent success, and as minimal as possible. Fortunately, there was no involvement of the lymph nodes, which would have meant a more complicated surgery, a longer recovery and an iffier prognosis. Of course everyone wanted to visit Sylvia in the hospital. Doris and I did visit.

When we got up to Oncology, Tommy, her nurse colleague from Emergency, was just coming out of Sylvia's room.

"The nurses on floor say she's the patient from Hell," Tommy said.

"She thinks she runs the show up here too. They said next time she goes to Big Rapids, no matter what."

We were standing in the hall, just outside Sylvia's doorway, but he said it all loud enough that he knew she would hear.

"Fuck you, Tommy!" she yelled.

"Wonder why they've got her in a private room?" Tommy asked.

It was a short visit. Sylvia made it very clear she did not like being seen in a dependent state, and we stayed only long enough to give her the flowers and tell her we missed her.

She thanked us, but she also said we should tell any other potential visitors to please "stay the hell away."

CHAPTER 50, ED

THE ELEPHANT IN THE CLOSET

It helped that our forced hiatus came at a time when most of us had other things to busy ourselves with. The Fosters were getting the resort ready for the fishing opener, Matt and Sylvia were occupied with Sylvia's recovery, and the four of us who worked for the school system were gearing up for all the year-end activities. Over that winter, I'd honored my vow to try and rid us of our mascot albatross, but by spring it turned out to be a discouraging task. The committee I put together held two open meetings to try to get citizens involved in making a change. I really hoped people would finally be ready to dump our humiliating, violence-provoking turkey. They weren't. Apparently a lot of local alumni felt nostalgic about the name. Either that, or maybe they felt they had suffered through it and why shouldn't their kids feel a little of the pain too?

One opponent of change pointed out that our University of Minnesota sports teams are "The Gophers," in honor of a timid little animal that lives mostly underground, eating roots and ruining crops. I agree that a gopher is a dumb mascot—there's still a bounty on them, for god's sake. But what was the guy's point? Because the university had their stupid mascot we should be happy with our stupid mascot? Somebody else in favor of keeping "Gobblers" dug up that Benjamin Franklin wanted the turkey to be our National Bird. Not

Ben's best thinking, but I forgive him; his praise for older women as sex partners more than makes up for his foolish national bird notion. Finally, there were the deniers, mostly older people, who argued that only depraved minds would associate "Gobblers" with sex. I could have pointed out that "depraved" is the actual medical description of a teenage boy's mind, but by that time I could see my campaign was already lost. In our final committee meeting, we couldn't even agree on a recommendation. It wasn't a good spring; the turkey survived, and B&G seemed doomed.

No one had any ideas about how we would get back in business again, and it looked doubtful that we ever would. With Joey on our scent, it was beyond risky to continue. But the idea of giving the whole thing up was hard to take. It wasn't just the sex, though of course I would miss that—especially Sylvia squirming underneath me, quacking about what someone was probably doing to Doris. I also missed all the rest of the fun, and I'm sure everyone else did too. Someone on the outside would likely guess that we were more serious and single-minded than we really were. They wouldn't have imagined our giant dentist with straws up his nose, doing a walrus impression, or Doris in a limbo contest with Matt Heikkela. Sex wasn't exactly secondary, but an audio recording of one of our get-togethers would probably sound more like the second or third drink stage of a successful party among friends than like a focused sex orgy. I didn't want to lose any of it, but there didn't seem to be any way we could continue.

Then, three weeks into our voluntary suspension of club

activities, another Sunday afternoon visit by Ned pushed my worries about the future of B&G into the background. He'd called that morning, saying he had something important for me, but that I might not want to share it with Doris.

The first photo was of Pete and a guy who couldn't have been more than thirty or so, half a century too young to be one of the "army buddies" that Pete said he visited on his trips to the cities. They're on a dance floor. Pete's eyes are closed and he's leaning back with his arms stretched straight out, his fingers interlaced behind the young guy's neck—the same position you see sixteen-year-old steadies in at a high school sock hop. The people in the background are all men, some in leather getups. There wasn't any doubt about the setting, or the clientele. I knew exactly where they were—The Gay '90s in Minneapolis.

The '90s has been around since Prohibition, and it's the biggest and best-known gay night club in the Midwest. It's also considered cool by lots of straight people, especially young people. When we were at the U, one of Doris's girlfriends held her bachelorette party at the '90s, and I'd been there on a couple occasions myself.

The other photo looked to have been taken in an apartment. The hustler—I assume he was a hustler, unless he had a grandfather fetish—is sitting on sofa, his shirt open to his waist and he's resting his arms on the sofa back. Uncle Pete's face is buried in the hustler's lap. It was the tackle box letters all over again, one more time that I had to reinterpret everything I thought I'd known. Dad's story that war injuries were responsible for Pete's lack of girlfriends was just another time bomb he'd let me carry through life.

Ned said he found the photos when he and Sharon were inventorying the contents of Joey's safe, deciding what to take with them and what to destroy when they made their exit. Sharon told Ned she'd used a connection from her dancing days to find a locksmith who was available for the kind of work they're not supposed to do. On a day when Joey was out of town she had the guy come over to check out the safe. She said the wall safe was an old one that had come with the house, and that it took the locksmith only a few minutes to feel out the combination and open it up for her.

The material inside was mostly unlabeled, Ned said. Sharon had seen the pictures of Pete before, but she had never seen Pete, so to her the photos had just been of an unnamed old man Joey had something on. Until Ned filled her in, she had no idea they related to the Albino Point battle.

Ned said most of the other compromising material in the safe was videos or photos shot in Joey's Mississippi riverfront condo, in the gentrified former milling district at the edge of downtown Minneapolis. Joey lived there with his second wife, but he kept the place even after he took up with Sharon and bought the mansion on Lake of the Isles, in the Kenwood neighborhood. Kenwood was "old money" and Joey liked that association. In his Minneapolis life he sometimes let on that his family was part of the nineteenth-century lumber aristocracy—at least that was the background he favored if he wasn't telling his Horatio Alger, barefoot-through-the-snow version. The Little Shit was whoever he needed to be.

The condo didn't sit entirely empty after Joey moved out. He used it as his own sexual playground, but he also made it available to a select group of politicians, business associates, and professional athletes—anybody he wanted something from, or might want something from in the future. Ned said the place was impressively furnished and that the view up and down the river was spectacular. I'm sure the surroundings helped convince young female visitors that sex with married men in that setting was way classier than it would have been in a motel. But according to Ned, a motel would have been a lot more private. The condo had "security system" cameras that no visitor ever noticed. Ned wasn't sure the videos were ever used to blackmail anyone other than Pete, but at the least they were an insurance policy if any guest ever tried to cross Joey, or if Joey needed a major favor.

Ned said Joey played a couple of X-rated condo clips for him, including one of a high-visibility local coach and family man, a guy who spoke at Promise Keepers events. In the video, the coach was bare-ass naked on a bed, face down in four-point restraints, with a ball gag in his mouth. A woman dressed only in a referee's shirt was disciplining him with a riding crop. I always thought the guy was a little too good to be true. I believe I've already mentioned my "no great men" theory.

Ned told me he was sorry to be the one who revealed Pete's secret life, but he also knew why Pete agreed to sell to Joey—sexual blackmail.

"I thought maybe you knew Pete was gay," Ned said.

I told him the idea had never crossed my mind. Ned said he'd always sort of known. He said that in the summer he worked part time with Pete, he'd found a stash of muscle magazines hidden in a cardboard box in the back of the shop. He said there were also a few other magazines, of a kind you wouldn't find on the rack in Grudee's drugstore. I asked Ned if it hadn't made him uncomfortable working with Pete.

"*Nah,*" he said. "Pete knew I was straight. He wasn't going to come on to me. As far as I was concerned, he was a great teacher and a great guy. Finding out he was gay didn't change my feelings."

The photos Ned showed me were copies. He said the originals were still in Joey's safe, but that when he and Sharon split they would destroy them. I didn't think the stuff was very dangerous now that Pete was gone, but it felt good to know they would disappear forever.

By the late twentieth century, even in Big Pine, being gay didn't carry the quite the same baggage it had forty or fifty years earlier. Most younger people no longer considered it to be someone's sole defining characteristic. We'd even had a couple kids come out to their classmates, something that would never have happened when I was in high school, or even in my earlier years of teaching.

Back then, Doris and I had a friend, Phil, who taught second grade at Big Pine Elementary. After Phil had been teaching for a couple of years, it was hard not to notice that such a good-looking and personable guy seemed to have no romantic doings that he ever mentioned, and that he spent a lot of weekends down in the Cities. Most people eventually assumed he was gay, and Doris and I knew he was. On one of his weekend trips to Minneapolis, Phil was arrested for propositioning a male undercover cop in Loring Park, a gay meet-up spot on the edge of downtown Minneapolis. It was only a misdemeanor charge—lewd conduct—but word of it got back to our town's enemies of sin. One blockhead started a "protect our children" petition, got a few other blockheads to sign it, and brought it to the school board. Phil could have fought it, but he decided it wasn't worth the hassle, and that it was time to find a job down in the city—Minneapolis has always been known as a gay-friendly town.

A year after he resigned, Phil stopped to visit Doris and me on his way to a canoe trip in the Boundary Waters, the wilderness area on the Minnesota/Canada border. His new partner was with him—a burly, bearded guy. They seemed happy together. After they left, Doris told me gay men sometimes refer to guys who look like Phil's partner as "bears." The cop who arrested Phil had also qualified as a bear. It probably would have been a relief to the blockhead crew to know that the only Big Pine second graders Phil was attracted to were the hairy 220-pounders.

For sure people's attitudes about gays had changed by the time of Joey's blackmail, but that wouldn't have been any consolation to Pete. To him the group that mattered were his peers at the VFW, the guys he drank beer with and traded stories with, and the Big Pine VFW was on record in opposition to gays serving in the military. Being seen as a "homo," especially by the older members, would have blown Pete's world apart.

I could imagine the terror he felt when Joey threatened him with the photos. The last weeks of Pete's life must have been a running nightmare over the potential exposure of his secret. No wonder he'd started drinking early in the day. He probably imagined his buddies gathered around, passing the pictures between them. His disabled combat veteran status wouldn't have saved him the way it did in the snowmobile shootings. I never showed the photos to Doris, but I did tell her about them, and that Joey used them in his campaign to get Pete to sell.

Doris' wanted to bring in law enforcement and have Joey charged with blackmail, but I pointed out that it would be hard to prove, and that even if Joey was charged it would mean "outing" Pete, posthumously.

My solution was more straightforward: I would kill Joey.

I had a plan. I'd tell him I wanted to sell Pete's property after all, and ask him to meet me there. I would kill him slowly, with my hands, in Pete's shop. I'd strangle him until his fucking eyes rolled back in his head, then slap him back to life so I could do it again and again. I'd ask him if he thought he was as terrified as Pete was when he got the pictures. Then I'd squeeze some more. I wanted his death to take hours. I've never hated that completely, and I know it was a trial for Doris. Usually I'm a good sleeper, but for weeks after I saw the photos I had to dip into her sleeping pills just to escape my anger for a few hours. I'm sure I was trying to escape my own guilt as well—if I hadn't goaded Joey on Success day, Pete probably would have been with us a little longer. I'll always have to live with that.

CHAPTER 51, ED

RESOLUTION

Spring weather arrived early that year. White Deer was open water by the first week of April, meaning walleye spawning would likely be finished before the fishing opener in May. I always pull for an early spawn. Otherwise the big females are still assembled in the shallows when the season opens, and too many of them are easily caught and removed from the population. After spawning they disperse into deeper water, where catching them requires more fishing skill.

The unusual weather also gave us a head start on the garden, and it looked like we might set a new house record for earliest edible radish, but neither the fishing opener nor gardening were my top concerns that spring. Book and Garden was in limbo, Joey was moving ahead with his plan to desecrate the Point, and I hadn't yet figured out a way to kill him without limiting my time with Doris to Visiting Days.

I couldn't stop thinking about killing him; I went to bed thinking about it; I woke up in the morning thinking about it. Doris said I needed psychiatric help. I probably did, and I'm sure it was even worse for her than it was for me.

But then, suddenly, it was over.

I'm always amazed when people who are already rich cross legal lines they don't need to cross. A few years back, two multimillionaires from a suburb of Minneapolis got charged for tampering with the electric meters on their own homes. Meter tampering? What the hell were they going to save? A hundred bucks a month? Two hundred, maybe? They didn't go to jail, but they both had to plead guilty to misdemeanors. If they'd been Joe Blows nobody would have been interested, but because they were well-known business guys it made the papers and exposed them as the selfish assholes they were. How do you face people after doing something that chickenshit for almost nothing?

Joey's downfall came over larger stakes, but it was just as foolish. He could have lived the rest of his life on what he'd already accumulated but, like the electric meter cheaters, he couldn't stop himself from taking just a little bit more, and he made the stupid moves that brought a shit storm sweeping over his world.

His end had nothing to do with the evil he'd done to Pete, the pain he tried to inflict on Book and Garden, or most of the other ugliness he'd delivered to the world. Instead, Joey was just collateral damage from an exploded love affair, and he probably didn't even know the name of the young woman who tossed the grenade.

Joey's lobbying job paid well, but he'd figured out a twist that would make it pay even better. During his deer season visit, Ned had mentioned his puzzlement about the money Joey'd been pushing across the poker table toward legislators—legislators who already supported Indian gaming. As it turned out, support wasn't what Joey was paying them for.

Indian gaming has always been a contentious issue in

Minnesota. Some of our citizens are simply opposed to legalized gambling in general, either as a moral issue, or because it disproportionately drains the pockets of our lower-income citizens—which it does. Others resent what they see as the Indians getting "something for nothing." Then there are those who just want a piece of the pie. The last group included people already in the gambling business elsewhere, and who wanted to see Minnesota opened up to non-Indian casinos. The stakes were high.

The monopoly on casino gambling was worth hundreds of millions of dollars a year to the tribes. Likewise, changing state law to license gambling to non-Indian casinos would be worth hundreds of millions to private license holders. It was a group of would-be licensees, already in the gambling business out West, who provided Joey with the cash he lost at the poker table.

Ned later figured out who they were, after he realized Joey always stayed in one of their Las Vegas properties—second-tier casinos, not the top-end places Joey would be expected to choose. The untraceable thousands in cash they gave Joey to "lose" was a relatively low cost investment designed to bring a few key legislators around to changing their opposition to non-Indian casino operations. For Joey, the potential danger of playing both ends was huge, but I'm sure he figured he would skate by, just like he'd done his whole life.

Not surprisingly, the biggest winner at Joey's card games was the guy with the most influence, a committee chairman who, for years, had skillfully kept any non-Indian gaming proposals from getting to floor votes. Unfortunately for Joey, the winning legislator had the usual "great man" affliction in the form of a hot young staff assistant who was gullible enough to believe her boss when he said he was going to leave his wife. After he called "April Fool" on her, she took her revenge in the form of a chat with a *Star Tribune* reporter, filling him in on the poker games and their purpose, and also her former lover's planned change of heart on keeping the casino business Indian-only. The resulting article didn't directly accuse Joey and the legislators of criminal behavior, but there was really no other way to read it.

The day the story ran, Joey's world ended. He must have known it. He was an idiot, but he wasn't stupid. He knew the tribes would sue him, and of course the state attorney general, and likely the IRS, would be in line for their pieces of his evil carcass. In addition to the criminal penalties there would also likely be "disgorgement" of his ill-gotten loot. I love that word. It calls up an image of the guilty person vomiting up the stolen money.

And painful as all those prospects must have been, Joey's biggest worry had to be how his silent partners would react. That was also Ned's first thought, and he realized that he and Sharon could easily become collateral damage. He decided they needed to move out of the line of fire immediately. Less than an hour after the morning *Tribune* arrived on his doorstep, Joey headed for a conference with Minneapolis's best known criminal defense attorney. As soon as he was gone, Ned and Sharon cleaned out the safe, loaded what possessions they could into his Ford pickup and Sharon's SUV, and headed to her anonymous riverfront apartment.

The next day, Ned drove up to Big Pine. He told me he had the contents of Joey's safe in a bag and that most of it, including the Pete photos, would go in his mom's trash burner that evening. He said there had also been four packets of hundreds in the safe and that Sharon said she was sure Joey would want Ned to have some severance pay, and also want her to have an extra little stake for her new life. She determined the forty grand would be Joey's contribution to those causes.

When I asked him about his plans, Ned said he was still working on an idea for Pete's place, and that the involuntary bonus from Joey meant he'd have a proposal for me and Doris soon. Meanwhile, he said, he'd somehow risen to the top of Sharon's potential roommate list, and he was going take her up on the offer while he figured things out.

"I think I told you," he said, "she's been growing on me."

~

On the day of Joey's indictment, his attorney announced that "Mr. Hamer strongly denies all allegations of wrongdoing," and he would offer a "vigorous defense."

Does any attorney ever say he plans to offer any other kind of defense? You'd think with all the money they're paid, they could come up with some original language once in a while. Anyway, that was just attorney talk. In truth, Joey was as terrified as a five-year-old watching a zombie movie. He didn't even try to present the bribery as "I'm just a bad judge of poker hands." I think he was desperate to cut a deal that would keep him alive and give him some hope of a life after he got out of prison. He even threw himself at the mercy of his estranged sisters. May got a couple independent appraisals for Albino Point then purchased it from Joey for ten percent over the higher of the two—she knew Joey's assets were all likely going to be seized or sued for, and her over-market payment was to make sure the sale was a transaction the courts wouldn't find fault with in the future.

My guess is that Joey's motivation for doing the deal came in the form of some promise from his sisters that when he got out they would toss him enough scraps that he wouldn't starve. But that's just a guess. The important thing was that the Point was in friendly hands. May Hamer to the rescue, one more time.

Despite the public bullshit from his attorney, Joey quickly negotiated a deal on the bribery charge. He reached a plea agreement that called for forty-four months in a medium security prison down in Rochester, and he agreed to begin his sentence immediately. He must have figured he'd be safer in prison than out on the street. Maybe he would have, but we'll never know. Joey didn't show up in court the morning the judge was scheduled to accept the plea. In fact, he's never shown up anywhere since.

Ned's prediction, even before Joey's plea agreement, was that Joey wouldn't rat on the West Coast people. The way things shook out I had to think Ned was right. Joey'd told the court that he didn't know who the money was coming from, and that his only contact was the anonymous guy who delivered the cash and the instructions. Ned had been present at a couple of the deliveries. He said he had a feeling that the delivery guy was a "serious person," and Ned isn't all that easily impressed. Reading between the lines of the plea, you could hear Joey screaming to the money people that he hadn't ratted, so please, please don't kill me. I don't think it worked.

For a few months after his disappearance there were supposed sightings of Joey in different parts of the country, and even in faraway places like Cuba and Rio. None of them panned out. My own guess is that Joey is someplace less exotic—maybe sending up putrid gas bubbles from under a tamarack swamp, or encased in cement, 300 feet below the surface of Lake Superior.

Almost everyone who ever knew The Little Shit wished him dead at least a few times. I'm in that category, along with his sisters, ex-wives, and 10,000 or so members of casino-owning tribes. But it's been a while now, and the longer it goes without any trace of him, the more I'm inclined to think his partners out West called in the same kind of professional magicians who waved a wand over Jimmy Hoffa. He hasn't been found either.

CHAPTER 52, ED

REUNION

We scheduled a B&G gathering for the first Saturday night after The Little Shit's predicament became public. We'd been out of business for only six weeks, but a lot had happened during the interim.

That first post-Joey meeting was at the Lodge, the week before it opened for fishing season. There were hugs and "so good to be backs" and all the happy expressions of welcome you might expect at a family reunion—though at a family reunion, Anne probably wouldn't have slipped her hand inside my robe and given me a little squeeze. It was "good to be back."

Everyone was relieved that the crisis was over, but the matter of Sylvia's surgery was hovering in the background. As usual, Anne took the lead. After a few minutes of celebration she sat us all down on the sofas surrounding the fireplace.

"Sylvia has something to show us." she said.

Sylvia stood up, dropped her robe to her waist, and did a slow 360 turn in the firelight.

"Asshole says I shouldn't bother with reconstruction," Sylvia said. "He says no one will notice the difference."

It seemed like everything was quiet for a long time, but it was probably only ten or fifteen seconds. Then Anne said the surgery looked so good she was going to sign off on it. She took a marker pen out of her robe pocket and drew a little heart with initials above Sylvia's scar.

"Come on people," Anne said. After we all signed, Sylvia looked down at the graffiti without saying anything. I think she was going to cry, but she ran into the dressing room before it happened. No one knew quite what to do; Sylvia crying was not something any of us expected to ever have to deal with. We needn't have worried. A minute or two later, she came back out, walked over to where I was sitting, and pretty much yanked me out of the chair.

"Your first chance to screw an Amazon," she said.

Our newly minted "Amazon" was just as exciting and efficient as ever. Book and Garden was truly back in business.

Perfect bodies are all alike; every imperfect body is imperfect in its own way. I apologize to Tolstoy, but it carries my point. When the pathetic geezer who started the girly magazine is in bed with his paid harem of nineteen-year-old "perfect" bodies, I doubt he can close his eyes and call up a separate mental image of any one of them—and I'll bet none of them ever want to close their eyes and call up an image of him. I find nineteen-year-olds attractive myself, but the idea of them as sex partners just feels too strange—like they're a different species, maybe. It's not that I'd see it as morally wrong, more like aesthetically wrong.

All of us in Book and Garden had what might be considered physical imperfections, and Sylvia's was just the latest one to appear. They were part of what made us real to each other. Sylvia opting out of reconstruction was a gift that helped confer grace on everyone's imperfections. Not that she saw it that way. One night I asked her about her decision.

"I didn't think it would make any difference," she said.

For some reason I still get a rush of desire for her every time I think about that statement. And she was right, it didn't make any difference.

Fortunately, we respond to a lot of things other than bodily perfection. Watching someone do just about anything they have a real passion for can grab us and transform the way we see them. When Maddie first saw Stan preaching against the war, it wasn't just his curly hair; it was the intensity of his conviction that drew her in.

I remember my buddy Elliot's account of seeing Janis Joplin in concert in Milwaukee. He said that when she walked out on stage, he was surprised at how plain she was—*homely* was the word he used. "But after she started singing," Elliot said, "I thought she was the most beautiful woman I'd ever seen."

My own thought about Janis was that seeing her performance wasn't necessary—just listen to "Me and Bobby McGee" or "Piece of my Heart" some time and try to imagine she isn't desirable—and I bet it isn't just men who react that way.

CHAPTER 53, ED

NEW RESIDENTS

A few weeks after B&G's rebirth, Ned called to talk to me about his plan for buying Pete's place and restarting the repair business. Automotive work had become so computer dependent, he said, that it wasn't as satisfying as it had been when he first started with the Ford dealer. He said he'd often thought how much more interesting Pete's operation had been, dealing with a wide range of equipment and solving problems that called for creativity on the part of the mechanic. Pete had also sparked Ned's initial interest in welding and, even though it wasn't much required at the Ford dealership, Ned had taken a number of welding courses over the years. He said it was a skill that had brought in a lot of Pete's business, and he figured it would do the same for him when word got around that the shop was open again. Then, at the end of our conversation, he dropped what they call on TV, "breaking news": he wouldn't be moving back to Big Pine as a bachelor. And he said he had a favor to ask of me and Doris.

When I told Doris that Ned and Sharon wanted us to stand up for them, she thought it might be too awkward.

"They've seen me doing things," she said, "doing things most women only do at home . . . at night . . . with their husbands."

I thought that was quite comical, coming from the mastermind behind Big Pine's only free-love society, but once in a while I do know to keep my mouth shut. Instead, I told her I understood her discomfort, but I pointed out that it was because of the bride and groom that no one else had seen her "doing things."

She came around pretty quick. I called Ned back and said we'd be delighted to help them set sail together—at our house, if they hadn't already picked a venue.

As it turned out, the Fosters insisted on hosting the event at the Lodge. Good old Anne. Having been seen naked by the prospective bride and groom was absolutely no problem for her.

The wedding was simple. All the Book and Gardeners were there, along with Ned's mom, and most of the guests, including the Swedish guy, shed some tears. Jim took wedding photos that turned out really nice, including some of the bride and groom standing on the lake shore. You can see White Deer Point in the background, looking just like it has for the last thousand years.

~

It's been a while now, and the group is still going. We're all getting older, but it turns out that after you've learned to appreciate the sensual possibilities of sixty-year-olds, seventy-year-olds start coming into focus through the same lens.

Hopefully, eighty-year-olds will follow.

One benefit of aging is that we worry less about scandal. Young people mentally neuter old people, and with every passing year they're less likely to see us as sexual beings. These days, if Maddie and I were discovered screwing in the post office lobby, most younger Big Pine-ites would probably assume we'd taken a fall and landed on each other.

If there's been a change it's that our gatherings are a little less focused on sex than they were the first couple of years. Some nights half of us just play games or hang out in the hot tub and talk. We laugh a lot, too. In a way, it's like a marriage; the sexual intensity falls off some, and you reach an equilibrium.

We do still meet as a complete group and it's always fun, but now it's more like once a month, not every week. It isn't that we've lost enthusiasm, but rather that subgroups have developed. Doris and I have a special friendship with the Heikkelas, and we spend a lot of time with just the two of them. Matt and I are now also regular fishing partners. He knows what he's doing out on the water, even to the point that I've picked up a few tricks from him. And vice versa. Better yet, we've become good friends. That's a real piece of late life luck for me—Matt has some of the cynicism and the wry sense of humor that I valued so much in Stan. The four of us usually get together at least once a week, and it's always a good time. Both Matt and Sylvia share my pessimism about the future of our species, but they're funnier about it than I am, so Doris doesn't mind. And because we all line up on pretty much the same side of most political and social issues, we're able to laugh together at whatever idiocy is taking place in the world around us.

We usually head for separate bedrooms for sex, though Sylvia's been a little more adventurous than she was at the full-group gatherings. It started with her peeking in on Matt and Doris one night. They're very hot together—even if they're just making out, you can tell they mean it. It was contagious enough that night that Sylvia ordered them to "slide over." That was fun, but it's not a regular thing.

Part of the preference for privacy is that sex with each other's spouses can be so intimate and affectionate that it's not comfortable to be within sight or earshot of our lifetime partners. I know that Doris has strong feelings for Matt—pretty much loves him, I guess—but then Sylvia and I are in the same neighborhood. At the beginning of our adventure we all assumed that would be disaster, but somehow it's working, and I don't think any of us would say we love our spouses any less for it. Apparently we're capable of more kinds of living than I once thought.

The other two clusters are Chip and the Petersons, and Maddie and the Fosters. The Petersons did buy a place on St. John and, as we expected, Chip goes down there with them. Most of the rest of us join them for a week or two. Chip also pretty much lives with Cal and Carolyn here in Big Pine, at least most of the time. He'd sell his house, except that he'd have to somehow explain his new living arrangement to his children and grandchildren. Maddie doesn't live with Jim and Anne, but the three of them spend a lot of time together. They also have the honor of being the only B&Gers who've been "outed."

CHAPTER 54, MADDIE

OUTED

Yes, Anne and Jim and I were found out—not quite caught in the act, but not long after. It happened a year ago, though it wasn't the result of anyone's sleuthing. Since the end of B&G's first year, the three of us are seen together a lot, but I don't think there's been any sexual gossip the way there might have been if we were younger, or if we lived together. I still own my home, and usually I sleep there. On Saturday nights, though, when there isn't a larger gathering, Jim and Anne and I have a standing date that almost always includes an overnight stay. I consider the relationship we've worked out to be a small miracle.

When Anne and I started seeing each other privately, during the Joey Hamer "time out," I began having the same feelings for her that I'd had for Sissy and Stan, my other real loves. In another life, Anne and I might have become full partners, but in this life she also has Jim, the husband she loves. Fortunately we've found our way to a relationship that works for all three of us, and Jim is largely responsible for that. He's managed to make space for me without being threatened by the feelings Anne and I have for each other. The result is that Anne and I still spend some alone time together but now, on Saturdays, it's the three of us, and it's something I've come to love. So much for my previous feelings about threesomes. Things change.

On our Saturday dates we sometimes go out for dinner, but

more often I cook. During tourist season they come to my house; in winter we get together at the lodge. Most nights, we watch TV, play three-handed Hearts, or have a hot tub soak before heading to bed together. I don't sleep well at the Lodge, especially if I'm sandwiched between my host and hostess, but it's worth it. If I've ever felt warmer and more cared for, it was only in the womb. Sunday mornings are lovely, too. Jim drives into town early, picks up the *Tribune*, and then we all have breakfast and do the crossword.

We were found out on a Saturday night, last April. The three of us were in bed around midnight, and Jim and I were already dozing off. He was spooned up behind me, with his arm over me. Anne was on the other side of me, reading, when I heard her say, "Allie?"

I opened my eyes, and there was their daughter, Allie, standing in the bedroom doorway. She was looking straight at me.

"Maddie?" she said.

Stupid as it sounds, my first reaction was to try to pull the sheet up to my neck, but Jim was lying on part of it, so the best I could do was to get it halfway up my chest.

I said, "Hi, Allie, how nice to see you."

Dumb, but that's what came out of my mouth in the moment.

"We weren't expecting you until tomorrow, Honey," Anne said.

"I can see that," Allie said. "I know I said I'd be coming on Sunday, but I thought I'd drive up a day early and surprise you. Sorry."

"Well, Honey," Anne said, "you did surprise us, but you don't need to be sorry. It's late though, and probably a good time for us all to say good night. We can chat in the morning."

As soon as we heard Allie's door close, I said I thought it would be best if I headed home.

"Unless you're planning to walk," Anne said, "you *will* be sitting with us at the breakfast table. Should I have Jim hide your keys, or can we trust you?"

The next morning the three of us were up and at the kitchen table when Allie came into the kitchen. Without saying anything, she walked up behind each of her parents and gave them a hug from behind. Then she hugged me too.

"Did I ever tell you I have really cool parents?" she asked.

I said I did know that. I said those parents also had a very cool daughter.

Later, Allie told Anne that our secret was safe with her, but that it was going to be hard not to share it with her twin sister. Anne told her she had to check to see if that was alright with me. I was very touched that they considered my feelings in the decision. I said if it was okay with them, I was fine with it too. After that, the girls decided I needed a title to go with our unusual arrangement. Now I'm "Aunt Maddie."

CHAPTER 55, ED

WHAT NEXT?

We haven't had any other potential scandals, but there have been a few more medical situations. Doris had a small melanoma on her arm, which pissed her off enormously because she's never been a sunbather. We don't worry about it much because the prognosis is good at the stage hers was caught. Chip was out of commission for a few weeks after his prostate surgery, but it turns out this is a good time in medical history to deal with the consequences, and he remains fully functional. Likewise, Cal, after his bypass. And the sharp-tongued Finn witch has remained cancer-free since her mastectomy. The only big news is that Doris and I have fallen completely in love with two new people.

Margaret Cooley, "Maggie," arrived less than a year after the Lodge wedding, and brother Daniel (Daniel *Edward)* joined her two years later. Doris gave her retirement notice the day after Sharon told us she was pregnant with Danny. It wasn't a coincidence. I have never seen my beloved wife happier. This coming fall, Sharon will be attending classes in Hibbing three days a week, her start on an elementary teaching degree.

Doris denies it, but I believe she slyly planted the education notion in Sharon, just so there would be a need for someone to take care of Maggie and Danny. I don't blame her. I can't get enough of them myself. The plan is for them be dropped off at our house on Sharon's class days. We can't wait—we're finally real grandparents.

~

So that's our tale up to now. I suppose that someone reading the history of B&G could get the impression that sex has been the sole focus of our later years. But that isn't accurate. We all still have interests that any other random group of seniors might have—we just added an activity that led us into some different ways of living. I can't say that choice would work out so well for anyone else. Maybe we've just been lucky. Probably we have been. We've talked about that, and we know we took risks that could have ended in disaster. I guess they still could, and we might end up sending the message to our great-greats not to follow our example.

But at least we're leaving our story, which is more than anyone did for us.

Unfortunately, the Gobbler endures.